DATE DUE

D1267290

All about the
Border Terrier

Head studies of Ch Clipstone Cetchup ('73)
and Ch Clipstone Comma ('73), both home bred by
Jean and Frank Jackson.

All about the Border Terrier

Jean and Frank Jackson

PELHAM BOOKS/STEPHEN GREENE PRESS

PELHAM BOOKS/STEPHEN GREENE PRESS

Published by the Penguin Group
27 Wrights Lane, London W8 5TZ, England
Viking Penguin Inc., 40 West 23rd Street, New York, New York 10010, USA
The Stephen Greene Press, Inc., 15 Muzzey Street, Lexington, Massachusetts 02173, USA
Penguin Books Australia Ltd, Ringwood, Victoria, Australia
Penguin Books Canada Ltd, 2801 John Street, Markham, Ontario, Canada L3R 1B4
Penguin Books (NZ) Ltd, 182–190 Wairau Road, Auckland 10, New Zealand

Penguin Books Ltd, Registered Offices: Harmondsworth, Middlesex, England

First published 1989

Copyright © 1989 by Frank and Jean Jackson

Typeset in Monophoto 11/13 pt Plantin

Printed and bound by Butler and Tanner Ltd, Frome and London

ISBN 07207 18597

A CIP catalogue record for this book is available from the British Library

Credits

Jean and Frank Jackson are grateful to the following for permission to reproduce photographs in this book: Thomas Fall page 161; J. K. & E. A. McFarlane
page 153; Anne Roslin-Williams frontispiece, pages 119, 155, 170; Russell
Fine Art page 174; Ken Thomas pages 117, 121, 210, 213. Many of the early
photographs are from the archives of *Our Dogs* to whom grateful thanks are
due.

Contents

Introduction

All breeds are unique but the Border Terrier, the only recognised breed which, in Britain at least, has managed to combine a successful career as a show dog, both at Kennel Club licensed shows and at working terrier shows, with its original role as a working terrier and at the same time to remain a robust and reliable companion, can lay justified claim to a rather special place among the breeds. As a show dog he is among the most popular in the terrier group in Britain and he has also won substantial support in Scandinavia, Australasia, Holland, Germany and North America. His success in the show ring has been consistent rather than spectacular due, perhaps, to a determination among breeders and exhibitors not to sacrifice essential and functional qualities in order to achieve a greater level of show-ring success. The Border Terrier has remained in close touch with its original purpose and even in countries where foxhunting, of the type for which the breed was developed, does not exist there is a determination to ensure that the breed remains in close contact with its roots. The breed is perhaps now in wider demand as a sound sensible and reliable working terrier than it was before recognition in 1920. It is certainly in far greater demand as a companion in which role precisely the same qualities which have made it a good show dog and an outstanding working terrier are highly valued. In our, admittedly biased, opinion the Border Terrier is the ideal companion for a long country walk or an evening by the fireside.

This book attempts to examine the breed's origins and early development, its purpose and its history, and to offer some basic advice to new owners and breeders. We know that we have barely scratched its surface and that what we have achieved may, in the words of James Thurber's amiable Golux, be 'less than much and only little more than anything'. We hope nevertheless that it will interest and entertain those who share our enthusiasm for the breed.

Newcomers to be breed will see the strong links which exist, and must, between what the breed is essentially for and what it is. Those with more expertise, we hope, may find stimulus which will encourage them to greater interest and enquiry into the breed's past and purposes. Perhaps our efforts may even answer some questions, though inevitably many more will be asked. We have not attempted to lay down the law, to reveal the tablets of stone which claim to provide the only true guide to understanding the breed. Certainly we have, from time to time, expressed our opinions. We may sometimes have done so strongly but have tried always to differentiate between opinion and fact. Wherever possible we have relied on the statements of people whose experience of the breed is relevant to the time and circumstances which are being discussed. We have quoted at length from a number of sources, preferring to rely on what was actually said than on our own, possibly biased, interpretation of what we believe was meant.

The impetus for this book came from our own enthusiasm for the breed, which began in the 1940s while hunting with the Lakeland packs. It came also from the realisation that hidden in *Our Dogs* archives and, in our own library, was a wealth of material which had not been seen for many years. We were concerned too that the passage of time, our increasingly urbanised lives, and the growing possibility of legislation which will prohibit the breed's essential purpose, the reason for its very existence, might separate the breed from its roots. No book though can hope to be more than a very flimsy defence against unwelcome changes or hope to offer substantial protection against the damaging consequences of those changes. If we have renewed or encouraged a desire to know more about the breed's purpose and about the lessons to be learned from its history then we will have achieved more than we could reasonably have hoped for.

This book has not been the product of our own unaided efforts. We have been helped by many people, knowingly and unknowingly, directly and indirectly. To thank any is to expose ourselves to the risk that not all will be thanked. It is a risk we must accept. We must record our thanks to the editor of *Our Dogs* who has, in ways of which he may not always have been aware, been of immense assistance. The Kennel Club, too, have been kind and cooperative in allowing us access to their records. Our thanks are also due to Billy Campbell, Mike Homan and Brian Staveley who, in different ways, have provided valuable assistance.

We are indebted also to Beverley Stock, daughter-in-law elect, and Karen White, who turned a battered manuscript into something more legible. Steven Holt, Ken Thomas, Russell Fine Arts and, inevitably, Anne Roslin Williams have also earned our thanks. Without their help the book would have been almost devoid of illustrations.

Nigel Sisson provided advocacy of a very high order at a critical time. To him especial thanks are due.

Most of all we owe a debt to our family, Elspeth and Simon, who have grown, through tolerance, to share our enthusiasm for the breed they both grew up with. Without their help, criticism and encouragement the flaws in this book would have been even more apparent.

Finally, we must record our debt to the hospitality of the Marquis of Granby without which, long ago, the idea of writing a book or even at all might never have occurred to us.

Jean and Frank Jackson
Ashworth Moor
1988

1 In the Beginning

It is apparent that well before the end of the thirteenth century terriers existed which would bolt their fox or, if necessary, draw him from the earth, which were capable of running with hounds and helping them to work thick coverts and which 'shagged and straight legged ... do serve for two purposes, for they wyll hunts above the ground as well as other houndes, and enter the earth with more furie than others'. These terriers obviously had a number of attributes now to be found in, and were worked much in the same way as, modern Border Terriers, but to claim that they were Border Terriers would be to give the evidence a far greater load than it can reasonably be expected to carry. Nevertheless foxhunting was well established as a popular pastime and as early as 1219, the fourth year of the reign of Henry III, it was recorded that 'His Majesty the King hath granted permission to John Fitz-Robert to keep dogs of his own to hunt foxes and hares in the forest of Northumbria, as long as it shall please our Lord the King. And it is commenced to Hugo de Neville that he do permit him to keep them.' Foxhunting in Northumbria, the Border Terrier's birthplace, would be inconceivable without the services of reliable terriers. It is certain, therefore, that, at least by the middle of the thirteenth century, there were terriers in Border country and it is likely that these terriers were used in the same way as are Border Terriers and even that they shared some of their physical characteristics. In a general sense they were Border terriers but whether they can reasonably be regarded as of the breed we now know as Border Terriers is questionable. Perhaps it is sufficient simply to regard them as the root stock from which the modern breed evolved.

During the seventeenth century several authors described the way in which the terriers of the day were used. It was not until after the middle of the eighteenth century that anything appeared which showed what the terriers looked like. A painting of Arthur Wentworth, earth stopper to the Tufnell Joliffe hounds, was completed about the middle of the century before being published as a print which appeared in

A portrait of Arthur Wentworth, earth stopper, engraved from a painting completed in the 1750s. Neither of the two Terriers would be out of pláce in a modern Border Terrier show ring.

three versions. The first was published in 1767, the second in 1794 and the third, used to illustrate William Daniel's *Rural Sports*, appeared in 1807. Arthur Wentworth is shown mounted on a rugged old pony, well wrapped against the cold of a winter night. He carries a well worn spade under one arm and a mattock in his belt. A feeble glimmer of light is provided by the lamp which he carries in his warmly mittened left hand. From his flat cap to this stout boots Arthur Wentworth is little different from the terrier men and earth stoppers who have succeeded him.

At the pony's feet are two terriers. Both are of the same breed, somewhat on the leg, moderately long backed, with broad strong heads, dark uncut ears, good rather hound-like shoulders, deep briskets, strong loins, racy hindquarters and thick undocked tails. One terrier, larger than its companion, is self coloured with dark ears. The other is darker, though not black, with a typical pattern of tan marking on head, legs and undersides. Both have rough and apparently hard weather resisting jackets and either could appear among modern Border Terriers either at work or in the ring without seeming at all out of place.

Tufnell Joliffe's hounds hunted a country later taken over by the Holderness in East Yorkshire which is no more than one hundred miles from the area in which the Border Terrier originated. Even so it would be presumptuous to claim that these two terriers were Border Terriers. It is enough that they are of the type which still exists as the Border Terrier.

The type, however, was, then as now, subject to variations and to differing interpretations by different authors and artists. Thomas Bewick was born in 1753 at Eltringham, just a few miles from Hexham in the very heart of Border country. Many of his engravings contain hunting scenes and it is apparent that Bewick was familiar with hunting in Border country. In 1790 Bewick published his *History of Quadrupeds* in which is an illustration of a terrier of the type he would see out with hounds and during his long walks around the Borders. The terrier is a strange looking beast, though some allowance must be made for the limitations of the process by which the illustration was produced and for the small size of the engraving. It has no pretensions to quality, is heavy-boned, long-backed, gay-sterned and has a long, though strong, bewhiskered head which is surmounted by an ill-matched pair of ears. In spite of its strange appearance the terrier has a number of similarities with some modern Border Terriers, though perhaps our friends will not thank us for saying so. Apart from the engraving Thomas Bewick also provided a description of the sort of terriers with which he was familiar. 'The Terrier', he said, 'has a most acute smell, is generally attendant on every pack of Hounds, and is very fierce on forcing Foxes and other game out of their coverts. It is fierce, keen, and hardy; and

A field dog from Gesner of the type used, during the sixteenth and seventeenth centuries, to drive birds and other quarry from thickets in which they had taken refuge. The head and general outline are very reminiscent of a Border Terrier.

in its encounters with the Badger sometimes meets with very severe treatment, which it sustains with great courage and fortitude. A well trained veteran dog frequently proves more than a match for even that hard biting animal.

'There are two kinds of Terriers – one rough, short-coated, long-backed, very strong, and most commonly of a black or yellowish colour, mixed with white, the other is smooth, and beautifully formed; it is generally of a reddish brown colour, or black, with tanned legs; and is similar to the rough Terrier in disposition and faculties but inferior in size, strength and hardihood.'

Although the fox was not originally highly regarded as a quarry, though his skin was sufficiently attractive to give his carcass some monetary value, there developed in Border country, as elsewhere, two different reasons for hunting the fox. One was intent on the sport which an intelligent and resourceful quarry could provide; there can be no doubt that it was this activity which gave rise to the Border terrier. The killing of foxes as well as otters, martens, wild cats and other animals for their skins needed a different type of terrier while a terrier which might accompany its owner on expeditions in which the hope of sport was no more than equal to the need to provide a few rabbits for the pot needed yet another type of terrier. Hence then the Border, the Dandie Dinmont and the Bedlington.

One of the Border characters who eked out a precarious living by the sale of fox and other skins was James Allan. He has been credited with having a hand in the development of all three terrier breeds and is thus of some importance to our story. James Allan, often called Piper Allan because of hs skill with the Northumbrian pipes, was a shady character whose career has been imbued with a certain romanticism by the passage of time. It is doubtful if his contemporaries entertained any romantic notions about a sheep stealer, poacher, thief and wife deserter who, according to some reports, died in Durham Prison. Little is known with certainty about his life, though numerous tales, which differ in both minor and more important aspects, have been published. According to Ash, usually a reliable authority, James Allan was born about the year 1704, the son of William Allan with whom he is some-times confused.

'Piper Allan', Ash wrote, 'was a tinker-sportsman who lived near Rothbury at Holystone, spending much of his time hunting otters and playing the bagpipes. He owned a pack of terriers, among which were the three favourites "Hitchem", "Charlie", and "Phoebe". It was "Hitchem" (often printed as

"Peachem") of which Piper Allan would say, "When my 'Hitchem' gives mouth, I durst always sell the otter's skin". It was this "Charlie" for which the Piper refused broad acres with the ever-living answer, "His hale estate canna buy 'Charlie'!". And later, when the Duke of Northumberland offered, so it is related, a lease of a small farm to Mr Allan in exchange for his little terrier "Hitchem", the answer was, "Na, na, ma Lord, keep yir ferum; what would a piper do wi' a ferum?" So with his terriers the piper lived, collecting head-money and selling skins, now tinkering, now hunting, and playing his bagpipes, until the year 1779, when, on February 18 of that year, just when the country promised good hunting, and life awakening, the old man died at the age of seventy-five.'

Rawdon Lee, using *The Life of James Allan* as his source, said that:

'Allan was born in 1719 at a gipsy camp (A branch of the well-known Yetholm tribe) in Rothbury Forest, and was the youngest son of William Allan, whose ostensible mode of living was a cooper, tinker, etc, but he was also an excellent piper and a keen sportsman. William Allan was noted for his skill as an Otter-hunter, and was much in request among the Northumberland gentry as a man who could always show them good sport, and for this purpose he always kept a number of Terriers of this (Bedlington) breed. He owned two favourite Terriers – Peachem and Pincher by name. He had taken particular pains in training Peachem, and such was his confidence that when Peachem once gave mouth on the trail of an Otter, Old Willie would remark that "he would sell the Otter's skin".'

It is not clear why the Northumberland gentry should need to rely on a tinker and his terriers for their sport when the region already contained well established packs of hounds. It is even less clear why Bedlingtons should be thought appropriate for hunting otter and why a breed which is of necessity a silent hunter which relies on keen eyesight should give mouth on the trail of an otter. More importantly Ash and Lee disagree not only about which breed the Allans kept but even about whether it was the father or the son who has given rise to the enduring romantic stories. They even disagree about the names of the terriers themselves. It is not a very reliable basis on which to base the history of any breed but both Ash and Lee as well as other canine historians since seem to have been happy to accept the stories at face value and not to have been at all concerned about the inconsistencies they contain. There was, however, a less romantic story to be told and though it comes from the pen of George Borrow, who can seldom be accepted as a reliable disciple of the unadorned truth, it also has the advantage of coming from a man who knew far more about the people with whom the Allans lived than did either Ash or Lee. George Borrow visited Kirk Yetholm, near Kelso, in 1866 and, though his principal interest was in the language of the gypsies who lived there, Piper Allan soon became the subject of conversation.

'"Did you ever see Piper Allan?" said I: "he was a great friend of your grandfather's." "I never saw him," she replied: "But I have often heard of him. He married one of our people." "He did so," said I, "and the marriage-feast was held on the Green just behind us. He got a good clever wife, and she got a bad, rascally husband. One night, after taking an affectionate farewell of her, he left her on an expedition, with plenty of money in his pocket, which he had obtained from her, and which she had procured by her dexterity. After going about four miles he bethought himself that she still had some money, and returning crept up to the room in which she lay asleep, and stole her pocket, in which were eight guineas; then slunk away, and never returned, leaving her in poverty, from which she never recovered."'

The story contains at least as many improbabilities as do those of Ash and Lee but it does also illustrate a side of life which the Allans lived which is conveniently ignored by the more romantic stories. Both Willie and Jamie Allan existed. They were active during the second and third quarters of the eighteenth century and as inveterate hunters would have need of good terriers. Neither father nor son, however, enjoyed the sort of settled life which would enable them to breed their own strain of terriers and it is far more likely that they simply picked up any likely terrier which they happened to come across.

The absence of firm evidence does little to deter canine historians from accepting the most elaborate stories. It is said that Ned Dunn of Whitlea got his terriers from Jamie Allan and that he then supplied James Davidson of Hindlee with his terriers, James Davidson being, it is said, the model on which Sir Walter Scott based the character of Dandie Dinmont in *Guy Mannering*. Certainly the breed derived its name from the character who first appeared in 1815. However, Sir Walter Scott denied any connection between James Davidson and Dandie Dinmont. Writing from Abbotsford to Mr David Terry he said, 'I was introduced to a man whom I never saw in my life before, namely the proprietor of all the pepper and mustard family, in other words the genuine Dandie Dinmont. In truth I knew nothing of the man, except his odd humour of having only two names for twenty dogs. But there are lines of general resemblance among all these hillmen, which there is no missing, and James Davidson of Hindlee certainly looks Dandie Dinmont very well.'

During this relatively early phase in the development of the various British terrier breeds the term 'Scottish Terrier' and 'English Terrier' were not well defined and even well after dog shows had become popular towards the end of the nineteenth century were still used to embrace breeds which though of distinctive type still had no distinctive name. The situation was further complicated when the experts differed about which of the several types should be regarded as English and which Scottish. The Yorkshire terrier, for example, was often scheduled among the Scottish breeds. This confusion also exists among the early nineteenth century illustrations of terriers. There are several which depict terriers of recognisable Border Terrier type which, though described as Scotch terriers, have no resemblance to any existing Scottish breed, all of which are short legged.

Stonehenge illustrates what he regarded as the true Scotch terrier using Peto, a rather leggy animal, rough coated, broad in skull and short in foreface but with cropped ears and a docked tail. However, Sir Edwin Landseer, who provided the original from which the engraving was taken, was adamant that Peto was an English terrier. Perhaps Stonehenge himself provides a clue which might help to solve the problem when, in his *Dogs of the British Isles* (1867), he refers to 'another race of terriers, analogous to the real pepper-and-salt (which) was common on the Border. It is not yet extinct. It was nearly like a Dandie on long legs, but a shorter body, and in general a less head; it was exactly of the same colour-coat, body, head and legs being exactly as in the real pepper-and-mustard. Alliances with these were not uncommon with Dandie Dinmont himself; and Tuggin or Tuggim was of this race.'

So Stonehenge believed that the Border did indeed contain a third terrier breed but one which was less familiar to him than either the Bedlington or the Dandie, both of which had already made their début in the show ring by this time. The Border, however, did not have the usual physical features which might have made him attractive to those who were looking for new breeds for the show ring. He appeared at the Border agricultural shows and shepherds' gatherings but his main value remained his ability to bolt foxes, badgers, pine-martens and wild cats from the dangerous rocky clefts and long wet moss runnels in which they had taken refuge. It was as a terrier working with hounds and hunting the fox that the Border Terrier was to achieve wider recognition but already the Northumbrian packs had raised him to a high standard.

The old Border families of yeomen farmers have bred and worked terriers for many generations. Jacob Robson, whose mastership of the Border Foxhounds was preceded by that of his father, suggested that hunting acted as a substitute for the Border raids, the thieving and killing which had always occupied the menfolk of the Borders. Jacob Robson's attitude was echoed by Robert Surtees, himself born on the Borders of yeomen farming stock and familiar with the local hunts. It would be fascinating to discover which Border character was the basis for John Jorrock's Handley Cross huntsman, the Northumbrian James Pigg. Perhaps like Dandie Dinmont he was not more than a reflection of 'lines of general resemblance' which existed among several Border huntsmen and which are still clearly discernible. Certainly Surtees must have had his Border hunting companions in mind when he put Jacob Robson's philosophy into John Jorrock's mouth and described hunting as the 'image of war without its guilt, and only five-and-twenty percent of its danger!'

Outside the Borders and its own staunch band of supporters the Border Terrier remained comparatively unknown until in 1890 correspondence in *Canine World* attracted the attention of Thomson Gray whose *Dogs of Scotland* had been published in 1887 and who was preparing another edition. He wanted to know more about these terriers.

'Sir – On reading "Wanny's" report last week, it occurred to me that "Wanny" may be able to supply me with the information I am in search of. Some time ago I was in correspondence with Mr Thomas Robson, Bryners (sic), Otterburn, about the Terriers they use with their hounds, and which have been exhibited at some of our Southern shows as "Border Terriers". Could "Wanny" tell me the original of the Terrier, what size and colour they are, and if prick, drop or semi-erect eared? If I can get sufficient reliable information, I may give this variety a place in my book the *Dogs of Scotland* and would, therefore, be obliged to anyone who knows the breeds for a description of it.'

Gray had already been in correspondence with Thomas Robson and may already have been told that the Border was not a Scottish breed. Nevertheless by 1891 he felt sufficiently confident to include the breed in the new edition of his *Dogs of Scotland*.

'The ancestral home of the Dandie and Bedlington – the Borders of Scotland on being ransacked, produces another terrier, well known to all Border sportsmen, but seldom seen on the show bench being more at home on the moors and fells of Roxburgh and Northumberland. This dog, for want of a more distinctive name, is called the Border terrier. The Border terrier is by no means a rare animal although confined to a limited area, and to one part of the country, and as regards antiquity may claim to be the original terrier of the hills, from which the Dandie and Bedlington sprung. Unlike the Dandie and Bedlington, which are a compound of two or more breeds, the Border terrier still retains all its pristine purity. Bred for work and not for show, fancy points are not valued in proportion to working qualities, still the breed has many distinctive features which are carefully preserved; and when the Border terriers have been shown, as they are at some of the autumn Border shows, they always command attention. Their intelligent eyes, hard coat, and general activity, stamp them as an intelligent breed which has not yet been contaminated and "improved" by the fancier.'

Thomson Gray then quotes at some length from a letter he had received from Thomas Robson, soon to become Master of the North Tyne but at that time whipping in to his brother who hunted the Border Foxhounds of which their father was master. Notwithstanding Thomson Gray's flattering comments about the breed Thomas Robson's remarks must carry more weight.

'There were, some years ago two or three letters in *The Field* about the Border terrier, in which the descriptions were very true. I remember one thing was wrong; one letter said they had semi-erect or prick ears, whereas they are nearly all drop-eared.

'These terriers have been on the border for generations, and I fancy have as much original Dandie blood as the show Dandie of today. My father and the late Mr Dodd used these terriers with their hounds long ago. Crossed they may have been sometimes, when a good dog of any sort turned up, but they are still true to type.

'My father had a picture of Old Yeddie Jackson, the "Hunter King" of North Tyne and Liddesdale (which my brother John has at Newton Bellingham now), with a hound and a terrier (the date is about 1826, I think), which is the same as most of our terriers.

'The colours are red, grey, wheaten, pepper, and mustard, some with a little white on chest or a white foot, and I have seen (seldom) them with a white strip on the face; they are never black, white or fox-terrier marked.

'They are nearly always and ought to be small, many of them not half the weight of a Dandie. They should, of course, have a hard close coat, and good legs and feet, as those we use have three days a week with our hounds, and follow through most of the runs, and have some queer holes to get into.'

Thomas Robson's letter raises a number of interesting and still relevant points. His reference to colour is, if we accept that 'grey' refers to what we now know as blue, entirely in accord with the present standard. He was adamant that black, white or Fox-terrier coloured were equally objectionable. Modern breeders sometimes excuse black as being blue. White feet are no longer seen though they persisted in some strains until the late 1960s. White shirt fronts are still to be seen and are sometimes glaringly obvious. But it is, perhaps, Thomas Robson's reference to size which is of greatest interest. He said that Borders are 'nearly always and ought to be small . . . not half the weight of a Dandie'. The Dandie Dinmont standard at that time asked for a weight of from 'fourteen pounds to twenty-four pounds; the best weight as near eighteen pounds as possible'. So that, even if we take the maximum allowable weight for a Dandie, Robson was talking about Borders which were not twelve pounds in weight.

It is apparent from Thomas Robson's description that although there was, as yet, no formally agreed standard for the breed its supporters had a very clear and detailed picture of what was required and that this picture extended to points which were not essential to the breed's ability as a working terrier. It was against this consensus of opinion rather than against an agreed standard that the breed must have been judged in the ring.

Another tantalising glimpse into Border Terrier history was revealed when, on 25 February, 1921, the editor of *Our Dogs*, Theo Marples, published a letter from 'one of England's foremost sportsmen and philokuons', Hugh, Earl of Lonsdale. At that time Lord Lonsdale was Master of the Cottesmore which, then as now, hunted a country which lies in Leicestershire, Rutland and Lincolnshire and so at a distance from the Borders. However, the Cottesmore had its origins in a pack which its first master, Viscount Lowther, had brought from the family seat at Lowther Castle in 1666. Lowther Castle is just south of Penrith in country which is hunted by the Ullswater and is adjacent to Blencathra country. The Lowther family have connections with both packs and both are known to have associations with early Border Terrier history. It is known that the Blencathra, John Peel's pack, relied for some of their terrier work on Border Terriers while the Ullswater with its own legendary huntsman, Joe Bowman, produced some of the terriers which occur in early Border Terrier pedigrees. Lord Lonsdale wrote:

'Thank you very much indeed for your little booklet re the Border Terrier. I notice in the first page, under the description of "colour" that you restrict the colour to "red-wheaten, grizzle, or blue-and-tan". I do not know if you are aware that we have had these Terriers at Lowther since 1732 and have a continuance of pedigrees from that date, and that we have, and have always

North Tyne Gyp's ('17) working certificate was issued by short-lived Northumberland Border Terrier Club.

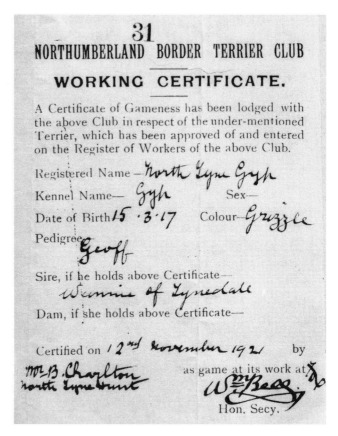

had a very considerable number of them white, and I often wonder whether the rough-haired terrier was not originated from this breed.

'We have always called these Terriers "Ullswater Terriers", and there is a place at Whale Moor, which is in Lowther Park, where there were at one time elaborate kennels for breeding them, and where the Cottesmore Hounds used to go for the summer, and these Terriers have been bred persistently, so I am quite sure there is no mistake about it. However, I only send you this for what it is worth, and may be of interest to you!'

Theo Marples used this letter to produce his own assessment of the place occupied by Border Terriers and, although he didn't say so in so many words, made it clear that there was reason to doubt whether the Ullswater terrier and the Border Terrier were in fact the same breed.

'It is quite easy to understand the variation in colour, and even in type, of say, the Border terrier of Northumberland and those of the English county – Cumberland – which together traverse and form the border lines of the English side between Scotland and England.

'The Border Terrier, therefore, is not like the Sealyham Terrier, a new creation, but a terrier of very ancient lineage, with great historical traditions of which those so generously given to the public by Lord Lonsdale form part.

'From these facts, therefore, there appears to be abundance of material for the new Border Terrier Club and its confrère in course of creation, the Northumberland Border Terrier Club, to evolve a sound, rationally built, and really utility underground dog which shall sustain the great traditions of gameness which it possesses, and at the same time commend itself to the modern and more educated eye in the way of make and shape, which nowadays is looked for in every description of livestock.

'In the old days, before dog shows came into being, the merit of terriers was gauged solely by their ability to perform the special functions assigned to them, whether it consisted of drawing a badger or fox or engaging in combat with other animals or vermin without any regard to his architecture, whether it be sound or angular. Make and shape, if they were ever thought of, were a negligible quantity, so that in the Border Terrier we have, without doubt, handed down to us a terrier which, weight for weight, has probably no equal for his specific avocation in the Border country. What the clubs which have been started to promote his particular interests and develop his traits have to do is to mould the material available into a terrier of more uniform type, more symmetrical in shape, sounder in limb, without in the least impairing his innate grit, gameness and tenacity. We are of opinion that it is possible to do all this, to eliminate the bad fronts, goggle eyes, long backs, light bone, flat ribs, one or more of which faults many otherwise good Border Terriers possess, and all of which are really a physical handicap to him in the performance of his legitimate sporting functions. Until this has been accomplished we fear the new aspirant to public esteem and favour will fail to rise to the popularity and classic stage of his brothers of the terrier persuasion – the Fox, Irish, Airedale, Scottish, Cairn and others of his ilk.'

What Theo Marples had done, doubtless unwittingly, was to catalogue many of the things which made the owners of working Border Terriers fearful of recognition. A terrier which was capable of running with hounds in Border country and of facing his fox below ground in some of the most fearful earths it is possible to imagine was hardly going to be made sounder by the demands of the show ring. Symmetry, popularity and an opportunity to share the fate of other terrier breeds, some of which had already been made useless for the purpose for which they were originally bred held few attractions for the breed's old supporters. Nevertheless what he had also done was to focus attention on a problem which was then exercising the minds of breeders.

For the history of terriers which irrefutably were Border Terriers it is necessary to examine the histories of the Border Foxhounds and its adjacent hunts, notably the Liddesdale and the North Tyne, as well as the histories of the dynastic families, principally the Robsons and the Dodds, which were, and remain, so closely associated with hunting in the Borders.

Jacob Robson kept hounds at East Kielder until 1857 when he moved to Byrness in Reedwater. These hounds, favourably noticed by Nimrod during his Northern tour in the early 1800s, were known as the 'Kielder Hounds'. At Byrness the pack was joined with that of a neighbour, Mr Dodd of Catcleugh, and the amalgamated pack were hunted as the Reedwater Hounds.

In 1869 John Robson, Jacob's son, took over the mastership and the name of the pack was once more changed, this time to the Border Foxhounds. Prior to this, terriers of the region had a number of names usually associated with the locality with which they were closest associated. Bedlingtons were referred to as Rothbury terriers, Borders were called Coquetdale terriers and the white terriers of the area, now extinct as a separate breed, were called the Redesdale terriers. However, as the fame of the Border Foxhounds began to spread so did that of the terriers on which they relied for their terrier work. It was not long before the breed became known as Border Terriers.

After his marriage in 1879 John handed the mastership to his brother Jacob who, with E. L. Dodd and Simon Dodd as successive joint masters, held the position until 1933, a period of fifty-four years during the latter part of which he was the oldest and longest serving huntsman in the country. In 1933 the mastership passed to his son, Jacob, who also held the position for a considerable time before handing over in 1954 to Ian Hedley. Jacob Robson died aged ninety-seven in 1985 having hunted with the Border Hounds for most of his long life. Nor was the influence of the Robsons, Dodds and Hedleys confined just to the Border Foxhounds. The North Tyne's predecessors were the hounds hunted by a succession of Dodds from Catcleugh. In 1878 the mastership of these hounds passed to Mr M. A. Hedley, one of whose family, William Hedley, had already appeared in the show ring with a Border Terrier called Bacchus. M. A. Hedley was soon joined by Thomas Robson, Tom O'Bridge Ford, brother of Jacob, Master of the Border pack, and together they held the mastership until 1901 when Hedley left Thomas Robson to carry on alone until his death in 1910. A third brother to the two masters was John, a noted breeder of sheep who lived at Newton, where hounds were kennelled when hunting the Bedlington side of the country. It was John, whose vociferous opposition to recognition which his two brothers actively supported, who had a hand in the formation of the short-lived Northumberland Border Terrier Club which tried to keep Borders only in the hands of Northumbrians and to roll back the tide which had swept the breed towards recognition.

The Liddesdale Foxhounds, which hunted a country to the west of the Border's and north of the North Tyne's, had been formed about 1800 and from 1860 had been hunted by John Ballantyne who handed over in 1881 to his son David Ballantyne who was joined in 1887 by John T. Dodd. Together they remained masters until 1900 from when until 1943 John T. Dodd carried on alone. He was once more joined by a joint master, Andrew Douglas, in 1943 and finally resigned only in 1947. None of the other hunts in the area, though using Border Terriers, had the same degree of influence over the breed's development as had these three Border hunts. Nevertheless mention must be made of these adjacent hunts which by using Borders and by continuing to use Borders for much of their terrier work helped the breed to remain a genuine working terrier. To the north of the Border and Liddesdale is the country hunted by the Jedforest, east of which is the Duke of Buccleuch's. The College Valley, the West Percy and the Morpeth lie to the east of the country hunted by the Border while the Tynesdale lies just to the south of it and adjacent to the North Tyne.

Perhaps the history of just one dog will suffice to show how Borders adapted from their traditional role as working terriers to a new career in the show ring and will also show how the resources of all the Border hunts were combined to produce the sort of terrier they needed. Perhaps too the story will go some way towards identifying a dog which might, with some justice, be regarded as the father of all show Borders and so of the modern breed itself. The dog in question was Flint, bred by John T. Dodd who, with David Ballantyne was joint Master of the Liddesdale. Flint was whelped in 1894 and was by Jacob Robson's Rock out of Tom Robson's Rat. Jacob Robson was at that time, with E. L. Dodd, joint Master of the Border Foxhounds while Tom Robson was, with M. A. Hedley, joint Master of the North Tyne. Rock, Flint's sire, was himself sired by M. A. Hedley's Rock, whelped in 1882. Hedley's Rock was by yet another Flint owned, we believe, by Tom Robson and whelped in 1878 which is, incidentally, the earliest date to which we have yet managed to trace any Border Terrier pedigree. Immediately then Flint demonstrates the way in which the Border, Liddesdale and North Tyne combined to produce their terriers. In 1898 Flint was mated to 'that good old bitch Vene' of which nothing more is known. From this mating came Fury who, in 1900, was mated to Twig, bred by John Dodd out of Daisy by Smith's Punch. This mating produced Bess I for John T. Dodd and the Liddesdale, and in due time she was mated to yet another Rock. There is some doubt about whether this was Tom Robson's Rock whelped in 1908 but it seems likely that it was the North Tyne's Master's dog which was used. In which case since Rocky was by John Dodd's Twig out of Pep we have an interesting early example of in-breeding.

Bess I was owned by Willie Barton, of whom more will be heard, and from her he bred, probably to Joe Bowman's Wasp, in 1909, a bitch called Nettle. However, before we go further it is necessary to examine Joe Bowman's Wasp. At that time Joe Bowman was huntsman to the Ullswater Foxhounds and there is no proof that he ever owned a Border Terrier. Wasp was by Ullswater Jack out of Ullswater Nellie who, from their names, sound as though they might well have been of the old Patterdale terrier breeding used much by the Ullswater. However, we do know that the nearby Blencathra at this time certainly used Border Terriers as did the West Cumberland Otterhounds. Wasp may well have been a Border and it seems more likely that Willie Barton would take a Border bitch to a Border than to a Patterdale dog. Be that as it may the mating produced Nettle who, in her turn, was mated to Jacob Robson's Pincher to produce J. S. Roddam's Wannie of Tynesdale. In 1917, when she was just over a year old Wannie was taken to Norman Crozier's Geoff of Fline, a son of Wasp who can with some certainty be regarded as the produce of Joe Bowman's terriers. This mating in 1917 produced a dog called Gyp which was sold to John Dodd, who changed his name to North Tyne Gyp. In 1919 North Tyne Gyp was mated to Daisy owned by Miss B. Bell-Irving, at that time Master of the Dumfriesshire Otterhounds. From this mating came Tinker who was to win the very first Challenge Certificate available to Border Terrier dogs. Interestingly enough the Bitch CC at this inaugural event was won by Liddlesdale Bess, owned by J. Davidson but bred by Willie Barton. She too can be traced back through Bess I to Tom Robson's Flint who thus has some claim to being the progenitor of the modern breed.

2 At Work

We recognise that not everyone will share the average Border Terrier's enthusiasm for hunting. There may even be Border Terrier owners who are actively opposed to hunting, a circumstance which seems to be analogous to a vegetarian keeping pigs. The unavoidable fact is that Border Terriers were developed to do a particular job of work associated with fox hunting in a particular part of England. It was the demands made by this work which formed the breed both physically and mentally; the standard itself is a response to them and was originally written by men who appreciated these demands.

The standard was their attempt to describe an ideal. It was an ideal which provided for the variations necessary in order to meet the varied demands met in the hunting field. The standard concentrated, almost to the exclusion of all else, on points which were essential to the breed's purpose. Where more trivial matters are mentioned they tend to allow for a latitude of interpretation which is indicative of the lack of importance which was originally attached to them. They allowed for individual tastes, for the changing demands of fad and fashion, without in any way interfering with the breed's ability to fulfil its essential purpose. During the years since the standard was written, and particularly during the early 1920s, the standard was revised and refined though never in such a way that essential points were changed. Sometimes changes responded to what was thought to be an ambiguity, sometimes to some undesirable feature which was creeping into the breed, but always changes were made by breeders in order to protect their breed, never to change it.

When the standard was first written all the breed's supporters would have been familiar with hunting in the Border countries. Nowadays only a minority of its supporters have any knowledge of hunting, many may not even have visited the breed's home country or experienced the Cheviots on a bleak winter's day. It is apparent, therefore, that the breed standard, no matter what form it might take, must assume a degree of knowledge which the majority of its readers will not possess.

The purpose of this chapter is to go some small way towards filling in the background.

An understanding of the breed's purpose is essential to a proper understanding of the standard and of the breed itself. It is essential to breeders, to exhibitors and to judges but is no less essential to those whose prime interest in the breed is as a companion. The breed's job of work formed its appearance, its character, its intelligence, its hardiness and its attitude to life.

In order to try to give some sort of idea of what hunting was like in Border country at the time when the campaign for recognition was being waged, we will rely largely on descriptions made at and prior to that time and by men whose experience of hunting in Border country is not only far greater than our own but probably can't be equalled.

Will Ogilvie writing *With the Border men* for *Bailey's Magazine* of April 1903 described both the Border country and the men who hunted it.

'Out of the heart of the Cheviots lies a little heard of territory, a terra incognita to most, a land of heath and moss, of rock and tussock and stone, where the whaups cry in the daytime and the foxes call at night – a realm of its own from Yeavering Bell to the Carter, where Robson, of Byrness, is King, and Elliott of Hindhope, Prime Minister; where the countries are Elliotts and Smiths and Douglases and Dodds all good men are true, breeders of sheep whose fame has crossed the seven seas, dispensers of hospitality, the name of which has reached the ends of the earth. But it is as Nimrods, as might hunters of the hills, that I would write of the Border men ... In Jacob Robson of Byrness they have an ideal huntsman, keen-eyed as ever to ride over the scars, and his love is a morning meet when the mists are lifting on College Water, and his pride the six or seven couple of grizzle-white hill-hounds that drive along the hillsides at the horse's feet ... It is the sight of a lifetime to see them drawing the glitters as they call the rubbly, rocky, patches on the face of the hill, over Grubbit or Wideopen, and besides them Robson and his henchmen cheering them to their work with the strange wild cries that belong exclusively to the Border men. Then, away in the lead a grizzled white hound owns the line, and then the hills are full of melody as one by one they take it up, and overall you hear the cheer "Forrit For-r-r-rit". It is always "For-rit" where the hillmen ride. You shake up your eager hunter who is clever enough to go forward when he can, but half a mile of climbing on a steep brae and you hear him already beginning to sob, and humanely you catch hold of his head and walk him, and then the hill ponies lob past you at a peculiar hopping canter, climbing without effort. Note the little chestnut as he goes by, breathing regularly and slow without the semblance of distress, with an ear forward to the music and a bright eye on this work, not a scramble or a slip nor half a hoof set wrong – a very master of his craft and glorying in it.

'See, here is somebody with a red Border terrier running lightly at his horse's heels for when the fox, hard pressed, goes to ground under some crags in Hen's Hole or above Kale Water, then comes the terrier's turn, and game with the gameness of everything well-bred, man and horse and fox and hound – the stout heart for the stey brae – will bolt the hunted rover from his refuge or bottle him up till spades arrive. But away on the misty hill top above you the last of the hill bred little horses has disappeared and when at length, after many scrambles and sideslips and girth-deep plunges in a soft place, you reach the crown of the ridge, you see far off on the next range the white hounds streaking up the brown hillside like flies up a window pane, and on the wind comes back their merry clamour and the ceaseless "For-rit, For-r-r-rit". Now the riders are dividing, some to the right, some to the left, riding hard, the white pack and those four men who are climbing straight behind them will be over and into Bowmont Water, or maybe streaking, tireless and keen over the very top of Grubbit with their heads to Kale. Between you and them lies a great gulf fixed, not only that half-mile of tussocked valley, but twenty to forty years of apprenticeship to riding in the hills – a gulf no years nor yearning love of sport can bridge. And so you sit and watch while your horse catches his breath in big gulping sobs, with his ears forward to the far-off music . . . You are not afraid of the fences in the low country, but not for all the gold of Klondyke are you going down over that precipice at a hard gallop.'

Such then is a generalised picture of hunting in Border country, a graphic description of the country but one which fails to mention that all this might have been carried out in the teeth of a damp and freezing easterly wind or against the background of a numbing sleet which saps the life from those not bred to withstand such conditions. All the while the hunt's Border Terriers will be scampering along, sometimes behind hounds, sometimes, having taken a short cut well up with them but always handy to eject Charlie from any place in which he might seek refuge. It is below ground that a terrier's work takes place and once more it is difficult to convey just what this means to those who are unfamiliar either with Border country or with hunting. Perhaps once more we may be allowed to rely on a pen more talented than our own and quote from T. Scott Anderson's *Hound and Horn in Jedforest*. From 1892 to 1903 Scott Anderson was Master of the Jedforest.

'You want for the country a terrier that can run with hounds, or, better still, that can follow up and run behind hounds – the sort that hunts a cover or darts away on a fox's line is useless. If he can be taught and trained to keep back with the second horseman so much the better. You want one that won't tire, but if forward to come up handy when he's wanted, and will "go in" right up to the fox below ground and will speak to him before he tries to tackle him. Jock here is great at this; he goes in like a bolt from a bow, and squeezes right up to the beggar without loss of time, and gives him notice to quit. If he can't get right up to him he will lie up and bark till he is hoarse, and this always lets one know where he is, and saves time if digging is required. He has the amiable habit of coming out then, and waiting and watching to see if his orders are going to be obeyed, for nothing makes a fox more likely and more anxious to bolt, if he has anything left in him at all, than, after having been well sworn at, to find his attacking enemy retire in silence. Then, if his orders are not obeyed, Jock goes in again with even more determination. How he manages I don't know. I think he only says and looks, "cut along out of this or I'll murder you". Anyhow his threats are nearly always promptly acted on, and the fox, feeling far safer above ground though pursued by the pack, than being niggled at and tormented by a little demon in the darkness below ground, once more faces the daylight and often gives a good chase, thanks to dauntless little Jock.' 'Yes,' said Bill, 'I think it's the most tremendous piece of pluck ever exhibited or possible to dream of. Think of it, to crawl up a long pitch dark tight hole right into the earth's bowels, and often filled with ice-cold water, and to boldly attack his unseen foe, a foe his equal in weight, equally savage, and most probably occupying a better position for repelling attack than he does. "Pon my word," it's equal to a man stalking a wounded tiger on foot.'

In 1903 W. D. Drury published *British Dogs: the various breeds* which contained a chapter on and perhaps more importantly illustrations of the Border Terrier. The chapter is important not just because of its early date but because it was written by two recognised authorities on the breed, John T. Dodd who was at that time Master of the Liddesdale and John Robson, ex-Master of the Border Foxhounds.

'When law and order were established on the Borders, the warlike and thieving instincts of its inhabitants found vent in fox-hunting, brock-hunting, etc. As the Cheviot Hills abound in craggy holes and wet moss-runners, good handy Terriers were an absolute necessity, and the result was the creation of two now extremely different varieties of dog – the Border Terrier and the Dandie Dinmont – though both originated in the same place. The latter, brought into prominence by Sir Walter Scott, became a fashionable pet, got into the hands of fanciers, and is now often useless for sporting purposes. The former were bred by the old Border yeomen and shepherd (who all kept their hounds or hound) purely for work. Nothing was used for breeding purposes that would not go to ground and face the hardest bitten fox in existence, and the Border Terriers have retained to a great extent the original characteristics of the late Ned Dunn's and Yeddie Jackson's dogs.

'They stand about 14 in high, are narrow in front, not more than 15 in round the girth, and weigh about 15 lb. They have hard coats, smooth or broken (the

former is preferable), as the case may be. In colour they are red or grey –
brindled, or with dark blue body and tank legs. Occasionally odd liver-
coloured ones are found, but the first named is the favourite colour. The head
is considerably shorter than and not so strong as that of the fox-terrier, and
the ears are half-pricked. As Border Terriers are wanted to bolt, not to worry,
foxes, their jaws do not require the strength of the fox-terrier. Bitches ought
not to average more than 14 lb weight and dogs 16 lb to 18 lb. The colour of
the nose should be black or flesh-coloured. The tail should be undocked.

'Nose (or scenting qualities) is one of the strongest attributes of the Border,
and a really good dog can tell by merely hunting round the strongest earth
whether or not there is a fox at home. Several have been known that would
not go to ground unless there was a fox at home, and some of the brightest
ornaments of the breed have never been known to make a mistake in this
connection.

'It is nothing out of the common for a Border Terrier to go down a vent in
a rock, and be unable to climb back, necessitating continued digging or
quarrying for three or four days. Of course many are never seen again. Whether
they venture farther than the fox and fall down some slit, or whether both are
lost, it is impossible to say.

'To face the moss holes (long runnels of water) formed at the bottom of the
mosses and often a quarter of a mile long, hard coats are a necessity. Many or
even the very hardiest die of starvation after coming out of these holes, and
before they can be carried to the shelter and warmth of the nearest fireside,
which may be five or six miles distant, so sparsely populated is that part of
the Borderland.

'Border Terriers are often left in an earth at a fox many miles from home,
but are generally found to have returned next morning, though sometimes
they do not arrive for several days, and then are frequently badly bitten.

'As stated, the Border Terrier has a good nose, is a keen holer, and will go
to ground in places that almost any other terrier would not look at. He can
follow a horse over the roughest ground of his native country, and yet he is
small enough to follow a fox through any rocky earth. He can stand wet and
cold as well as any breed, and better than most, is very sharp with rats and
other vermin, and at the same time is a sensible, affectionate, and cleanly
companion.'

Let's just imagine a cold November morning at Otterburn, with a
biting easterly wind blowing carrying a Siberian chill. Hounds are put
into a thick covert of gorse and whin, eventually a hound speaks as he
owns Charlie's line.

As the pack gathers about his line, Charlie decides it is time to be
leaving the covert in which he has spent the night. He makes toward
higher ground and a refuge in which he knows he will be safe from
hounds. The way is across the valley bottom and up onto the hill with,

at its foot, the deep peat bogs through which the hounds will own his scent only fitfully and which will sap the stamina of even the fittest horse. As hounds jostle away on his scent they are followed by a couple of Border Terriers and another scampers along behind the first whip's horse. They do not follow the hounds, nor every twist and turn of Charlie's cunning course, but cut corners, seek out the short routes and use their remarkable intelligence to anticipate the line and so stay in contact with the pack. They pick their way through the peat bog and up into the hill, pushing through dense bracken and heather, scampering over sharp screes and over outcrops of rough rock. Charlie knows where he is going and the terriers too know the place. It is a deep earth with a narrow entrance between massive rocks giving into a series of tunnels between the rocks which go possibly forty or fifty feet into the hillside. Generations of foxes have used this place as a refuge. They know it is far too deep to be dug and they know that in it they are safe from both hounds and man. Even with the most resourceful team of terriers in pursuit the fox's knowledge of this deep earth will give him a distinct advantage.

He reaches one of the entrances to the earth and glances back contemptuously at the toiling pack and the tired white lathered horses. He too is panting but that deceptive easy loping stride and his intimate knowledge of the country have conserved his energy. He sees the first of the terriers coming over the brow of the hill, he too covering the ground with an easy, unhurried and economical stride. He knows that his work will soon begin. Charlie turns and squeezes his narrow shoulders and rangy body through the narrow entrance to the earth. Further down a drop of five or six feet worn by countless years of running water must be negotiated before he lies up on a rock shelf well above the earth floor and with a narrow route behind him which leads even deeper into the earth. Behind him he knows that the passages are narrow and tortuous and even for his narrow body not easy to negotiate. He knows that he can lie in one of these narrow, totally dark places and be protected by the enveloping solid rock with only a narrow aperture at his front to defend and the possibility still of further retreat to even greater depths or along a passage which will lead him once more to the hillside where he might again trust his speed to keep him away from hounds.

It is from this seemingly impregnable fortress that terriers have to eject him. They too have to follow where he has led. Through that narrow and complex entrance which would be effectively closed to a terrier which was in any way thickly built or which lacked the agility and suppleness to twist through its narrow confines. The terrier has to negotiate the sharp drop and then climb the other side knowing that Charlie will be waiting above. For a terrier which was short in the leg the task would be impossible and for one which was not totally game, the task would be too daunting. The major part of his work remains ahead; he must in these narrow Stygian passages, some dripping with icy water, others inches deep in freezing mud and all musky with the scent of successive generations of foxes, not only find his quarry but find some way of ejecting him from his retreat. The terrier too knows that should he get injured, should he be unable to get out of this labyrinth, there is no hope of effective help from above ground, he must rely entirely on his own resources. He knows too that Charlie may be in no hurry to move, he may have spent the night feasting on the carcass of a lamb and now will know that it is safer to stay in these passages than to face hounds. Nevertheless, the Border must make him move, farmers are not anxious to lose more lambs, and, even if the job takes many hours, it is a job which must be done.

Such then is the nature of a terrier's work in Border country and such are the demands which have shaped our breed. There is the need for a sociable nature to allow the terrier to work amicably alongside strange terriers, among hounds, among farmstock, and with the members of the hunt. There is also the need for intelligence to pick the best line across a difficult country and to conserve energy for the demanding task which lies ahead, and the need for stamina which can only be the product of total soundness and fitness.

Arthur Heinemann was no admirer of Border Terriers, the chief point against which like others since he said 'is their colour, which often costs them their life, hounds mistaking them for fox or otter in the melee, even white or whitish Terriers often meeting their death in this way'. In our experience it is very rare indeed that hounds make this sort of mistake. We have seen it occur just once and that with a predominantly white terrier and on that occasion it was not colour which was the problem but the scent of otter which clung to the terrier which emerged unexpectedly from a hole into the jaws of an excited and inexperienced hound. If there is any real objection to the use of coloured terriers it arises not from the likelihood of mistakes by hounds but from what Beckford succinctly described as 'awkward people' who may confuse a terrier, particularly a coloured terrier, with a fox. We have known 'awkward people' demonstrate an inability to differentiate between foxes, hares, rabbits, even pheasants and on one occasion heard a confident and stirring yell directed at a discarded tweed hat!

3 Towards Recognition

An application for recognition had been made to and was promptly rejected by the Kennel Club in 1914 and, according to Morris, even earlier attempts to put the breed's affairs on a more formal footing and to form a club had been made, by John Houliston, about the year 1895.

Fred W. Morris was *Our Dogs* terrier correspondent, the son of W. Morris, a noted breeder of Bedlingtons, and a doctor in general practice in Bardon-Mill-on-Tyne. He was said by Theo Marples, the paper's editor, to have 'dabbled' in Whippets, in which breed he produced Ch Black Bess, and in Bedlington Terriers. He was, however, better known for his Wansbeck Field Spaniels. In this breed he was closely associated with Mr F. E. Schofield, whose name will reappear in connection with Border Terriers. Nor was this the extent of Morris's interest in livestock. He was also an authority on Pouter Pigeons. In the north he was accepted as a judge of several breeds but seems, from what he wrote in *Our Dogs*, to have regarded an excursion into the south almost as something akin to a missionary expedition.

Early in 1918 Morris was appointed editor-in-chief of a new weekly column in *Our Dogs* which was to be devoted entirely to terriers. The column was called 'Terrier Tattle' and from 1918 was to provide a platform to put the Border Terrier before the public eye. After seventy years it is impossible to discover what motivated Morris' campaign. He was certainly a fierce advocate for all things British and, in particular, all things that were associated with Northern Britain. He was not, however, one of the breed's traditional supporters and although he made frequent reference to the breed's working abilities and to the importance of retaining these he frequently betrayed very limited practical experience of hunting. Nor can Morris be said to have been motivated by a desire to found a kennel of Border Terriers. He owned a dog called Harry Hotspur and one or two others but none made any sort of mark in the show ring. As far as judging was concerned he was

BORDER TERRIER CLUB.

Registered name of Terrier *Mick* (*Ivo Roisterer*)

Kennel name *Mick* Sex *Boy* Date of birth *Aug 12. 1915*

Breeder *Ursa Drummond* Owner *Mrs Hamilton Adams*

Colour (please describe very exactly) *Dark Red*

I hereby certify that the above Terrier is an efficient worker underground.

(Signed) *John O'Snaith*

Date *Sept 29th 1920* Master of *Coquetdale Fox* Hounds

Ch Ivo Roisterer ('15), one of the very few Border Terriers owned by Hamilton-Adams, the Border Terrier Club's first secretary, earned his working certificate with the Coquetdale Foxhounds when he was five years old. Most Border Terrier owners continue to place great emphasis on working ability.

already sufficiently well established not to need any additional impetus which a successful campaign might provide. Possibly he needed no other motivation than the desire to see a Northern terrier breed given the recognition he thought it deserved but quite possibly the campaign was also welcome because it provided copy for a voracious weekly column. Whatever the reason, the breed is very much in Fred Morris's debt.

Morris's 1915 article introduced a number of topics which have been interminably discussed ever since.

'That the Border Terrier is a very old breed there is little doubt and they are still bred on the Borders for bolting (not worrying) foxes.

'The Border Terrier should have a good nose and be able to go to 'ground' where other breeds could not enter. Border weather is nothing to them, wet and cold being all the same, for hardiness is one of his many assets. No day is too long. Veritable little demons, they live for sport and sport alone. There is no standard of points for the Border Terrier, but the following indicates the size, make and shape and character of the dog.'

Then followed Morris's attempt at a standard for the breed which we will discuss in detail in another chapter; suffice it now simply to record that the standard which Morris claimed had been produced with the help of some of the breed's old supporters was perhaps the first round in his campaign to get the breed recognised by the Kennel Club.

Five years later the campaign was to achieve its aims but unfortunately until mid-1918, the war interfered with the more important matter of published discussion about the breed. In August 1918, however, Morris returns to the major fray to say that 'a great effort is to be made after the war to bring the interests of the Border Terriers more to the notice of the general public. Already this matter is in the hands of several prominent North-country fanciers, who are most enthusiastic over the many pleasing qualities of this game little dog.'

'We in this district,' he wrote, 'and in Wooler, Otterburn and Morpeth, have such an "eye" for a Border Terrier that we may view with suspicion any fancy points being attached to the game little dog, for "little" he is, unlike the small Irish Terriers which to the ignorant pass as the "real native". True, there is no standard of points, although *Our Dogs* published a "standard" which I drew up a few years ago. With the help of such enthusiasts as Mr J. T. Dodd, Mr Strother, Mr O. Owen and Mr F. E. Schofield, I am hopeful that this Terrier will take up a strong position in Terrierdom.

'We understand that the Hexham August Bank Holiday Show will, as usual, give a few classes for Border Terriers. This show has for years now catered for the Borders, and a lady, resident in London, Miss Mary Rew, offers a challenge cup for competition'. That was on May 23 and the following week Morris wrote: 'The Dodd and Robson families are closely identified with the Border Terriers. Both families, who reside in the "wilds of Northumberland", are, we believe connected by marriage. It is good news to know that Mr S. Dodd has consented to judge the Border Terriers at Hexham August Bank Holiday Show, where no doubt a large and representative entry will be found.'

The Miss Mary Rew referred to as giving a trophy to be competed for at Hexham had, in the previous year, also given one to the Eskdale and Liddesdale Agricultural Society, at Langholm. The first winner of this trophy was William Barton's Venus who was declared 'The best Border Terrier in the Showyard', a rather quaint phrase which is engraved on the trophy itself and adds interest to it. After Venus had won the trophy seems not to have been awarded again until after the First World War but in 1920 the winner was Thomas Lawrence's Teri. In 1921 it was again William Barton's turn, this time with Liddesdale Bess. Teri and Liddesdale Bess were to become the breed's first two champions. Sometime in the 1920s the trophy found its way into the possession of the Border Terrier Club and is now awarded for Best in Show at its Open Show.

Pride in winning the trophy encouraged Willie Barton to place a half page advert in the *Illustrated Kennel News* in December 1913. The advert included a detailed review by 'Capsic' which suggested that

730 THE ILLUSTRATED KENNEL NEWS. DECEMBER 12, 1913.

Mr. W. BARTON'S Border Terriers,

at Whitrope, Newcastleton, Roxburghshire.

IN the wild, hilly country on the borders of Scotland and England this but too little known dog has his native home, as his name implies. Here this grand little fellow is appreciated at his true worth, and only needs to be better known in the canine world beyond to become one of the most popular Terriers in the universe, as he is, beyond dispute, the gamest and pluckiest. A small, alert, game-looking dog, 12 to 13 inches from the ground to top of shoulder, between 14 and 16 lbs. weight, with coat of thick-set, hard hair of a dark red colour, rather short in head, but of good width,

of her breed; her record on the show bench is unbeaten, and this year at Langholm she had the distinction of winning the silver challenge cup presented by Miss Mary Rew, the first ever offered for the breed at any show. Nailer, one of her kennel mates, is a great little dog, whose show career is equally good, but it is on the hillside he is seen at his best, where he promises to rival the prowess of his ill-fated sire Rock, whose gameness cost him his life when hunting with the Liddesdale Hounds. Mr. Barton has espoused their cause for many years, and owns the largest and most successful kennel in

run to ground in a moss hole. Bess entered, and after a severe fight, in which she got badly bitten, bolted her fox, who again holed a few miles further on. Another Terrier was entered, who made a game attempt, but failed to dislodge Reynard. Bess again went in, closed with the fox, and fought him for two hours before bolting him, and when he appeared she was hanging on to him. On another occasion, when crossing a linn, she marked an otter amongst some large boulders, and after a struggle, in which she again got badly bitten, she bolted him. A Foxhound who accompanied Mr.

Photos by]

NAILER.

NAILER AND VENUS.

[J. E. D. Murray, Hawick.
VENUS.

powerful jaw, small dark eye, with ears hanging more like those of a Foxhound than a Fox Terrier, narrow in shoulder, straight in leg, and small, round feet, with that "fear-no-foe" expression which stamps him as a Terrier beyond ordinary. This is no chance breed of a nondescript character, but has been bred and kept pure by the Border sportsmen for generations, and breeds as true to type as any of the better-known Terriers. Classes are generally given for the breed at the Border shows, and here Mr. Barton's splendid team has always proved invincible. In the bitch Venus, whose photo we reproduce, Mr. Barton owns the acknowledged best

the kingdom, not only on the show bench but in the realm of sport. In this wild country so many strongholds abound in which foxes take refuge when hunted, that without good Terriers fox-hunting would be impossible. These holes are generally either wet moss holes, often of great length, or slits in the rocks, sometimes 20 to 30 feet in depth. These are very dangerous, and to be of any use a Terrier must be small, active, hardy, with a good nose, and courage above suspicion, and in the Border Terrier these qualities are combined to perfection. Mr. Barton's bitch Bess (now thirteen years old), the dam of Venus, already mentioned, is one of the gamest that ever faced a fox. On one occasion when hunting with the Liddesdale pack a fox was

Barton was laid on, and between them the quarry was hunted up and down stream, Bess putting in some grand work in the deep pools, marking every dive the otter made, forcing him to dive or leave the water. He was eventually cornered, and Bess, watching her chance, closed with him, getting him by the throat, and hung on till he was dead. He proved to be a dog otter of 22 lbs. weight. Many similar incidents I could narrate did space permit, but these may serve to prove to the world of sport the existence and value of a dog whose equal for sterling pluck, gameness and determination has yet to be found; and I hope the day is not far distant when he will receive that recognition which he so richly deserves. CAPSIC.

among the high hopes that the Border Terrier would soon be recognised was also a determination that it would not be ruined as a working terrier by its new career in the show ring.

The review not only extolled Willie Barton's kennel but also provided the growing number of judges who were being called upon to pass judgement on the breed with a brief outline of its characteristics and purpose.

The advert is headed simply 'Mr W. Barton's Border Terriers, at Whitrope, Newcastleton, Roxburghshire' and says that

Not only was Willie Barton's kennel one of the most influential during the years prior to and just after recognition but the influence was to continue for an unusually prolonged period. The kennel's contribution to the breed's development has been consistently undervalued.

'In the wild, hilly country on the borders of Scotland and England this but too little known dog has his native home, as his name implies. Here this grand little fellow is appreciated at his true worth, and only needs to be better known in the canine world beyond to become one of the most popular terriers in the universe, as he is, beyond dispute, the gamest and pluckiest. A small, alert, game looking dog, 12 to 13 inches from the ground to the top of the shoulder, between 14 and 16 lb weight, with coat of thick-set, hard hair of a dark red colour, rather short in head, but of good width, powerful jaw, small dark eye, with ears hanging more like those of a Foxhound than a Fox Terrier, narrow in shoulder, straight in leg, and small, round feet, with that "fear-no-foe" expression which stamps him as a Terrier beyond ordinary. This is no chance breed of a nondescript character, but has been bred and kept pure by the Border sportsmen for generations, and breeds as true to type as any of the better-known terriers. Classes are generally given for the breed at the Border shows, and here Mr Barton's splendid team has always proved invincible. In the bitch Venus, whose photo we reproduce, Mr Barton owns the acknowledged best of her breed; her record on the show bench is unbeaten and this year at Langholm she had her distinction of winning the silver challenge cup presented by Miss Mary Row, the first ever offered for the breed at any show. Nailer, one of her kennel mates, is a great little dog, whose show career is equally good, but it is on the hillside he is seen at his best, where he promises to rival the prowess of his ill-fated sire Rock, whose gameness cost him his life hunting with the Liddesdale hounds. Mr Barton has espoused their causes for many years and owns the largest and most successful kennel in the kingdom, not only on the show bench but in the realm of sport. In this wild country so many strongholds abound in which foxes take refuge when hunted, that without good Terriers fox-hunting would be impossible. These holes are generally either wet moss holes, often of great length, or slits in the rocks, sometimes 20 or 30 feet in depth. These are very dangerous, and to be of any use a Terrier must be small, hardy, active, with a good nose, and courage above suspicion, and in the Border Terrier these qualities are combined to perfection. Mr Barton's bitch Bess (now thirteen years old), the dam of Venus, already mentioned, is one of the gamest that has ever faced a fox. On one occasion when hunting with the Liddesdale pack a fox was run to ground in a moss hole. Bess entered, and after a severe fight, in which she got badly bitten bolted her fox, who again holed a few miles further on. Another Terrier was entered, who made a game attempt, but failed to dislodge Reynard. Bess again went in, closed with the fox, and fought him for two hours before bolting him, and when he appeared she was hanging onto him. On another occasion, when crossing a line, she marked an otter amongst some large boulders; after a struggle, in which she again got badly bitten, she bolted him. A foxhound who accompanied Mr Barton was laid on, and between them the quarry was hunted up and down stream, Bess putting in some grand work in the deep pools, marking every dive the otter made, forcing him to dive or leave the water. He was eventually cornered, and Bess, watching her chance, closed with him, getting him by the throat, and hung on till he was dead. He proved to be a dog otter of 22 lb weight. Many similar incidents I could narrate did space permit, but these may serve to prove to the world of sport the existence and value of a dog whose equal for sterling pluck, gameness and determination has yet to be found; and I hope the day is not far distant when he will receive that recognition which he so richly deserves.'

It is interesting to see that the description of the breed repeats that which had appeared in the magazine just a few weeks earlier, a fact which surely reinforces any claim that may be made to it being the first published standard for the breed. However, Mary Rew, though a staunch and generous supporter of the breed's activities in the ring, felt it necessary in the following week's paper to voice a degree of concern. She expressed her delight in seeing the account and the photographs which she said were the first she had seen in the doggy paper but this delight was tempered by a belief that 'it would be very disastrous if they fell into the hands of such "fanciers" who would doubtless set to work to "improve" them until their heads were 12 in by 2 in wide, and all intelligence had disappeared and their legs either so long that they could no longer go to ground or else so short that half an hour's work on their native hills would tire them out; and, finally, I suppose their coats would have to be pulled out, as that seems the correct thing to do with Terriers of most other breeds. However, we will hope that these drastic measures will never be taken with these cheery little dogs.'

However, we run ahead of our story and must return to Miss Mary Rew, who, besides being remembered as the generous donor of a highly prized trophy, must also go down in Border Terrier history as the owner of Mosstrooper who, in 1913, became the first Border to be registered with the Kennel Club on their register for 'Any other breed or variety of British, Colonial or Foreign dog not classified.'

All was not plain sailing, there were disappointments in store and later, in August 1919, Morris had to record that:

'We understand that the Committee of the Kennel Club, at a meeting held recently, in answer to a correspondent, refused to provide a separate classification on the register for Border Terriers. This is a very great blow to the Border Terrier, and is no doubt the outcome of so many northern agricultural shows providing an extensive classification for the Border Terrier.'

The disappointment was quickly set aside and in the following month Morris was raising two questions which are still endlessly discussed today.

'We are often asked which is the better variety of Border Terrier, the large or the small. There is only one: the small, and one need not be surprised at such a question being asked when so many large ones, especially dogs, are seen at some of the shows. A Border Terrier is a small dog, and should be of the size to enable him to enter to fox, badger, or otter. He bolts the fox etc, and there are occasions when he holds on, and it is astonishing the "hold" a Border Terrier has.

'A difficult question to answer is: "Is trimming needed for show purposes?" No. The Border should be shown in natural coat. The question of a club has been mooted, but this requires careful consideration. Still, the writer will be glad to hear from fanciers on the matter. Possibly a club may get the much-desired "recognition" from the Kennel Club.'

In September too Morris makes mention of a show which had already established itself as an important gathering of Borders, and which eventually was to be regarded as one of the most important shows in the breed's calendar, but sadly has now disappeared from the Border Terrier scene:

'Bellingham show always ran Hexham show very closely for the patronage of the Border Terrier. At Bellingham show the Borderer is always one of the "sights", for here, as at Hexham, many fanciers exhibit only at these shows. The show will be held on Saturday, September 27, and all who admire wild and romantic scenery cannot do better than visit Bellingham.'

In October, Morris again returned to his campaign to get the Border Terrier accepted as a recognised British breed.

'Meeting our Border Terrier friend, Mr John Haddon, the other day, a gentleman who is deeply versed in Border Terrier history, a keen fancier and judge, "bred and born" in the Borderer's country, where he still resides, he made an allusion to a canine matter which is certainly giving much "food for thought" to many Border Terrier fanciers. It is this: Why does the Kennel Club "amend" their classification for "foreigners" – the Alsatian Wolf-dog – and to the writer's knowledge, refuse to "recognise" by classifying in the breed list such a true British dog as the Border Terrier?

'Northerners do no like such "class" distinctions, and are wondering if the so-called Alsatian wolf-dog has got such "recognition" because he has gained the favour of the so-called "upper classes". Let us in all things, even in dogs, be patriotic and let us recognise something of our own manufacture rather than a foreign make.'

In November 1919, Morris received what may be the first public acknowledgement of the success of his campaign but, since this was coupled with a well argued case disagreeing with his arguments about size, the response may well have been received with very mixed feelings and particularly so since the pseudonym of Teri was only a thin veil over the name of Tommie Lawrence, an acknowledged authority on the breed.

'Fanciers of the Border Terrier should be indebted to Mr Morris for the way in which he has brought the breed into prominence through "Terrier Tattle", but in one point I cannot agree with him, and that is re: size. In a recent article from his pen he mentioned that the leading winners were too big. This, in my opinion, is not the case, although I should not advocate any further increase of size than what at present is winning. Their natural quarry are the fox, the otter and the badger, each of which in ordinary circumstances weighs over 18 lb. Add to this the latter's wild life, where agility, cunning and teeth are continuously being brought into play, and then think: "Is it fair that a small Terrier, scaling probably 12 lb or 13 lb should be asked to evict any of the animals named from its lair?" The gameness is certainly in the Terrier, but what is it worth, coupled with a snipey and weak face, which one bite often destroys. The weakness in head is the worst point in most of the Borders, and if we have to add weight to increase the strength of jaw, then weight let it be. I should fix the maximum at about 18 lb for dogs; bitches slightly less.

'The present-day winners scale about that, and I can vouch for their being able to get to ground, having handled several of them at hunts this last season or two. Exhibition of the breed this year has been a strong point, no fewer than 20 entries in one class at Langholm, and 35 in three classes at Bellingham, being recorded, and these shows on the same day. Surely it is time the Kennel Club awoke to the fact that the variety needs recognition, and it is to be hoped

Ch Teri ('16), owned and bred by Tommie Lawrence, was the breed's first champion dog.

all interested fanciers will sign the petitions at present out for this purpose. We should then have something tangible to work upon for framing size-points, etc, and not have so many different types on the bench. Such recognition would also do away with misleading pedigrees and borrowing of dogs for show purposes, which undoubtedly meantime takes place.

'Do not, however, let us forget the original character of the breed – namely gameness, – but if other sporting varieties of dogs can be used in a dual sense, I fail to see how the same cannot be managed with the Border.

TERI.'

However, Morris was anxious to ensure that the identity of his assailant should be known and to the foot of Teri's argument added:

'Mr Thomas Lawrence has placed at the service of breeders his winning Border Terrier, Teri (late Jack). This should be an opportunity to fanciers of this variety which should be eagerly accepted.'

The following week Morris was able to publish a letter from an ally:

'As a fancier of the Border Terrier who has kept working Terriers for the last forty years, I take exception to "Teri's" remarks in your last issue as regards the size of the present-day "Borders", and endorse every word that Mr Morris has said, namely, that they are too big. A dog should not weigh more than 15 lb at most, and the very outside weight for a bitch 12 lb. It is almost impossible for an 18 lb dog of any description to follow a fox, and my experience is that either a fox or an otter bolt ten times better to a little game Terrier than a big one. As for using Borders for badgers, they were never intended for this work, and never bred for it. I would never allow a "Border" of mine in a badger earth if I knew it. They are too hard, as I know to my cost. I am afraid I cannot agree with our old friend Mr Morris as to recognition of the Border by the Kennel Club. What have they done to improve the other Terriers that were used for work?

"A LITTLE GAME 'UN".'

Once more, however, Morris's ally turns out to have feet of clay by arguing against the whole idea of Kennel Club recognition for the breed. Morris typically rises to the challenge and in the following week, 21 November 1919, attempts to down all his adversaries.

'I am sorry that "Teri" who is an ardent Border Terrier fancier, cannot agree with me that many of the Border Terriers are too big, but at the same time "Teri" would not advocate any further increase of size than what is at present winning. On the other hand, "A Little Game 'Un" endorses every word that I have said – namely, that they are too big. "Teri" would no doubt see the "cutting" from "lay" papers on a report of a show where two exceptional judges officiated, and this is a very strong proof that my remarks on "size" are quite acknowledged. At Hexham Show I made it my business to see every Border Terrier there that day, and in conferring with many Border Terrier fanciers we found all agreed that "size" must be curtailed. If "Teri" met many Border Terrier fanciers he would quite easily be convinced, for it is the "cry" at present: "Too big!" I like a dog about 15 lb and a bitch about 12 lb. Another point not to be overlooked is that the Border Terrier should be narrow in front, well ribbed, and not too deep in brisket, as this prevents the dog from getting into a small hole. A good point (if I may call it so) is that the Border Terrier should be easily gripped with the hands behind the shoulders. At one show I noticed that nearly all the competitors were too wide in front. Such dogs could never "enter", and let it be understood that the Border Terrier should not be used to worry but to bolt their fox, etc. I agree with "A Little Game 'Un" that the Border Terrier should not be used for badgers. I have a letter before me in which the writer says: "I got an otter last Thursday. It weighs 19 lb. I thought my bitch was going to be bad, but she is looking better now, although the otter tore her mouth and front paw very badly." The Border Terrier is fast making headway, and I only ask for "recognition" because the Border Terrier deserves it. At the same time I do hope that he will not be "carted" about from show to show, and be nothing else but a "show" dog. My idea is: Recognition by the Kennel Club, a Border Terrier Club, and a club show, say at Hexham, once a year.'

In December Morris returned to his battle for recognition.

'I am adding the names of those who are wishful for their names to appear on the "recognition" petition for the Border Terrier to the Kennel Club. There is still time to add more, and I shall be glad to hear from those who desire their names to go forward. Londoners will get an opportunity to see the game little Border Terrier at the National Terrier Club Show, Westminster (January 15). Three classes are provided, and one thing is certain, no gamer Terrier will be benched.'

Then right at the end of 1919, Thomas Lawrence discards his thin pseudonym and writes to Morris.

'As the writer of the note which you published on Border Terriers in your issue of November 1, under the nom de plume of "Teri", I was gratified to find some criticisms appear on it in your papers of the 14th and 21st ult. I cannot agree with "A Little Game 'Un" as to maximum weight being fixed at 15 lb for dogs and 12 lb for bitches. Certainly foxes can at times be easily bolted with small-weight Terriers, but it will be generally found that in the case of a run fox going to ground, a good strong Terrier is required to evict it. Terriers at the maximum weight mentioned by me (18 lb) can at any time be seen working, and working well, with North-country packs. In fact, I have a letter before me now from the Hon. Whip of the Blencathra Hunt, one of the most famous of hill packs, in which he endorses all I previously wrote on the breed, and also mentions that their Border Terrier bitch scales 16 lb and has never failed them in finding and beating her quarry.

'Further, I might state that the peculiar nature of the ground over which the Hounds, with which these Terriers are used, hunt does not permit of the Terriers being carried on horseback, and it is therefore essential that they have strength to force themselves through rough heather, etc, and reach earths if need be, in a condition to successfully tackle Reynard. You cannot get this with lightweights. The Borders are often used at Badgers, and I would as soon try mine at them as at an otter.

'Regarding recognition by the Kennel Club which is undoubtedly coming, it is not a case of "what have they done to improve other sporting Terriers?" but "what have fanciers done to spoil them?" It is for the latter to say what is required, and the Kennel Club will faithfully carry out the arrangement, and, incidentally safeguard fanciers against irregular practices. Border Terriers, since their inception, have been kept in too few hands, and it is time all admirers of the breed had a chance of obtaining them.

'Now, as to Mr Morris's contributions of the 21st ult. I did see the paragraphs in the local papers re: a certain show, and might inform him that an 18 lb dog could have won there had the entry been in time. This is from one of the judges, who examined him a day or two later. I had also obtained various fanciers' opinions on Borders at Hexham, and they all endorsed Mr Dodds' judging. His decisions, to a certain extent, were a replica of Mr Jacob Robson's awards at Hawick, and this gentleman is recognised all over the Borderland as perhaps the greatest authority on the variety. It is now considerably over twenty years since I had my first hunt with the North Tyne Foxhounds.

'I agree with Mr Morris that a few of the Terriers show a tendency to be wide-fronted and also deep in brisket. This could easily be remedied if care were taken not to overfeed and to give them plenty of exercise. No one, I think, wishes Borders carted from show to show, but if we loan Terriers to hunts during the winter season, we certainly wish some sport with them in summer, and how else can we obtain it than in friendly rivalry in the show ring? Personally I would make it a rule in cup awards, such as Hexham and Langholm, that the Terriers competing for them should be proved as having been at least three times to ground during the hunting season with any recognised pack of Hounds. In neither of the criticisms to which I have referred is mention made of head point. Why should this not be tackled?

Thos. Lawrence.'

With more and more shows beginning to schedule classes for Border Terriers, the problem of finding judges who were genuinely interested in the breed and had at least a working knowledge of it became acute, nor has the problem become any less acute since 1920. A great many Border Terrier exhibitors today would give a heartfelt 'Amen' to the sentiments which came from Morris's pen in March 1920.

'The appointing of judges is now being considered by many of the Border Terrier fanciers, who certainly object to the variety being judged by gentlemen who have no knowledge of the breed and who only see the breed for the first time upon its appearance in the judging ring before them. The matter of appointing judges of the breed at South Country shows must be attended to, and I appeal to those ladies and gentlemen who guarantee classes at South Country shows to insist upon a judge being appointed who has some knowledge of the breed. We in the North are to set the type where we know the dog, his characteristics, and his work.

'I know on this vital point I have the support of all the Border Terrier fanciers.'

Though Morris recognised the dangers of appointing judges who lacked knowledge of the breed he, for the time being at least, remained anxious to welcome to the breed those whose reputations were already well established in other breeds.

In May he was championing the cause of Mrs Lesmoir Gordon, who had an eye for any breed which was increasing in popularity and might therefore be sold from her Bond Street pet shop. The lady appears not to have been completely satisfied with the breed's potential as a saleable item and so took it upon herself to write a standard which, while doubtless well supplied with the characteristics which would have increased the breed's appeal to her pet shop's customers, betrays at best an ignorance and at worst a contempt for the breed's purpose as a working terrier.

'Mrs Lesmoir Gordon writes that she is simply inundated with applications for them at her Dog Bureau in the New Bond Street and very kindly sends us a list of summarised points of the breed as follows:

POINTS OF THE BORDER TERRIER

'Reds are the most-desired colour. To breed dark reds, mate a blue with rich tan legs to a red dog. The puppies from this mating should be mostly dark-reds.

'My fancy for a typical Border is:

'Height 12–13 in, narrow in brisket, straight in shoulder and forelegs, 13 in round the girth, 13–15 lb weight, hard coat either smooth or broken, undercoat fine and dense. Head is shorter and not so strong in appearance as a Fox-terrier, with half-pricked ears carried over the eye. Eyes round medium, black or hazel. Nose black. The jaw, especially the underjaw, is the strongest point and the most powerful of all the Terriers. The teeth must be strong, sound and level in front. Backs should be short and compact and strongly coupled. Tail short and gaily carried. A Border should be alert, smart and perky and full of life.'

Morris must have been torn between his sycophancy and a more honest reaction to what he might well have regarded as a bid to undermine the standard he had published some five years earlier. What the reaction of the breed's traditional supporters was to this extraordinary 'list of summarised points' we cannot now know, but if the editor received any letters on the subject they were not of a sort which he could print. The whole idea of a straight shouldered terrier, with a head not so strong as a Fox-Terrier, with half-pricked ears, round eyes and a short back is not one which would make any sense as a working terrier and to add to this the word 'perky' really was adding insult to injury.

Morris felt that the threat of Mrs Lesmoir Gordon's summary of points was sufficiently strong to warrant a re-appearance of the standard which he had first produced in 1915 but he did make one change to his previous draft, possibly in order to make the breed more widely acceptable, by inserting in the clause on General Appearance the phrase 'that of a small Irish Terrier'. The change illustrates just one of Morris's many inconsistencies about the breed for it had only been in the previous year that he had forcefully expressed his contempt for the 'ignorant' who regarded the Border as like a 'small Irish Terrier'.

In subsequent weeks it was to become apparent that Morris's standard did not enjoy universal support. He was called to task by William Bell of Tweedmouth who was to remain a source of discomfort for Morris.

'Dear Sir,

'As one who breeds and keeps Border Terriers for their work I have been much astonished at times to see some of the correspondence under "Terrier Tattle".

'I noticed on November 4, 1919 that it was made out that they were not fit for badger digging, but here I most strongly disagree, as I have proved by working mine at a badger as well as fox whenever I can, and find that they soon learn the art as well as any other breed.

'Again on January 6, 1920 you say that you agree that the head wants improving. Does this mean that we are to go in for long and narrow heads? If so, I again disagree, as we do not intend them to kill, but to bolt the fox etc.

'Now last week you published a summarised list of points by Mrs Lesmoir Gordon, of the Dog Bureau in London, and I find that some of the said points are the very opposite to what that greatest of all experts on Border Terriers, Mr Jacob Robson, late of Byrness, gave in a letter quoted by Juteopolis in *Our Dogs* of December 10, 1909.

'Mrs Gordon: Colour, red. Height, 12–13 in. Weight, 13–15 lb. Nose black. Ears, half-pricked carried over the eye.

'Mr J Robson: Colour, red or mustard; plenty of the breed are pepper coloured, and some are black-and-tan. Should be able to follow hounds all day. Weight, 15–18 lb. Nose either red or black, but the red-nosed ones are often the keenest scented. Ears ought to hang like a Fox-Terrier.

'I have always myself found that the red-nosed ones are best at finding and marking, though I have had black-nosed ones very hard to beat at work.

'Now surely we sportsmen of the Border are not going to allow a South-Country person to lay down the points when we have such an expert in the breed and requirements of a Working Terrier as the great Veteran sportsman of the Border, Mr Jacob Robson or we may see the down of the breed.

Yours etc

Wm. Bell'

Bell's reply disposed of Mrs Lesmoir Gordon's summary of points and used the opportunity to criticise Morris's own standard. Morris adopted a singular line of defence by agreeing with all his critics.

'The question of experts for judging Border Terriers arouses much interest. For a great number of years now I have attended Hexham show as a judge, exhibitor and spectator. At every show I have paid particular attention to the judging of Border Terriers, and never once have I seen one of the "expert judges" of Border Terriers look or examine the mouth and teeth of any Border Terrier.

'Mr J. R. Haddon writes me that he is taken up with the idea (standard) every way, except size, which is far too big for present-day fox hunting men.

'I agree with Mr Haddon. Captain Pirie says that the only thing he does not like in my standard is "general appearance" – that of a small Irish Terrier.

'Here I also agree with Captain Pirie, but what breed can I suggest for general appearance? I do not wish the Border Terrier to be judged as an Irish Terrier. Nothing of the kind! Lieutenant E. C. Spencer writes, and I feel sure we all agree with his suggestion that what is required is for a club to draw up a scale of points and fix on a definite type, and every scope given to get the opinions of the breeders, the main object being to keep the dog, and not to drift away from working capabilities.'

Morris, having changed his mind about Border Terriers looking like 'small Irish Terriers', in July was trying to improve fronts by suggesting they should have fronts like Fox-terriers, 'real Redmond fronts' he calls them, Francis Redmond being at that time one of the most successful exhibitors of Fox-terriers. The suggestion, redolent of Mrs Lesmoir Gordon's 'straight in shoulder and forelegs' demonstrates how little Morris cared or even knew about the breed's purpose and can hardly have endeared him to the breed's traditional supporters.

Throughout the Summer of 1920 the idea of forming a club began to make progress. Morris suggested that it would be appropriate to hold a meeting to discuss the idea at Richmond on 2 July, where Morris, by no means incidentally, happened to be judging the breed. Not surprisingly the idea seems not to have received enthusiastic support from the breed's northern strongholds and so Morris, though refusing to relinquish the idea of a meeting at Richmond, which, he said, 'is already meeting with strong approval', had to accept that 'it is, of course, quite proper that a meeting shall be called for some suitable venue in the North, probably the Hexham show, so that Northerners may give their valuable suggestions'. But Morris was not going to have things all his own way and on 2 July we find the indomitable Tommy Lawrence writing to the editor of *Our Dogs* to say that 'a meeting would be held at the Hawick Show on 24 July when it is hoped to have an attendance of all the leading breeders, also a representative of the Kennel Club Committee'. Under these circumstances he said there was no point in proceeding with the Richmond meeting, neither will it be in the interests of the breed that Southern Country fanciers 'who know practically nothing about them should have the initial say in the matter'. On 16 July Morris wrote: 'The Border Terrier Club which was first mentioned just on the outbreak of war, is now established, and a meeting will be held at Hexham Show on 2 August. I am now in communication with Mr E. J. Jaquet to have certain particulars brought to the notice of the Kennel Club. In the meanwhile will all those ladies and gentlemen who wrote me kindly do so again.'

By the following week he seems to have got wind of other attempts to form a club. 'It will', he said, 'do the breed a great deal of harm if there are "two Richmonds in the field". The little Britisher must not suffer by falling between two enthusiastic camps. Northerners are entitled to have a voice in all things. In pre-war days it was suggested that a club be formed, which the war only prevented. Therefore the fault is not mine if another club is formed. Why not amalgamate?' The mystery of this other 'Richmond's' identity was solved by Morris's notes the following week.

'A meeting of the Border Terrier Club will be held at Hexham Show on Monday. It will take place outside the judging ring of the Borderers immediately after the variety is judged. From letters to hand I am glad to hear that many fanciers from the "wilds of Northumberland" will be present. I wish fanciers to particularly notice that the game little Britisher will be at Hexham represented by gentlemen who, in many cases, are Borderers themselves, and have known the little dog long before many who now attempt to claim him as their own, and who have during their life probably not seen more than a dozen representatives of the variety.

'From the *Kennel Gazette* it will be seen that Mr T. Hamilton-Adams has applied to the Kennel Club for registration of the title of the Border Terrier Club. I have not the pleasure of knowing Mr Adams, who, I think, was an onlooker at my judging ring at the late Richmond show. If Mr Adams has the welfare of the Border Terrier at heart, he surely should have, at least in the first place, communicated with those who already have the promotion of the Border Terrier Club in hand, and are doing their best for the Border Terrier.'

Thomas Hamilton-Adams was the 'second Richmond', a man who, in spite of being a well known Sealyham exhibitor and having been present at Morris's ringside at the Richmond show, had 'probably not seen more than a dozen representatives of the variety'. It seems that he had simply jumped the gun and without any discussion with any of the breed's supporters had already approached the Kennel Club. But why, we wonder, had the Kennel Club Secretary, E. J. Jaquet, with whom Morris had already established contact in early July, not informed Morris of this second development?

The long awaited Hawick meeting took place on 24 July and, according to Morris, the Border Terrier Club became a reality. 'Provost J. C. Dalgeish was', Morris reported, 'voted to the chair, and there was a large attendance of fanciers present who have the interests of this game little Terrier at heart. After a considerable discussion it was agreed to form a club to be called the Border Terrier Club, and to make representation to the Kennel Club to have the same registered and the breed recognised and admitted to take its place among the various other breeds of Terriers now enjoying that privilege. Mr Jasper Dodd, one of the most experienced breeders of the variety, was appointed president of the new club, Mr Hamilton-Adams secretary, together with a strong and influential committee, composed largely of Border men.'

The report, with its lack of detailed information, only partly hides Morris's disappointment that, after all his hard work, he had been ignored but Morris was nothing if not resilient and, in spite of occasional bouts of petulance, he could rise above personal disappointment in order to further the cause of the breed. Within a couple of weeks he wrote that 'the meeting of Border Terrier fanciers at Hexham did much to clear the air, and after the "Tattle" there we all "buried the hatchet" and are now a united army'.

Meetings at Hawick, Wooler and Hexham had already been held but at none of them had the standard been discussed. The fact is not without importance because the Bellingham meeting was not to take place until 25 September whereas Hamilton-Adams, perhaps again acting on his own initiative, was present at a meeting at the Kennel Club on 1 September at which approval was given not just to the formation of a club and to recognition of the breed but to a breed standard. A report of the meeting appeared in the September issue of the Kennel Gazette.

'The Committee considered the following applications:

1   To grant a separate classification on the registers for Border Terriers.
2   To register the title, "The Border Terrier Club". Mr Hamilton-Adams was in attendance.'

The Secretary read what occurred at a Committee meeting in 1914, when an application was received for a separate classification.

MR HAMILTON-ADAMS (addressing the Committee): Since the beginning of the year over 150 registrations have been made, and here, for instance is a Show at Wooler which I attended, where there was a big entry. (Catalogue of the Show was put in.) I should think there must be between 1,100 and 1,200 dogs on the border. The dogs are mostly local.

A MEMBER: What was the first show?

MR HAMILTON-ADAMS: That was at Hawick, but I have not got a catalogue with me. Great difficulty is experienced in getting people to register their dogs, as they seem to think they cannot be registered if the parents are unregistered.

THE CHAIRMAN: It is an old breed revived?

Yes

What are the points of the Border Terrier?

Weight about 14 lb, head otter shaped, comparatively wide in skull, short broad muzzle with even teeth, ears drop, eyes dark and small. Body medium length, deep ribs, well carried back, but not so sprung as those of a Fox Terrier. Front straight and narrow. Forelegs straight, but with less bone than those of a Fox Terrier. Hindquarters galloping. Coat dense, harsh, with good undercoat. Skin, thick, and colour red, wheaten or grizzle. These dogs run with the pack.

How many members have you?

About 122 (list of vice presidents were read out). They are all Masters of Foxhounds.

Have you got any rules framed yet?

Not yet; I am waiting for the standard of points to be approved.

You want us to give you a separate classification on the register?

Yes, but

A MEMBER: You say about 150 registrations?

Yes but there would be more but for the difficulty of registrations.

Mr Hamilton-Adams then withdrew.

The Committee decided that the application be granted.

The application for the registration of the title, The Border Terrier Club, was granted, subject to the regulations for the Registration and Maintenance of Title of Associations, Clubs and Societies.'

When Mr Morris saw the report he was not slow to offer his far from critical comments but strangely these did not include any comment on Hamilton-Adams's statement that the breed was an old one being revived; perhaps it was better that such a statement should be kept from the breed's old supporters on the Borders for fear that Hamilton-Adams too might require revival.

'The *Kennel Gazette* for September is to hand. It is especially interesting to Border Terrier and Kerry Blue Terrier enthusiasts, in as much as our intrepid friend, Mr T. Hamilton-Adams, who has taken the former under his wing, and been the means of promptly founding a club for this game sporting little Terrier, ably placed its claims before the Kennel Club, which has given official recognition to it as a distinct breed and placed it upon its register. The K.C. has also acknowledged the club of which Mr Hamilton-Adams is Hon. Sec., pro tem., subject to confirmation to the regulations for the registration and maintenance of such clubs. Great credit is due to Mr Hamilton-Adams for his efforts in bringing this old huntsman's Terrier, which has existed in the Border districts for centuries, to the front, and obtaining for it and its new club official Kennel Club Recognition.

'We believe that a few zealots, under the leadership of the Mr F. W. Morris were, before the war and since, banding themselves together with a view of bringing the claims of this game little dog before the general public but whilst they were considering a *modus operandi*, Mr Hamilton-Adams seems to have swooped down on the enterprise, and, Napoleon-like, formulated the framework of a club, and his followers a rough draft scale of points for the breed, and at once gone to the foundation head to get his scheme sanctioned and ratified.

'Mr Morris subsequently lodged an objection against the title being granted to the club of Mr Hamilton-Adams' pioneering, but the K.C. pointed out to him that this objection came too late, as the latter's application had been duly advertised in the *Gazette* and no demur received from anybody.

'These "points" of the Border Terrier, which were submitted by Mr Hamilton-Adams to the Kennel Club, and which are set out in the *Gazette*, no doubt generally fairly represent the desired points in the breed, but are not, we should say, complete or irrevocable in all their details. For instance, it strikes us as being a little irrational that a Border Terrier, which is in the habit of drawing swords with that hard-bitten animal, the otter, as well as the fox, should not require as much bone or heart room as a Fox-Terrier; if, under the circumstances, the scale had provided for a little more in each case instead of a little less, we should have applauded it.'

Morris then saw a chance to put his own claim forward for recognition by the Club and later in September wrote:

'Why should the Border Terrier Club have a secretary residing in Eastbourne? Like scores of others, I hoped that the secretary of such a club would reside in the North.

'I thank that Great Scotch contemporary *The Scottish Field* for its kind allusions to my work for "more years than I care to look back upon", and I say now without any hesitation that unless a resident of the north country is appointed as hon. secretary, another club will be formed.'

It was not until 8 October however that Morris felt at all inclined to give details of the new Club's officers and even then he did so only after the Secretary had provided these details and with them, perhaps, a gentle reminder that they had not previously been published.

'We have been favoured by the Hon. Secretary of the Border Terrier Club, Mr T. Hamilton-Adams, with a list of the officials and standard of points adopted by the Club. They are as follows:

'Vice Presidents: The Duke of Beaufort, M.F.H.; The Lord Charles

Bentinck, M.F.H.; The Lord Chesham, M.F.H.; The Earl of Essex, M.F.H.; The Duke of Hamilton and Brandon; The Earl of Kenmare, M.F.H.; The Earl of Lonsdale, M.F.H.; The Lord Middleton, M.F.H.; The Duke of Northumberland; The Lord Poltimore, M.F.H.; The Lord Southampton, M.F.H.; The Lord Redegor, M.F.H.

'The Committee: Messrs W. Barton, W. Bell, J. Carruthers, Jasper Dodd, R. T. Elliott, J. R. Haddon, T. Hamilton-Adams, T. Lawrence (Moorhouse), T. Lawrence (Scawmill), J. Mowitt, G. Sordy and J. M. Strother.

'Hon. Secretary and Treasurer, Mr Thos. Hamilton-Adams.

'Hon. Assistant Secretary, Mr J. M. Strother (Wooler).'

Here then are those who assumed responsibility for the breed during its early days as a show dog. The Vice-Presidents, without a mere 'Mister' among them, then included a number of masters of foxhounds. The 9th Duke of Beaufort was Master of the Beaufort from 1899 to 1924, Lord Charles Bentinck Master of the Blakeney from 1906 to 1909 and then Master of the South Wold from 1914 to 1920. Lord Chesham was Master of the Old Berkeley from 1918 to 1921 and then the Bicester and Warden Hill from 1922 to 1925. The Earl of Essex was Master of the North Herefordshire from 1919 to 1923 and then the Fitzwilliam from 1923 to 1924.

Hugh, Earl of Lonsdale was Master of the Cottesmore from 1915 to 1921. The 9th Lord Middleton was Master of the Middleton from 1917 and 1921. Lord Poltimore was joint Master of the Dulverton from 1920 to 1940 and it was the previous Lord Poltimore, Master of the Tiverton from 1858 to 1866, who had appointed the Reverend Jack Russell to the living at Black Torrington as a means of helping to solve the old man's financial problems and to ease his remaining years. The family's interest in terriers was therefore well established. Lord Southampton was Master of the Hurworth from 1911 until 1924.

Thus the Vice-Presidents represented a wide section of the English hunting countries but strangely, and perhaps significantly, not the countries which actually gave birth to the Border Terrier.

It is not now possible to be sure of just how far Hamilton-Adams had acted off his own bat before and during the formation of a club and over the business of recognition. It seems very likely that the application for recognition had been made independently of that for which Morris had been collecting signatures during the early part of the year. The list of Vice-Presidents too cannot be said to reflect any sort of contact with or even desire to please the breed's old supporters. Where was Jacob Robson, joint Master and huntsman of the Border, and where was E. L. Dodd, his joint Master? Where was John Straker,

Master of the Tynesdale and where Bartholomew Charlton, Master of the North Tyne? Where indeed was J. G. Dodd, Master and huntsman of the Liddesdale? These were the men who had supported the breed at Border shows, who knew more than anyone about its purpose and who had, in their kennels, the bloodlines which were going to be needed if the breed was to progress. They were all, each and every one ignored and it is to their credit that none seems to have taken offence but continued, just as they had in the past, to work for the betterment of the breed while the aristocratic and sporting 'Johnny-come-latelies' whom Hamilton-Adams had gathered around him quickly and quietly faded from the scene.

Of far more importance than the list of Vice-Presidents was the standard which was approved by the Kennel Club without demur and which appears not to have enjoyed the whole-hearted support of the Bellingham meeting. John Dodd had raised objections to the size. The standard had, according to Morris, called for dogs which were between 14 lb and 17 lb in weight and 13 in and 16 in in height at the shoulder. Bitches were to be not more than 15 lb in weight and 15 in at the shoulder. Apparently John Dodd had argued, in words which have since become very familiar to all Border Terrier breeders 'The Border Terrier is essentially a working terrier, and, being of necessity able to follow a horse, must combine great activity with gameness. We do not desire', he is reported to have said, 'to breed whippets. Do fanciers realise what a dog 16 in at the shoulder and 17 lb in weight is? The Border terrier is to bolt foxes, otters and badgers, and at such a weight and size he would be perfectly useless.' The warning was heeded and what appeared in the standard approved by the Kennel Club was 'weight about 14 lb'.

F. E. Schofield, Morris's old Field Spaniel colleague, also had something to say about the proposed standard. According to Morris he 'voiced a matter which brought forth great laughter. Was it', asked Morris rising indignantly to the defence of his old friend, 'the laugh of the ignorant? – for Mr Schofield was right in his question. He asked what about the "moustache" for the Border Terrier should have what cannot be better termed than a "moustache" for "moustache" it is. Are we to lose sight of this characteristic? I was amazed to hear such laughter, but Mr Schofield has certainly the laugh on his side, and I again say that this characteristic of the Border Terrier must not be overlooked or lost. Border Terriers do not require trimming and this "tuft of hair" or "moustache" must not be "trimmed out" like some other varieties of Terrier. Do not forget this fact, that quite fifty years ago Mr Schofield was breeding Border terriers, and to my certain knowledge – and few know him better than I – Mr Schofield has kept himself in touch with the Border terrier ever since.' We are tempted to wonder whether the laughter might not have come from those who knew the breed in the field and whose prime concern was to preserve its working qualities on which moustaches had little or no influence. But the meeting was prepared for a while at least, to go along with their Napoleon and, as a result, the breed became recognised in the Autumn of 1920.

At the end of the year Morris took stock and he wrote:

'The year 1920 will ever be red-letter year in the history of the Border Terrier, for in 1920 this game British Terrier has been "recognised" by the Kennel Club, a special club has been formed to further the interests of the breed, and a standard of points has been drawn up and accepted. So far so good. It is in the recollection of many how for years I have fought for this "recognition", and advocated a club being formed. With all the above results – and do not forget that *Our Dogs* was the first and only paper which took up the question years before any other doggie paper gave even one line to advocate the claims of the Border Terrier – we Border Terrier fanciers are pleased, and realise that this little dog is now making headway in the fancy.

'We have had classes at several of the best shows in the London district and large provincial cities, and at all these shows much interest has been aroused. At Richmond, where I judged, a very large number of ladies and gentlemen asked me many questions on the breed, and I felt that my propaganda visit to the royal borough had not been in vain. We have had challenge certificates allotted to the breed at Carlisle, Edinburgh and the K.C. show; and every week proves that the Border Terrier has come to stay; but he must be protected from some of his friends ... He is making progress. We have had some remarkable entries at Wooler, Hexham, Bellingham etc, shows, and with a club of over 100 members the day is not far distant when the Border Terrier will have a show of his own – a club show – where there should be a great "gathering of the clans".'

4 Evolution of the Standard

The earliest description of the breed we have yet found is that written by Thomas Robson and quoted by Thomson Gray in 1891. He said that 'they are nearly all drop eared ... colours are red, grey, wheaten, pepper and mustard ... never black, white or fox terrier marked ... (and are) ... nearly always and ought to be small, many of them not half the weight of a Dandie. They should, of course, have a hard, close coat, and good legs and feet.'

In 1909 a more detailed description, provided by Jacob Robson, appeared in *Our Dogs*. 'The favourite colour', he said, 'is red or mustard, although there are plenty of the variety pepper coloured and a few black-and-tan. Their coat or hair should be hard, wiry, and close, so as to enable them to withstand wet and cold. They should stand straight on their legs, and have a short back, not made like a Dandie Dinmont, long backed and crooked. Their ears ought to hang like a Fox Terrier's but this is not a *sine qua non*. A strong jaw is a good point; not nearly so long in the nose as a Dandie or a Scottish Terrier. They may be either red or black nosed, but the red-nosed ones are often the keenest scented.'

There is not much in either description to provide guidance for a judge who was unfamiliar with the breed. Nevertheless the two descriptions do show that the breed's traditional supporters placed some importance on characteristics which were not vital to the breed's essential purpose. They were interested in appearance as well as function.

In September 1913 *The Illustrated Kennel News* published a description of the breed which contains much of the information needed in a standard and which certainly comes closer to being a standard than anything which had previously been published. Even so it is difficult to know how much support it had among breeders and we will show that at least one prominent breeder seemed to have reservations about some of its requirements.

The description read: 'The Border Terrier is not unlike a small Irish Terrier, 12 to 13 inches high, and weighing fom 14 lb to 16 lb. He has a short, well-knit body, with a hard wiry coat, of a rich reddish hue for preference, though blues, too, are frequently seen. His head is rather short, but of good width, with jaws of tremendous power. The ears are carried well back, like those of a foxhound, with a dark, piercing eye. The shoulders should be narrow with a straight front, and the feet small and round. He must not be too low to ground, as he frequently has to gallop many miles with the huntsmen.' The description then goes on to explain that 'the Border Terrier has been very little exploited though several of the Border shows for some years past have provided classes which always fill well. Many owners of these gallant little dogs are loath to see him benched, as in their opinion his value as a game and sturdy sportsman, the foxhunter's friend, would be prejudicially affected, and the game, hard-bitten little Terrier, the hero of many a fight in craig and moss, become "my lady's lapdog".'

As a basis for making decisions at shows the description has several and obvious defects. It offers no guidance about the ideal build for a Border, it says nothing about size or about temperament. Nor does the description appear to have had the whole-hearted support of one of the leading breeders. Willie Barton advertised in the magazine in December and in his advert made use of the description though he omitted both the reference to small Irish Terriers and to a short, well-

Harold Chadwick's grandly named King of the Borders whelped about 1912.

knit body. We can only assume that he did not agree with these parts of the description.

In 1915 Fred Morris published his attempt at a standard. It was radically different from anything which had gone before and, according to Morris, had been written with the help of some of the breed's old supporters, though he did not go so far as to claim that the finished product had their support. The 1915 'Morris' standard said that:

'Head very much shorter and stronger than that of a fox-terrier in jaw. Skull moderately strong and not flat on top. Eyes not too small; bright and keen. Ears rather small, filbert shaped, dropping close to the head, neck fairly long, strong and arched somewhat.

'Body medium length, narrow in front, well ribbed, not too deep in brisket, as this prevents the dog from getting into a small hole, strong hindquarters. The largest sized dogs should easily be gripped with the hands behind the shoulders. Tail rather short, undocked, set on low and slightly curved, but not curled.

'Legs and feet. Straight forelegs, cat-like feet with good pads and toes closely knit together. Coat wiry and weather resisting with the hair not too long and lying fairly close to the body with a good undercoat. This class of coat is to be preferred for the moss or peat holes. Old fanciers prefer the dog free from topknot and do not care for the very broken coat. Colours: red or grey-brindled, with a dark blue body and tan legs. Livers are often found but red is the favourite colour, with dark muzzle and dark velvety ears.

'Size about 14 inches high at the shoulders and weighing about 14 or 15 pounds.

'The Border Terrier is clean in his habits, very intelligent, affectionate and as a companion cannot be surpassed. Of late many fanciers in the South of England have "taken up" this game little terrier.'

The main body of the standard displays a far greater awareness of the essentials of a working terrier than is usually to be found in Morris's writing. The stress which is laid on the need for a strong jaw, and neck, on a straight, narrow front; on the difficulties which can be encountered by a terrier with an over deep brisket and on the importance of a weather resisting jacket and good undercoat all add weight to Morris's claim that the breed's old supporters had had a hand in producing the standard. Perhaps Morris's own priorities can be seen in the references to filbert shaped, velvety ears; to the breed's clean habits and its affectionate nature. Perhaps too Morris's influence can be seen in the fact that he chose to refer to the importance of a good nose, to its hardiness, its stamina and its love of sport not in the standard itself but in a preamble to it. Such matters would have little bearing on the breed as a show dog but are absolutely vital to its role as a working terrier.

The next standard to appear in print was that which accompanied Hamilton-Adams's successful application to the Kennel Club for recognition. However, this standard was never used, being immediately set aside in favour of that produced at the Bellingham meeting which was then adopted by the newly formed Border Terrier Club. Nevertheless the Hamilton-Adams standard is not without interest and appears to have been every bit as influential on subsequent standards as was the Morris standard.

The Hamilton-Adams standard said 'weight about 14 lb, head otter shaped, comparatively wide in skull, short broad muzzle with even teeth, ears drop, eyes dark and small. Body medium length, deep ribs, well carried back, but not so sprung as those of a Fox Terrier. Front straight and narrow. Forelegs straight but with less bone than those of a Fox Terrier. Hindquarters galloping. Coat dense, harsh, with good undercoat. Skin, thick, and colour red, wheaten or grizzle. These dogs run with the packs.' The standard introduces for the first time both the comparison with the head of an otter and the need for a thick skin; both are still part of the standard. The description of the hindquarters as 'galloping' has now been changed to 'racy', hardly a major change. Comparison with Fox Terriers has, however, been dropped. In 1920 Fox Terriers were a very popular breed familiar to all who attended shows and so provided a reasonable point of reference. Nowadays they have fallen from popularity and have moved very much further away from their role as working terriers. Comparisons between the two breeds would no longer be helpful.

Then in 1920 came the Border Terrier Club's own standard, which said:

The Border Terrier is essentially a working terrier and being of necessity able to follow a horse, must combine great activity with gameness.

N.B. The points following are placed in their order of importance.

Size: Dogs should be between 14 lb and 17 lb in weight and 13 inches and 16 inches in height at shoulder. Bitches should not exceed 15 lb in weight and 15 inches in height at shoulder.

Head: Like that of an otter, moderately broad in skull, with short, strong muzzle, level teeth, black nose preferred, but liver and flesh coloured not to disqualify.

Eyes: Dark with keen expression.

Body: Deep, narrow, and fairly long, ribs carried well back, but not over-sprung, as a terrier should be capable of being spanned by both hands behind the shoulder.

Forelegs: Straight, not too heavy in bone.

Feet: Small and cat-like.

Stern: Short, undocked, thick at base, then tapering, set high, carried gaily, but not curled over the back.

Hindquarters: Racing.

Coat: Harsh and dense with close undercoat.

Skin: Thick. Colour red, wheaten, grizzle or blue and tan.

Disqualifications: Mouth undershot, or much overshot.

This standard introduced requirements which had not previously been mentioned or which were different from what had previously been required. The description of the body introduced the word 'deep' and relied on whether or not the terrier could be spanned as the only control over depth. Earlier descriptions had placed some stress on the problems which would arise if a terrier was too deep in brisket. Previous descriptions had also favoured low set tails whereas now they were required to be set high. Pictures of terriers of the period invariably show low set tails. As far as size is concerned it appears that the school of Tommie Lawrence had prevailed the preferred weights were considerably greater than some previous descriptions had favoured and were associated with heights which would have produced a very racy terrier. They were, however, compatible with the classic 14 lb/14 inches touchstone which had for so long been used as a guide by many who bred terriers intended to run with hounds and to work primarily to fox.

Jacob Robson had said that Borders should be short backed but was comparing them with the exceptionally long backed Dandie Dinmont. Morris had said the back should be of medium length as had Hamilton-Adams while the Border Terrier Club suggested that a 'fairly long' body was correct. In fact the differences are far more apparent than real and do not suggest any real disagreement about the necessity of avoiding a short back which would not give the terrier the flexibility it needs underground.

It was, however, on the question of size that there seemed to have been most disagreement. John Dodd, joint Master of the Liddesdale and a vociferous antagonist of the entire idea of recognition, had voiced his objections to the size clause saying that Border Terriers should not be Whippets. He was to play a major role in the formation of the short-lived Northumberland Border Terrier Club and doubtless had a considerable influence on the standard which the club drew up:

The Border Terrier should be a real sporting terrier, and not too big.

1 Dogs 14 lb. Bitches 13 lb maximum.

2 Head, otter shaped. The skull should be flat and wide.

3 The jaws powerful and not pointed.

4 Nose, black or flesh coloured.

5 Ears, small and curved rather to the side of the cheek.

6 Neck, moderate length, slightly arched and sloping gracefully into the shoulder.

7 Not too long and well ribbed up body.

8 Chest narrow.

9 Shoulders long, sloping and set well back.

10 Legs, true and muscular and not out at the elbow.

11 Coat, wiry and hard with good undercoat.

12 Tail, well carried and not curled over the back.

13 Mouth, level: under shot or pig jaw no use.

It is temptingly easy to concentrate on the differences between the two clubs' standards but their similarities are of far greater significance. Both standards agreed that the head should be broad and otter-like, the jaws strong. They agreed too that the ears should be small and the coat hard and wiry with a close undercoat. They both thought that the forelegs should be straight and the shoulders narrow and the body of fair length. Both too were adamant that faulty mouths should not be tolerated.

It was in their attitude to size that disagreement was concentrated. Tommie Lawrence's arguments had led the Border Terrier Club to adopt a top weight of 17 lb while the Northumberland Club responded to John Dodd's determination 'not to breed Whippets' by setting the maximum weight at 14 lb. Both clubs quickly realised that they had been pushed into opposing extremes and within a very short time the Border Terrier Club standard had been changed to 13 lb to $15\frac{1}{2}$ lb for dogs and $11\frac{1}{2}$ lb to 14 lb for bitches. The Northumberland Club changed their standard to 'dogs 15 lb, bitches 14 lb' and so the major difference between the two had disappeared.

The Border Terrier Club's standard was again revised sometime prior to 1926 when Rowland Johns was able to include the new version in his book *Our Friends the Lakeland and Border Terriers*.

The Border Terrier is essentially a working terrier and, it being necessary that it should be able to follow a horse, must combine activity with gameness.

Weight: Dogs 13 to $15\frac{1}{2}$ lb, bitches between $13\frac{1}{2}$ and 14 lb.

Head: Like that of an otter, moderately broad in skull with a short strong muzzle, level teeth, a black nose is preferred, but a liver or flesh coloured one is not objectionable.

Eyes: Dark with keen expression.

Ears: Small V-shaped of moderate thickness and dropping forward close to the cheek.

Loin: Strong.

Body: Deep and narrow and fairly long, ribs carried well back, but not oversprung, as a terrier should be capable of being spanned by both hands behind the shoulders.

Forelegs: Straight and not too heavy in bone, feet small with thick pads, stern moderately short and fairly thick at base, then tapering, set high and carried gaily but not curled over the back.

Hindquarters: Racing.

Coat: Harsh and dense with close undercoat.

Skin: Thick.

Colour: Red, wheaten grizzle and tan, or blue and tan.

	Points
Head, ears, neck and teeth	20
Legs and feet	15
Coat and skin	10
Shoulders and chest	10
Eyes and expression	10
Back and loin	10
Hindquarters	10
Tail	5
General appearance	10
TOTAL	100

Apart from the fact that the description of the mouth had been made very much less forceful than either the Border Terrier Club's previous standard or that of the Northumberland Club, a change which cannot have pleased working people or had any beneficial effect on the breed, the major change was the introduction of a scale of points. This was intended to ease the task of judges and is a method still used in some countries, but not in Britain.

Once more, the change was one which had been entirely prompted by the needs of the show ring and had nothing whatsoever to do with the breed's work. Indeed the scale of points suggests that the priorities of those who had approved the Border Terrier Club's original standard less than six years previously were already being set aside. The original standard had emphatically placed size as the most important of all the breed's characteristics whereas this new scale of points did not even mention size and presumably expected it to be included among the 10 points allocated to General Appearance.

The next change, which took place some time during the 1930s was the last undertaken by the breed to be of any real significance and resulted in a standard which was to remain unchanged for over fifty years. Such a period of stability is by no means unusual, though few, if any, have maintained faith with their original purpose or with the primary intention of their standard in the way in which have Border Terriers. In spite of all the problems and counter attractions, Border Terriers are still genuine working terriers not only capable of doing the job for which they were intended but still actively associated with work.

The revised standard was:

Characteristics: The Border Terrier is essentially a working Terrier, it should be able to follow a horse and must combine activity with gameness.

Head and Skull: Head like that of an otter, moderately broad in skull, with a short, strong muzzle, a black nose is preferable but a liver or flesh coloured one is not a serious fault.

Eyes: Dark with keen expression.

Ears: Small V shaped of moderate thickness and dropping forward close to the cheek.

Mouth: Teeth should have a scissor like grip with the top teeth slightly in front of the lower, but a level mouth is quite acceptable. An undershot or overshot mouth is a major fault and highly undesirable.

Neck: Of moderate length.

Forequarters: Forelegs straight and not too heavy in bone.

Body: Deep and narrow and fairly long, ribs carried well back, but not over sprung as a terrier should be capable of being spanned by both hands behind the shoulders.

Hindquarters: Racy, loin strong.

Feet: Small with thick pads.

Tail: Moderately short and fairly thick at the base then tapering, set high and carried gaily but not curled over the back.

Coat: Harsh and dense with close undercoat. The skin must be thick.

Colour: Red wheaten, grizzle and tan, or blue and tan.

Weight and Size: Weight dogs between 13 and $15\frac{1}{2}$ lb, bitches $11\frac{1}{2}$–14 lb.

	Points
Head, Ears, Neck and Teeth	20
Legs and Feet	15
Coat and Skin	10
Shoulders and Chest	10
Eyes and Expression	10
Back and Loin	10
Hindquarters	10
Tail	5
General Appearance	10
	100

In 1980, what at first appeared to be a threat to the standard which had served the breed so well for so many years appeared. It was the result of a hasty decision taken at a World Conference of kennel clubs which was intended to promote international unity of breed standards. The basis of the decision was that all standards should comply with an order of clauses favoured by the American Kennel Club, though not adhered to by many American standards. It eventually transpired that the Kennel Club was the only body which took action as a result of the decision and so the cause of international unity of standards was probably hindered rather than promoted. However, the Kennel Club had already begun to examine standards with the intention of removing or modifying any requirements which might predispose a breed to hereditary problems. There was no suggestion that the Border Terrier standard contained any such clauses, but, in spite of the wish of all the breed clubs that the standard should not be changed, it quickly became apparent that the breed could not escape the effects of the exercise.

Fortunately, the clauses in the breed standard were already arranged in the required order but three, those covering General Appearance, Temperament and Movement, were missing. All were adequately covered by the existing standard but the Kennel Club nevertheless insisted that each should appear as a separate clause.

In addition, the Kennel Club, much as they had done when adding the clause which covered, for every breed, the question of dogs which were not entire, insisted on adding a clause which gave guidance on how faults should be assessed. Advantage was taken of this clause to further reinforce the importance of faults which might detract from the breed's essential purpose and the changes were therefore such as might have received the approval of the standard's authors.

In fairness to the old Northumbrian farmers, who wrote the original standard, and to the present breed clubs it should be pointed out that the pidgin English used in the revised version of the standard, as approved by the Kennel Club at their meeting on 15 April 1986, is not theirs. The phrasing was imposed by the Kennel Club in an effort to achieve brevity.

Breed Standard of the Border Terrier

General Appearance: Essentially a working terrier.

Characteristics: Capable of following a horse, combining activity with gameness.

Temperament: Active and game as previously stated.

Head and Skull: Head like that of an otter. Moderately broad in skull, with short strong muzzle. Black nose preferable, but liver or flesh coloured one not a serious fault.

Eyes: Dark with keen expression.

Ears: Small, V-shaped; of moderate thickness, and dropping forward close to the cheek.

Mouth: Scissor bite, i.e., upper teeth closely overlapping lower teeth and set square to the jaws. Level bite acceptable. Undershot or overshot a major fault and highly undesirable.

Neck: Of moderate length.

Forequarters: Forelegs straight, not too heavy in bone.

Body: Deep, narrow, fairly long. Ribs carried well back, but not over-sprung, as a terrier should be capable of being spanned by both hands behind the shoulder. Loins strong.

Hindquarters: Racy.

Feet: Small with thick pads.

Tail: Moderately short; fairly thick at base, then tapering. Set high, carried gaily, but not curled over back.

Gait: Has the soundness to follow a horse.

Coat: Harsh and dense; with close undercoat. Skin must be thick.

Colour: Red, wheaten, grizzle and tan or blue and tan.

Size: Dogs 5.9–7.1 kg (13–15½ lb); Bitches 5.1–6.4 kg (11½–14 lb)

Faults: Any departure from the foregoing points should be considered a fault and the seriousness with which the fault should be regarded should be in exact proportion to its degree and its effect on the terrier's ability to work.

Note: Male animals should have two apparently normal testicles fully descended into the scrotum.

© The Kennel Club 1986

The clause which describes the breed's general appearance states, quite simply, 'essentially a working terrier' which is to say that everything about its appearance should be suggestive of its function and should both reflect and contribute to the job for which it is bred. The clause demonstrates the importance of function, which is also emphasised elsewhere in the standard, and suggests that the Border Terrier should not be glamorous, pretty or dandified but should rely for its appeal on the sort of beauty to be found in any animal which has been superbly constructed for a particular job of work. In our opinion, the clause remains remarkably similar to the standard presented at Bellingham in 1920. It is only by a close relationship between form and function that the excesses of fashion can be avoided and, even if the day comes when Border Terriers will no longer be allowed to follow their original calling, it will be necessary to understand all that the phrase implies if the breed is to be protected from well meant but destructive 'improvement'.

It is sometimes suggested that the phrase 'able to follow a horse' is on the one hand asking too much and on the other too vague. It is argued that no terrier could hope to keep pace with a horse. The suggestion betrays an ignorance of the way terriers are used in Border country.

Border Terriers running with hounds are expected to 'follow a horse' in much the same way as a mounted follower follows hounds. They use their intelligence, experience and awareness of their own capabilities to find a way across country which will keep them in touch with hounds. A Border Terrier does not slavishly follow hounds any more than a mounted follower slavishly follows every twist and turn which hounds may take. As for the standard's lack of precise reference to the type of horse which a Border Terrier is expected to follow we may assume that since anyone hunting in Border country is as unlikely to be mounted on a Shetland pony as on a Shire carthorse. The type of horse referred to is the type likely to be used when hunting in Border country.

All the versions of the standard are unanimous in their requirement that the Border Terrier must combine 'activity with gameness'. The 1920 standard emphasised the point by referring to 'great activity'.

The standard also calls for 'gameness' but this is a quality which can only be properly assessed in the field. Gameness should never be confused with a quarrelsome or aggressive nature. A terrier which will not amicably accept the presence of other dogs would be useless as a working terrier and particularly for the way in which Border Terriers are traditionally used. A terrier which did not have a reliable and sociable disposition simply couldn't be run freely with hounds or among farm stock and could not be worked alongside other terriers. The 'terrier spirit' which is often commended in some other terrier breeds is in fact little more than a perversion of the temperaments needed in any genuine working terrier and is, more often than not, also an indication of cowardice and stupidity. In the ring, all that a judge can hope to do is look for some indication that a terrier, when faced with a fox, might respond gamely. An intelligent curiosity, a lively manner and a refusal to be disturbed by unexpected sights and sounds coupled with an air of confidence and quiet determination are perhaps the best indications.

The new clause which describes the breed's temperament is, perhaps, the least satisfactory in the standard. It says little about temperament and exists only, on the one hand, because of Kennel Club determination to have a temperament clause and, on the other, because the clubs were equally determined that no new phrases should be added to the standard.

Once it is accepted that the breed is 'essentially a working terrier' then all is known that needs to be known about its temperament. It must be able to mix amicably with other dogs and with farm stock. It must readily accept being handled by strangers.

Morris's very first standard gave the impression that he was anticipating the description of head and skull which appeared in 1920 and which has remained essentially unchanged to this day. He described the head as much shorter and stronger than that of a Fox-terrier in jaw, and the skull as moderately strong. By 1920 the head was being described in the standards of the rival clubs as 'like that of an otter', surely an inspired description. The head is perhaps the physical characteristic which most obviously differentiates the Border from all other terrier breeds. Without the characteristic otter-like head, the Border might be just another little brown terrier.

The skull throughout has been described as 'moderately broad', while the description of the muzzle has been unequivocally 'short and strong'. There have been times when some breeders have sacrificed strength in an attempt to produce extreme shortness while others have sometimes argued that a longer muzzle imparts greater leverage and so improves strength. We need do no more than reiterate that the standard has always called for a muzzle which is both short and strong.

The likeness to an otter is not something which can be carried down to the last detail of the head. Border's and otter's ears are, for example, very different. The similarity stems from the flow of line from the nose, across a short, broad and strong muzzle, up a shallow and rather sloping stop and over a skull which is broad and flat. The smooth line then continues into a very slightly arched neck. Sometimes the otter-like appearance is enhanced by carefully sculpted hair and whiskers. It should not rely on furnishings but rather on the basic shape of the head itself. There is almost something reptilian about the smooth lines of both a Border's and an otter's head which also share an expression which is at times fiery, sometimes rather soft, seldom, if ever, hard, never mean and always giving an impression of implacable determination.

In the 1920 standard the bite was described as 'level' though an 'undershot or much overshot' mouth was regarded as a disqualification. By 1926, this disqualification had been dropped and it is not difficult to imagine the troubles which arose as some breeders used this as an excuse to breed from and to show terriers with less than perfect mouths. Nowadays, the clause has again been tightened, though not to the point where a Border with an imperfect mouth may be disqualified.

Eyes in 1920, in 1926 and nowadays are succinctly described as 'dark with keen expression', in 1915 Jacob Robson had described the

Otter heads showing the characteristic, almost reptilian, line from nose to neck which contributes so much to the Border Terrier's otter-like appearance.

expression as piercing but the only reference to size is Morris's 'not too small'. There has been no attempt to describe their shape.

The description of ears has, even from Morris's rudimentary 1915 standard, remained essentially unchanged as far as size and shape are concerned. We must admit to an affection for Morris's reference to the ears as 'filbert' shaped but perhaps the shape of a filbert nut is no longer universally known and so would contribute little to our knowledge of the desired ear shape. We remember, some years ago, John Renton describing the ideal tail as shaped like the tine of a harrow. He was surprised when we suggested that there may be some Border Terrier owners whose lives were not enriched by a daily familiarity with harrows let alone tines but was nevertheless prepared to amend his analogy. After thinking for some time, he suggested that a more readily understood comparison might be with the shape of a Dobies Intermediate carrot with which, we suspect, many Border Terrier owners will be no more familiar than with filberts or harrows.

It is interesting that nowhere in the standard does there appear to have been any reference to the colour of the ears. Such a cosmetic point would simply not have interested the working people who produced the original standard but even Morris whose concern for working ability was perhaps more apparent than real did not think the point of sufficient importance to warrant a mention.

As far as the shape of the ear is concerned, V-shaped ears of moderate thickness are less likely to be damaged than are rounded ears or ears which are paper thin. Equally fleshy ears would heal more slowly should they be damaged while a small ear or one which did not lie snugly against the cheek would not provide the required degree of protection to the inner ear when a terrier was working below ground.

The present standard describes the necks as 'of moderate length', reintroducing the word 'moderate' which recurs throughout the standard. Morris's description was possibly more meaningful in that it said 'fairly long, strong and arched somewhat'. Strangely neither the 1920 nor the 1926 standards contained any reference to the neck though the importance of an adequate description is obvious. The length of the neck is, to some extent, a product of shoulder construction. An upright shoulder tends to shorten the neck while a well-laid shoulder imparts length. An upright shoulder would also restrict a terrier's range of movement and agility as well as impairing its ability to traverse difficult terrain. For a working terrier, there is also another disadvantage. In a narrow earth a terrier has little room for manoeuvre. One with a short neck resulting from poor shoulders may find it difficult to get into a restricted space and once there might be unable to retract its feet behind protective jaws.

Forelegs are and were required to be 'straight, not too heavy in bone'; again the requirement has not been changed over the years, and is, in its terse way, perfectly adequate to describe the feature. It is true that some pedantic souls have asked how heavy is too heavy. The word 'moderate' would seem appropriate.

Lord Henry Bentinck and 'Ikey' Bell, perhaps the two greatest breeders of Foxhounds, were adamant that the excessive bone with which old fashioned Foxhounds were furnished was a 'useless appendage' which greatly restricted their speed and activity. Modern methods of rearing, especially when compared with those which Border Terriers had to endure during their early development, have a strong tendency to increase size and substance and perhaps to an extent would reduce their ability to do the job for which the breed is intended.

The body is described as 'deep, narrow, fairly long', another description which has stood the test of time though, once more, one which requires a modicum of background knowledge and commonsense in fathoming its precise meaning. We might, in the light of what nowadays appears to be happening in the ring, draw particular attention to the word 'narrow' and particularly associate it with correct shoulder construction and ribs which are not over sprung, again a phrase which has appeared in successive standards and which in its turn can be associated with the fact that a Border 'should be capable of being spanned by both hands behind the shoulder'.

When the standard was written, by hunting men living in a very masculine world, there seems to have been no thought that the Borders might one day be judged by ladies, some of whom would have small, lady-like hands. Of course the phrase refers to the span of a grown man's hands but is nevertheless still a very good way of assessing a terrier's ability to negotiate tight places. The process of spanning also gives a perceptive judge a great deal of other information. Many judges will span a dog after they have completed their examination on the table. They will lift the dog off the table and place it on the floor. Doing so not only allows them to measure the ribcage but also gives information about the terrier's balance, of the way it 'comes to hand'. The phrase is one which is difficult to define. It refers to a quality of overall balance, of ease and a lack of exaggeration. Lifting a dog off the table while spanning it also tells a judge something about the way it will submit to being handled by strangers and thus of its temperament.

A terrier with a weak or short loin would not have the strength necessary to stay with hounds or the flexibility to manoeuvre underground. Some schools of thought like a level topline, others a slight arch over the loin but if this arch is a roach, resulting from a weak loin which also produces the pronounced tuck-up to be found in a Bedlington or Whippet, it must be regarded as wrong. Both these breeds are built for sprinting speed, not for stamina, and stamina is essential to a Border Terrier. Once more the Foxhound may be used as a guide to what is required.

Reference to hindquarters as 'racy' may possibly be regarded as too terse yet successive amendments have not found it necessary to change the description in any way at all. In order to appreciate what is mean by 'racy' we would suggest that a Foxhound's quarters should be examined. The similarity is remarkable and perhaps essentially so since both are expected to traverse the same ground. There are interminable discussions about what should be regarded as the correct degree of angulation of the hind leg. Similar discussions go on among Foxhound

Ch Ivo Roisterer ('15), the only champion owned by Hamilton-Adams and, like so many of the period, out of unregistered and largely untried stock.

breeders and we can do no better than refer to Daphne Moore on the subject. In her *Book of the Foxhound*, she wrote: 'there are two schools of thought regarding the hindleg, some people liking a rather straight variety comparable with that of a horse, whilst others advocate a hindleg with a degree of angulation, though this does not of course, refer to the weak 'sickle' hock occasionally met with, and which may be described as the divergence from a straight line which, in a good hock, should extend from the point of the hock to the ground. In either case, the hock should be well let down; the nearer to the ground the Os Clacis (or the point of the hock) the faster the hound.'

The degree of angulation to be found in a cart horse intended for pulling heavy loads and not for moving at speed across a difficult terrain is not wanted. Equally a straight stifle would deprive a terrier of the drive and agility it would need to travel across country. Once more we would commend the word 'moderate' to describe the appropriate degree of angulation.

The 'racy' quality is partly a product of the position of the hock joint. In one such as Daphne Moore describes, low to the ground would produce a racy hindleg while a higher joint would tend to produce a greater bend of stifle and less raciness.

The feet are described as being 'small with thick pads' though the original standard used the word 'cat-like' as did Morris. The need for thick pads, for any animal required to cross a rough country, is obvious;

thin pads or open feet would quickly be damaged and would thus lame the terrier. The terrier's weight should be evenly distributed over the whole foot, the nails should wear evenly and themselves be sound, not hollow. The foot should be arched and muscular not thin or fleshy.

The word 'moderately' reappears in the description of the correct tail, more appropriately, perhaps, referred to in earlier standards as the 'stern', which has not materially changed since the first standard was written. The important words are 'moderately short and thick', a long, thin tail, though arguably having little or no effect on a terrier's ability to work, detracts considerably from the overall appearance, especially since, as so often seems to happen, it is excessively proud of this untypical appendage and carries it curled over its back in the position which Foxhound breeders describe with such vehemence as a 'gay stern'. Strangely the standard has never said whether the tail should be docked or not. It should not. Border Terrier breeders are expected to have the skill to breed tails of the required length without having recourse to surgery in order to produce a desirable appendage.

Another clause which has been added is one which describes the breed's movement. The standard has always said that the Border Terrier should be capable of following a horse. The new clause which describes gait repeats this and so avoids the trap of attempting the impossible and unnecessary by trying to describe movement in detail. It takes only a little commonsense to realise that a terrier expected to stay with hounds must be able to move quickly, efficiently and economically. Any which move in an exaggerated way plaiting, dishing, weaving or with a hackney action in front or with weak or excessive drive behind would be unlikely to stay with hounds. Exaggerated movement may look attractive going round the ring but would certainly limit a terrier's ability to go further or over rougher ground. As Daphne Moore says of hounds 'flashiness should never be mistaken for drive'.

The correct coat is described as 'harsh and dense with close under-coat' and the description is another which has survived through successive standards. A jacket which will withstand the worst of Northumbrian winter weather is an obvious must for any dog expected to spend its working life in just such conditions and for a terrier which will often be called up on to work below ground in freezing cold water the difference between a good jacket and a poor one may in fact mean the difference between life and death.

But a harsh, double coat is not the only protection needed by a working Border Terrier. He also needs a thick skin, as, in a somewhat different sense, do judges and successful exhibitors. The standard says the 'skin must be thick', the requirement having remained unchanged since it first appeared in the 1929 standard. The operative word is 'must', a fact which is too often ignored by judges, some of whom seem unable to differentiate between a thick skin and one underlain by fat.

Colour in the Border Terrier is perhaps of little functional importance but in the ring a good, rich colour can help attract the judge's eye and in the hunting field there is at least an equal degree of appreciation for a richly coloured turnout. Nowadays the dark grizzles seem to predominate while the clear foxy reds are, temporarily we hope, taking a back seat. Wheaten, true wheaten not to be confused with a mousey grizzle or a pale tan, seems to have been lost or at least misplaced.

The earliest attempts to produce a standard for the breed found their greatest difficulties in arriving at a size and weight range which could be accepted throughout the breed and when after a few years this had been achieved there remained the problem that a number of terriers, including some of the best, were larger than the standard allowed. After more than sixty years, this problem has not been solved but has, for a number of reasons, been aggravated.

The Border Terrier Club's original standard allowed a range from 14 to 17 lb. The Northumberland Club, however, said that 14 lb for dogs and 13 lb for bitches should be regarded as maximum weights. These weights were very much closer to Thomas Robson's 'less than half the weight of a Dandie' but were, nevertheless, very soon set aside in favour of the heavier range. What the standard seems to do is identify the range of size within which Border Terriers capable of doing their job should fall. There is no uniformity about the size of foxes and still less about the places in which they might take refuge. It follows, therefore, that it would be quite wrong to insist that all Border Terriers should be the same size. A small bitch might be needed to thread her way between tree roots or through a very narrow rock cleft while a larger dog, capable of negotiating the deep steps to be found in some rocky chasms or of forcing his way through the obstacles to be met in a deep moss hole, would be better in other circumstances. Size, therefore, is, like much of the rest of the standard, a product of function and is not subject to arbitrary changes of fashion.

In our experience, foxes share with fishes a tendency to grow larger in the minds and imaginations of those who may have had no more than a fleeting glimpse of them. Weighing foxes over a period of years in the Home Counties we seldom found one which exceeded 18 lb and the average was probably little more than 14 lb. In Border country, however, foxes are undoubtedly bigger and stronger; they have to be to survive the conditions in which they exist. Nor have they been subjected to the mass import of small foxes from Europe which took place at the end of the nineteenth century and was concentrated on the more fashionable hunting countries. Border foxes are still very much of the old hill stock. A number have been weighed for us by people on whose veracity we can rely. This admittedly small and by no means scientific survey produced a number of foxes which exceeded 20 lb in weight and the average weight was probably nearer 18 lb than 14 lb.

Size, however, is not just a project of weight. The most important measure of a Border Terrier's size is its ability to follow wherever a fox may lead. A tall, rangy dog may look big from the ringside but could negotiate tighter places than an apparently smaller dumpy terrier.

Then follow two clauses which appear in every standard. The first replaces the list of faults and disqualifications which used to appear in so many standards and is intended to encourage a more positive attitude to judging than is to be found in merely finding faults. In the case of the Border Terrier the Kennel Club were persuaded of the importance of the breed's work and have accepted a modification to the faults clause which stresses that faults which detract from the terrier's ability to do the job for which the breed is intended should be more seriously regarded than those which do not affect its ability to work. Inclusion of this modification effectively refutes the erroneous but commonly held view that the Kennel Club have little interest in maintaining a contact between a breed and the job for which it was intended.

The final clause, again common to all standards, defines an attitude to a serious hereditary fault which could threaten a breed's future and which, in the past, has been rather lightly regarded by some Border Terrier breeders and judges. The condition is known as cryptorchidism. A cryptorchid is a male whose testicles are abnormally retained in the abdominal cavity. Such a dog is infertile. A unilateral cryptorchid is a dog which has one apparently normally descended testicle and one retained in the abdominal cavity. Dogs also occur which have one or both testicles only partially descended or which have no testicles.

5 American Standard

The standard as it nowadays exists in Britain and which has, with only minor changes, served the breed well for over sixty years is the one against which Border Terriers are judged in all parts of the world except in America. Only in America was it thought necessary to have a standard which differs both in form and content from that used throughout the rest of the world.

The American Border Terrier standard was approved by the American Kennel Club in March 1950 and, though broadly based on the British standard, differs from it in some important points.

Since the Border Terrier is a working terrier of a size to go to ground and able, within reason, to follow a horse, his conformation should be such that he be ideally built to do his job. No deviations from this ideal conformation should be permitted which would impair his usefulness in running his quarry to earth and in bolting it therefrom. For this work he must be alert, active, and agile, and capable of squeezing through narrow apertures and rapidly traversing any kind of terrain. His head 'like that of an otter' is distinctive and his temperament ideally exemplifies that of a terrier. By nature he is good tempered, affectionate, obedient and easily trained. In the field he is hard as nails, 'game as they come' and driving in attack.

It should be the aim of Border Terrier breeders to avoid such over emphasis of any point in the standard as might lead to unbalanced exaggeration.

General Appearance: He is an active terrier of medium bone, strongly put together, suggesting endurance and agility, but rather narrow in shoulder, body and quarter. The body is covered with a somewhat broken though close fitting and intensely wiry jacket. The characteristic 'otter' head with its keen eye, combined with a body poise which is at the alert, gives a look of fearless and implacable determination characteristic of the breed. The proportions should be the height at the withers should be slightly greater than the distance from the withers to the tail, i.e., by possibly $1\frac{1}{2}$ inches in a 14 lb dog.

Weight: Dogs 13–15½ lbs; Bitches 11½–14 lb. These are appropriate weights for the Border Terriers in hard working conditions.

Head: Similar to that of an otter. Moderately broad and flat in skull with plenty of width between the eyes and between the ears. A slight, moderately broad curve at the stop rather than a pronounced indentation. Cheeks slightly full.

Ears: Small V shaped and of moderate thickness, dark preferred. Not set high on the head but somewhat on the side, and dropping forward close to the cheeks. They should not break above the level of the skull.

Eyes: Dark hazel and full of fire and intelligence. Moderate in size, neither prominent nor small and beady.

Muzzle: Short and well filled. A dark muzzle is characteristic and desirable. A few short whiskers are natural to the breed.

Teeth: Strong with a scissor bite, large in proportion to the size of the dog.

Nose: Black and of good size.

Neck: Clean, muscular and only long enough to give a well balanced appearance. It would gradually widen into the shoulder.

Shoulders: Well laid back and of good length, the blades converging to the withers gradually from a brisket not excessively deep or narrow.

Forelegs: Straight and not too heavy in bone and placed slightly wider than in a Fox Terrier.

Feet: Small and compact. Toes should point forward and be moderately arched with thick pads.

Body: Deep, fairly narrow and of sufficient length to avoid any suggestion of lack of range and agility. Deep ribs carried well back and not oversprung in view of the desired depth and narrowness of the body. The body should be capable of being spanned by a man's hands behind the shoulders. Back strong but laterally supple, with no suspicion of a dip behind the shoulder.

Loin: Strong and the underline fairly straight.

Tail: Moderately short, thick at base, then tapering. Not set on too high. Carried gaily when at the alert, but not over the back. When at ease a Border may drop his stern.

Hindquarters: Muscular and racy with the thighs long and nicely moulded. Stifles well bent and hocks well let down.

Coat: A short and dense undercoat covered with a very wiry and somewhat broken top coat which should lie closely, but it must not show any tendency to curl or wave. With such a coat, a Border should be able to be exhibited almost in his natural state, nothing more in the way of trimming being needed than a tidying up of the head, neck and feet.

Hide: Very thick and loose fitting.

Movement: Straight and rhythmical before and behind, with good length of stride and flexing of stifle and hock. The dog should respond to his handler with a gait which is free, agile and quick.

Colour: Red, grizzle and tan, blue and tan or wheaten. Small amount of white may be allowed on the chest but white on the feet should be penalised.

Scale of points

Head, ears, neck and teeth	20
Legs and feet	15
Coat and skin	10
Shoulders and chest	10
Eyes and expression	10
Back and loin	10
Hindquarters	10
Tail	5
General appearance	10
	100

The standard is considerably more verbose than the British standard and perhaps this is understandable in a country so far removed from the Border's origins and without any tradition of the sort of terrier work which the Border was originated to undertake. However, there are parts of the standard which differ appreciably from that of the breed in its native country.

The preamble to the American standard very properly places great emphasis on the breed's role as a working terrier but sadly does so in a way which misrepresents this role and what it demands of a terrier. It is not, and never has been, part of a terrier's task to run his quarry to earth.

That foxes do from time to time gain the refuge afforded by their earths is not something achieved with the help and encouragement of hounds and terriers but in spite of their best efforts to prevent such a thing happening. When a fox does manage to gain such a refuge, then it is the terrier's job to persuade him to leave using no more force than is absolutely necessary. A terrier which was as 'hard as nails ... and driving into attack' would not long be welcome as an adjunct of a pack of Foxhounds. It is not the terrier's job to murder his fox, but to eject him from whatever retreat in which he might seek refuge.

In the General Appearance clause, the reference to the qualities of the coat emphasises just those points on which breeders, particularly the early breeders, set such importance but about which the British standard is silent. The ideal coat should need no expert trimming to hide its faults or enhance its qualities but it must be admitted that both in Britain and, in spite of the emphasis in the standard, in America hairdressing sometimes assumes a greater importance than is desirable.

The American standard seeks both dark ears and a dark muzzle, though not, it should be noted, necessarily black.

The nose is required to be black, in contrast to the more lax requirement of the British standard.

The bite is as in the British standard except that the teeth are required to be large in proportion to the size of the dog, an essential requirement of a working terrier, but one which is not mentioned in the British standard, though one on which British breeders should place considerable emphasis.

The forelegs are said to be 'placed slightly wider than in a Fox Terrier'. The Fox-terrier standard makes no mention of the placement of forelegs. It is possibly better to compare a Border with a fox, the quarry which he has to follow to ground, a task which he would be unable to accomplish unless he was built on narrow lines.

The description of the body is fuller than that found in the British standard and we particularly like the phrases 'of sufficient length to avoid any suggestion of lack of range and activity' and 'back strong but laterally supple', both of which contain a wealth of meaning.

The American standard differs from the British standard in its reference to the tail only in that it mentions that 'when at ease, a Border may drop his stern'. If for no better reason than that this serves to introduce the word 'stern', we like this reference.

The mention of coat in the clause on General Appearance is repeated and amplified in a way which provides a very much fuller guide than that found in the British standard. We might query whether it is objectionable if a Border's coat has a wave in it, and we wonder just how many American exhibitors and handlers put their dogs in the ring with 'nothing more in the way of trimming . . . than a tidying up of the head, neck and feet'.

The reference to the hide (and could any word be more apt than that for a Border's skin?) says 'very thick and loose fitting' which is precisely all it needs to say.

The differences which exist between the American and British standards may reasonably be accounted for by the distance which separates American breeders from any real contact with or experience of the work for which the breed was intended and which remains its essential purpose. There are, we believe, valid reasons for having a fuller more graphic standard than has been found to be necessary in Britain.

6 Early Shows

It may well have been the hound shows which John Warde ran during the mid-1770s, while he was hunting the country around Westerham in Kent, which gave rise to the famous Holkham Sheep Shearings. These, in their turn, were to provide some of the impetus which led to the formation of agricultural societies. It would have been surprising if in the early days they did not include a few classes for sheepdogs, gundogs, hounds and terriers. Certainly the Cleveland Agricultural Society were running shows for hounds and, probably, terriers as early as 1857.

The agricultural shows in the Borders were providing classes for sheepdogs, hounds and terriers by 1880; it was not until the 1890s that the results of the shows began to be published and by this time a number of Border shows were regularly providing separate classes for the breed.

During the 1870s, a dog called Bacchus was successfully campaigned in the Borders by William Hedley, Master of the North Tyne Foxhounds. In 1880, Mr George Davidson competed successfully in the variety classes at the Border Union Agricultural Show at Kelso. Then, according to Morris, Byrness followed by Bellingham, and Hexham, gave the breed its own separate classes.

In 1892 the breed had no classes at Bellingham, Hawick, Hexham or Kelso schedules because Mr Thomson Gray was judging and his recently published book had exposed a lack of awareness about the breed. No such excuse is available for Hexham where the Dodd/Robson partnership was in the money with Fox-terriers. In the following year, 1893, the Tyneside Agricultural Society at Hexham provided a class for Dandie Dinmont, Scotch or Border Terriers in which both Bill Hedley and Jacob Robson were placed. There were no classes for the breed at Bellingham, Hawick or Kelso.

In 1895, the position appears to have begun to improve, though the change may be more apparent than real due to the fact that in that year *Our Dogs* superseded the *Fanciers Gazette* and could devote more attention to dog shows. On August 5, the Border Union Agricultural Society scheduled the breed at Kelso under Mr James Locke. The *Our Dogs* report was less than flattering to the breed.

'Border Terriers formed a heterogeneous lot, whose lineage we would not care to unravel. If the little beggars are as game as they look, it is little wonder that they have many admirers.' The winner was G. Bolam's Spink, T. Robson was second with Wasp and third was T. W. R. Scott. Neither Hawick nor Hexham seem to have scheduled the breed though, at Hawick, J. Dodd judged the Sheepdog trials. On September 25, the North Tyne and Redesdale Agricultural Society at Bellingham also provided a class for 'the Border Terrier – as distinct from the Dandie – of which there is seldom a class, but which seem to have some sort of uniform type about them. We hope to refer to this breed on a future occasion.' Of the show itself, *Our Dogs* reported that 'Border Terriers were numerous, and certainly have a type of their own, though we can't see much in them. The winner scored in face, legs and feet.' This time the reporter was Saxon. The award list reported that G. Bolam's Spink was again first, J. Sisterson's Pincher second, with J. Robson and J. Taylor's unidentified terriers being highly commended. In the following year, the Tyneside Agricultural Society at Hexham again offered a mixed Dandie and Border Terrier class judged by James Hedley and John Shorthose. 'The winner', it was reported, 'is a good pepper, of the former persuasion. Second, a fair mustard. Third, a Border Terrier, rather nondescript, owned by Thomas Robson.' On this occasion, the unimpressed reporter was Strebor.

Two days later, on August 5, Mr R. Chapman judged a class for Border Terriers at the Border Union Agricultural Society, Kelso. The winner was again Spink and second was J. Elliott's Border. On September 23, the North Tyne and Redesdale Agricultural Society at Bellingham provided a class, judged by Mr G. H. Proctor, and on this occasion Jacob Robson's Flint beat Spink.

Show reports for 1897 made it seem that, as a show dog, the breed was going backwards rather than forwards. No reports were filed for either Kelso or Hawick, there were no classes at Hexham where Mr R. Marshall judged and, even at Bellingham on September 22, George Raper, a very well known judge of Fox-terriers, had a less than overwhelming entry which Northumbrian said 'hardly called for comment'. In the single class A. Dodd's Rosy was first, J. Robson's Flint second and T. Robson's Border suffered the indignity of being placed not third but V.H.C. Things were only slightly better in 1898, with no report filed for Kelso and no classes at either Hawick or Hexham. The Jedforest Sheep and Dog Show on August 13, when Messrs W. Hedley and A. Charlton judged Sheepdogs, Dandie Dinmonts, Borders and working terriers only improved the situation slightly. 'Boxer', *Our Dogs* reporter, was unimpressed. 'Border Terriers', he wrote, 'were a mixed lot, and not two alike. I am at a loss how they are judged, as all kinds of types won; and they didn't look a useful lot either but I may be wrong.' The first three places were occupied by J. T. Dodd, T. W. R. Scott and J. Robson.

John Dodd was then joint Master of the Liddesdale with David Ballentyne, Jacob Robson was joint Master of the Border with E. L. Dodd and, within a very few years, T. W. Robson Scott was to become Master of the Jedforest; none were likely to keep a terrier, let alone show one, which wasn't better than merely useful. It is interesting how often, during these early years, classes for Border Terriers were judged by and frequently won by masters of the various packs of Border Foxhounds. There was a very close link between the early show dog and the terriers which were relied upon to do the work in the Borders. Often, they were the same animals and sometimes it was the workers which had produced the winners. No other terrier breed has had, still less attempted to maintain, this close link between their working origins and their new career in the ring.

Competition ended for the season with the North Tyne and Redesdale at Bellingham where J. T. Dodd's Flint beat J. Charlton's Daisy, the only two entries.

A pattern was beginning to emerge, with Border Terriers scheduled only when knowledgeable people from the area were available to judge them; these judges placed great emphasis on working qualities and were frequently also asked to judge working terriers, foxhounds and sheepdogs. However, when the appointed judge was from outside the Border counties and so had no knowledge of the breed and probably very little knowledge about working terriers, the classes, no matter what his fame as a judge, tended to be quietly dropped for the year. It seems that the Border Terrier owners were more interested in an opinion which had some real value than in the actual competition.

The pattern continued in 1898 when the Border Union Agricultural Society show at Kelso provided just one class, under Mr T. T. Charlton, for Border Terriers and another for Shepherd's Dogs. Borders were said to have been 'not strong' with Mr T. Robson's terriers filling the first three places. At Hexham there were no classes for Borders though a number of familiar names were to the fore in both Fox-terriers and Collies. At Bellingham Messrs Robson and Elliott judged both Collies and Border Terriers, placing H. E. Thompson's Pep first and R. E. Thompson's Daisy second. As the century closed, Hawick, Hexham and Kelso had no classes and no reports were filed for Bellingham or Jedburgh.

Five years later, in 1905, Hawick, Hexham and Kelso were still without classes though the one class provided at the Jedforest Sheep and Dog Show on August 12 was well filled. It was judged by Thomas Murray and T. T. Charlton and won by T. Carruther's Floss; J. T. Dodd's Flint was second and W. J. Elliott's Tip third. Bim reported that 'Border Terriers are getting very popular in this district; there being 15 entries in the class. First to Floss; was lucky to beat Flint, who is about the most perfect Border we have seen. Third to Tip, a hardy little specimen, and a likely worker.' The Bellingham Show on September 14 had Mr J. T. Dodd judging working Collies and Border Terriers. The winner of the dog class was J. Thompson's Rap with B. Charlton's Twig second and Miss E. Hedley's Lancey third. The bitch class had D. Sergent's Pep as the winner; J. Smith's Kitty II was second and T. Robson's Clip third.

The situation seems to have continued virtually unchanged for another five years with, in 1910, only Hexham apparently deemed worthy of a report. Here, Mr W. Hedley, the owner of Bacchus, was the judge of both Border and working terriers. 'Border Terriers', Victrix said, 'were from what one knows of this exclusive breed, a nice collection. Mouths, coats, legs and feet are said to be great points, but as no accepted standard is drawn up, it is at the present time the "opinion" of the elected judge. One we noticed, Yettan, was very much to our liking and would please a fastidious Terrier man.' In fact, William Hedley had placed F. E. Scholfield's Yettan third to J. S. Roddam's Nettle and A. Elliott's Iky. J. Smith's Newton Rock was reserve. The local class for dogs was won by Miss N. Dixon's Ben who beat Mrs O. H. Owen's Teddy and J. Dodd's Pincher. In bitches Nettle was the winner, Yettan was second and third was Mrs Henderson's Trim.

In 1920, with recognition just around the corner, the breed began to be scheduled regularly at southern shows. The first of these, appropriately enough, was the National Terrier Club show held at the Royal Horticultural Hall, Westminster. The judge was James Hagate, who wrote for *Our Dogs* under the pseudonym of Victrix and so, unusually, provided his own report of the breed's southern debut.

'Border Terriers: A new variety to the Southern shows that created some interest. As so few of these game Terriers have been benched further South than Hexham they were no doubt a new breed to many; but once known, and the type definitely fixed, they will no doubt catch on, and be as big a favourite as the now popular Cairns. Like this breed, they require no trimming; in fact, it is doubtful if any of the rough coated Terrier family can equal them in either texture or denseness of coat, and certainly not in general soundness, especially in hocks and hindquarters. In the Novice class Towser won well; a typical-headed dog, nice skull, ears and eyes, cuts away a little in jaw, well-placed shoulders, shade light in bone but clean and straight; rather thin in pads, good body; excellent hindquarters and set-on of tail, which is rather too fine and plenty long enough; he also shows rather more daylight than I like; good texture and pleasing colour. Flaxhead Flame, a better sized Terrier, and with rather more substance and compactness; a typical head, which bears traces of his numerous combats; he has hardly the positive front of his more useful competitor; excellent coat and lots of character. Heather Bell; nice type and sort, not quite so pleasing in colour, and out of coat. Open Dogs; Teri is full up to size, but a real good-headed dog; shade big in ears, good neck, shoulders, legs and feet, capital body, an ideal coat, good bright colour. Towser, the Novice winner close up. Open Bitches; A very smart Terrier in Yettan headed this class; nice head and ears, fair eyes, good front, body and coat; a shade too light in colour. Cheekie has also the right head, with capital legs and feet; little plain over the loin, good quarters and tail, good texture of coat, but not enough of it. Flaxhead Flame and Heather Bell followed on. The winning dog gained *Our Dogs* special for the best of the breed, having a slight advantage in jaw power, and a denser and harder coat.'

On March 24 came another southern show, this time in Kensington and judged by Mr W. J. Nicholls. In the novice class, the winner was Mrs Lesmoir Gordon's Hadley Hobble de Hoy which Nicholls described as 'a rare made little chap, grand coat and colour, nice front and just right for his work'. Second in the novice class was Captain and Mrs H. V. Pirie's Flaxhead Flame, 'a smart little bitch, extra good bone, front and body', and third was J. M. Strothers's Sportsman. The open dog class had just one exhibit, Hobble de Hoy, and the bitch was won by Flaxhead Flame with Mrs Lesmoir Gordon's Hadley Happy Go Lucky which Nicholls thought to be on the big side though better than Captain Pirie's Flaxhead Flicker, 'a raw promising puppy'.

At the end of April Nicholls was again in the Border ring, this time at Ayr where he judged one class for Borders, placing Tinker, Bunty, Rip and Tib in that order.

In May, the spotlight again moved south to the Ladies' Kennel Association Show at Ranelagh. Mr W. S. Glynn judged and the report for *Our Dogs* was written by Frank Butler who reported that 'Border Terriers do not seem (to be) catching on in the south. Only five entries in three classes. Flaxhead Flame had the Novice class to himself; a blue and tan, with good body and bone. Open dogs: Hadley Hotspur came first; a smart little red dog, looks all over a workman. Second Flaxhead Flame. Open Bitches: Flaxhead Dlaame and Flaxhead Flicker 1st and 2nd; a couple of useful reds.'

In July, the Richmond Show scheduled four classes for the breed and these were judged by F. M. Morris, who had given the show extensive publicity in his column, but the entry was again poor with only one in puppy, two in novice, one in open dog and two in open bitch. Morris thought the solitary puppy, Flaxhead Flicker, to be 'small, neat bodied, with good quarters, not a bad head and good coat'. Flicker also won the novice class to beat Hadley Hussey who had 'a good otter head, but is too light in hindquarters', where Hadley Hotspur, the solitary open dog, also failed. In bitches Flaxhead Flame was described as 'a beautiful bitch, low, short-backed, big bone, with a nice class of head and is the sort we like in the North. Keep this type in one's head, and you have a Border Terrier.'

It is hard to imagine that any 'low, short-backed, big boned' terrier would do the job for which the breed was intended or that such an animal would be appreciated in the north.

As summer turned to autumn, the breed entered what for some years had been its traditional show season among the Border agricultural societies. First, on July 24, came Hawick where Mr J. R. Hall and David Ballantyne judged working collies, in which John Ballantyne won with Moss, and Border Terriers which the report said 'made a representative lot. In Open Dogs, Rock won, a rare sized one, with capital body, good class of head; his "worn" appearance did not handicap his chances, and rightly so, as they are essentially working terriers. Hyndlee is a trifle leggy, but otherwise a nice sorty one. Third Teri, bigger than those placed over him, but exceptionally sound. Doctor, res., is quite nice except his front, which is doubtful. In a good class of bitches, Bess won; good in head, front and body but shown out of coat. Nearly all the others were up to a good show standard, but as this is a breed practically in the making, with no fixed standard of points, it is rather dangerous to criticize them closely.' The award list showed that Willie Barton owned Rock, T. Thornton Hyndlee, Tommy Lawrence Teri and Miss S. D. Robson Doctor. E. Thompson owned Jess, J. T. Dodd the unnamed second in the bitch class, Willie Barton Tibbie the third prize winner and A. Anderson was reserve.

On August 2, it was Hexham and the Tyneside Agricultural Society show where Mr M. Robson judged Border and working terriers. Fred Morris did the report and said that

'Puppies: 1st, Dan, a neat-sized dog, "otter-headed", good bone and coat. 2nd Jimmy, very nice dog; good class of head, good coat, a sound one. 3rd Jackie, neat good coat and bone, nice sort of head. Special Limit: Local: Dogs: 1st Noted. 2nd North Tyne Gyp, a good useful sort; nice in head, body, legs and feet. 3rd Newton Rock, shows a bit of age. Bitches: 1st Dot, a nice little bitch, on working like lines; good head, coat and body. 2nd Vixen, neat and small, good body shape. 3rd Blanche, looks a worker; nice bone, head, tail, coat and expression, a good sort of Terrier. Mick is a good one; excellent all round, one of the best I have seen, and am not astonished to hear he was awarded the special for best at Wooler Show; here he was without a card, another case of "many men, many minds"; he was the sire of the cup winner. The Working Terriers looked "workmen".'

Just three days later, on August 5, it was the Border Union Show at Kelso and here the judge was James Holgate whose entry, according to Glasguensis, was adversely affected by an indifferent schedule. 'Open Dogs: T. Lawrence's Teri, the old favourite again maintained his superiority; bar being full up to size, is quite the soundest and most typical of this breed that has yet graced the show bench, and the type and pattern that should be taken by the recently formed club in fixing their standard of points. 2nd to Towser (Mrs Robertson), a nice stamp, with good body. Bitches: 1st E. M. Robertson's Cheekie, a wonderful coated one, was closely pressed by Betty (Mrs Roughead), whose faulty mouth prevented her getting the premier award.'

Two days later, Simon Dodd was judging Working Collies and J. T. Dodd was judging all the other classes at the Jedforest Sheep and Dog Show at Jedburgh. Once more Glasguensis was on hand and reported that '1st W. M. Barton's Rock, the Hawick winner, in fine form: he also won the special for the best of this variety. 2nd T. Lawrence's Teri, now well known; his size handicaps, otherwise the best of the lot. 3rd Mrs E. W. Robertson's Cheeky, a good headed one; nice body and front, fair coat'.

On August 13, another of the traditional Border shows took place; again Glasguensis wrote the report.

'Jedburgh Show, held on Saturday last, was a happy gathering, the Sporting Dogs and Border Terriers being the features. Provost Dalgleish's red-roan Field Spaniel puppy, Ellwyn Queen, again won. Mr William Barton headed the Border Terrier section. The Cheviot hill men were forward in force, all keenly interested in the game little Border dog. Mr Jacob Robson, the Master of the Border Counties Hounds, was looking on and many other keen followers of the chase were enjoying the judging of Mr John Dodd, who is one of the oldest and best judges of this breed. Many of the sporting men left early to be present at the Duke of Buccleuch's puppy show at the kennels, St Boswell's, another fine gathering.'

The season, as far as the Border shows were concerned, closed on September 25 when both the North Tyne Agricultural Society and the Eskdale and Liddesdale Agricultural Society provided classes for Border Terriers. Both shows appear to have been well supported but Morris, somewhat typically, had fault to find with the method of 'staking' dogs at Bellingham, a method which he condemns as 'quite out of date' but which was still in use nearly forty years later when we first showed at Bellingham.

'Bellingham September 25 – 76 entries. Judges: Mr S. Dodds (Border Terriers) and Mr F. Barnett (the remainder). A dog show in conjunction with the North Tyne and Redesdale Agricultural Society was held at Bellingham. The arrangements for the dogs were quite out of date, the old "stake" principle being adopted, and during the great heat of the day dogs lay panting on the ground. It is to be hoped that another year better arrangements will be made for the exhibits.

'Border Terriers made a magnificent show, there being 54 entered, a great compliment to Mr S. Dodds. In the dog class: 1st W. Forster's Dan, was, I think, the winner of the Puppy and other classes at Hexham, and like 2nd, J. W. Carruther's Flint, was taller than 3rd, J. Dodds' North Tyne Gyp, who is a grand specimen, for in head he scores all the way, he has a beautifully balanced body, nice bone, good coat, ears and eyes. 1st and 2nd have good coats and perhaps better fronts. Mrs Appleyard's Dash, the Hexham winner, is a nice red dog, but gives one the impression that at times he does not place his feet in an orthodox position. Mrs Sordy's Tattler is a splendidly balanced dog of nice size, capital head, bone and body, and he should go far in the future; he is one of the best I have seen. Mrs Smith won the bitch class with Dot, the Hexham winner; a good bitch; she is small, nice body, and capital type and a pleasing head; her tail is also good and not too long. 2nd, A. Dodds' Vic, was, I think, last year's winner at this show; nice size, good tail and coat with well turned body. 3rd, J. D. Potts' Bridge End Beauty, is certainly one of the best Border Terriers I have ever seen; she is beautifully balanced all round, head, body, bone and ears excellent, some may consider she had too much hair on her short and well-shaped tail, but even considering this she is the beau ideal of a Border Terrier. In the under 12 months class, the 1st, Mr

Sordy's puppy is too light all round and carries the tail like a whippet. 2nd, George Dagg's bitch, is on nice lines; neat in size, good class of head and coat, nice ears and tail and good eyes. I could not find if a 3rd prize had been awarded. J. Strother's puppy, Sis, is at present promising; nice size, grand jaw and promising head. J. Allgood's Beele is the Whittington winner, and today, like the Hexham Cup winner, received no recognition. J. Strother's Jean now shows signs of age and was thus handicapped. Not a really bad one was benched and from today a great epoch opens out in the history of the Border Terrier.'

The Eskdale and Liddesdale Agricultural Society at Langholm held its 82nd show with Frank Noble judging Collies and Border Terriers. Once more Teri was first but was hard pressed by Willie Barton's Rock and Miss Paterson's Peter was third. In a class devoted to Blues there were no less than fifteen entries, the winner being Tommy Lawrence's Sting; second was R. Stewart's Langholm Lady and third J. J. Dodd's Billy. By this time all those who had supported the north country agricultural shows as well as a number of southern newcomers to the breed knew that later in the year there would be, for the first time, the opportunity to compete for Challenge Certificates; it must have been an exciting time.

The Border Terrier entries at these long established northern shows were growing and Morris published a league table to underline the support which breed classes were receiving at these shows.

'Bellingham is quite in the wilds of Northumberland, and all lovers of the Border Terrier who journeyed there last Saturday will not readily forget the fine collection of the breed they saw. Still Bellingham with its 55 entries does not establish a record for the year. Wooler stands first with 60, Bellingham second, Whittington (54) third, Hexham (31) fourth and Glanton (28) fifth.'

Then came the first of the breed's championship shows, held at the Carlisle Open Championship show which no longer exists as a championship show.

Carlisle (Championship) September 30. Held in the Markets. 720 entries. Mr Simon Dodd: Border Terriers.
   The Carlisle Open Championship Show was held as above. Old Calabar benched and fed the exhibits.

Border Terriers: A nice class of eight to cheer the enthusiasts. Dan, the winner, we caught once or twice with a dip in his back, and in addition he is quite enough on the leg; fairly good front, first-rate Border head, dense coat and

F. E. Schofield had a good entry at the Alwinton Shepherds Show in 1923. From left to right, George Sordy with Titlington Tartar ('21) who went on to win one CC, John Carruthers with Flint ('19), by Ch Ivo Roisterer, John Dodds with Sambo ('21) and Mrs Adam Forster with Harbadle (*sic*) who, in the bitch class, had been beaten by David Jackson's Daphne ('21) who, alone of the five, went on to become a champion.

shows well. 2nd Ivo Roisterer is absolutely built for his work; a hardy, natty little fellow, with a plump straight front and perfect feet, he is a little strong in shoulders, stern well set, and coat, what there was of it, on the day was dense and weather resisting. 3rd Red Gauntlet, has a moderate pair of shoulders and front, nice class of head and best of bodies but again quite big enough. Res. Jimmie, good rich red, and coat is harsh, capital feet and head, and typical of the breed. Graduate: 1st and 2nd as in the preceding class. 3rd North Tyne Gyp, scored in front, legs and feet. Junior: Tinker, came out of the best; shade better than some, with fair amount of timber; elsewhere very nice, including body, coat, head and general style. In a capital Mixed Limit we have to notice Teri, 3rd; is surely up to size, and his head did not appeal to us; his make, shape, and movement are decidedly good, as is his coat, which doubtless appealed to the judge. We next come to the Bitches. Liddesdale Bess 1st, a neat one; quite the size, nice coat. She beat 2nd Nett, on form, the last-named absolutely refusing to show.

W. Nicholls

Awards: Novice: 1. W. Forster, Dan: 2. Hamilton-Adams, Ivo Roisterer: 3. W. Barton, Red Gauntlet: Res. I. A. Paterson, Jimmie. Graduate: 1. Dan: 2. I. Roisterer: 3. J. Dodd, North Tyne Gyp: Res. R. Gauntlet. Junior: 1. Miss Bell-Irving, Tinker: 2. Dan: 3. Jimmie: Res. G. Boynes, Gill. Limit: 1. N. T. Gyp: 2. Dan: 3. T. Lawrence, Teri: Res. I. Roisterer.
Bitches: 1. and Ch. W. Barton, Liddesdale Bess; 2. F. Cowlson, Nett.

Morris does not appear to have been impressed by Simon Dodd's judging for on October 2 he wrote:

'The awards in the Border Terrier classes at the Carlisle Show will doubtless give many of us food for thought, but first let me congratulate Mr W. Barton on his great successes, for this old and tried breeder won the bitch championship with Liddesdale Bess, was 3rd with Red Gauntlet, and he also bred Miss Bell-Irving's Tinker, the winner of the dog Championship.

'Now let us look at the decisions and at the same time bear in mind that Mr S. Dodd also officiated as judge at Bellingham on Saturday, where he placed Mr W. Forster's Dan 1st. At Carlisle Dan notched two 1sts and two 2nds, and in the Open class did not "touch". Now I wish fanciers to compare his type with Mr J. Dodds' North Tyne Gyp, a beautiful type of Border Terrier, and Mr T. Hamilton-Adams' Ivo Roisterer, the Wooler sensation, a dog we all admired at Hexham. At Carlisle Roisterer was awarded two 2nds and two reserves, and Mr T. Lawrence's Teri, the Hexham and Langholm cup winner, had two 3rds to his credit at Carlisle. When fanciers get the chance to see the above-named dogs all together, let them compare them, and then I should like to hear which type they prefer.'

Next came the Edinburgh Championship Show:

Edinburgh (Championship) October 6 and 7. Held in the Waverley Market. 1378 entries. Border Terrier judge: Mr Jacob Robson.

Border Terriers were a nice even lot. In Open Dogs Teri won; he has a good head and plenty jaw, good eye, and capital ears, good body and coat, nice front and ample bone and a good showman. 2nd, Dan, nice body and good front, and good bone, fails to winner in coat and skull. 3rd, North Tyne Gyp; nice head, good eye and ears, good body, nice front and good bone, fails in mouth; still we fancied him for 2nd place. Res. Dash, nice in body and coat, but wants to be stronger in head. Open bitches: 1st Winnie, nice little Terrier, but far too small. 2nd, Bet, a better all-round Terrier than the winner; good texture of coat, nice body, and typical head. Teri won the challenge cup for best worker, also the K C Challenge Certificate. Winnie won the K C Challenge Certificate for bitches.

Sam Graham

Awards: Open: Dogs: 1. T. Lawrence, Teri; 2. W. Forster, Dan; 3. J. Dodd, North Tyne Gyp; Res. Mrs Monica M. Appleyard, Dash. Bitches: 1. H. C. Appleyard, Winnie; 2. T. Lawrence, Bet. Limit – Dog or Bitch: 1. T. Lawrence, Teri; 2. W. Forster, Dan; 3. N. T. Gyp; Res. Dash. Graduate: 1. Dan; 2. N. T. Gyp; 3. Bet. Novice: Bitches: 1. Winnie; 2. Bet; 3. G. C. Boys, Jill. Puppies – Dog or Bitch: 1. Jill. Brade: 1. T. Lawrence.

Then finally came the Kennel Club's own Championship Show at Crystal Palace which, in common with other southern events, was when compared with northern shows very badly supported.

Crystal Palace (London) The Kennel Club (Championship) November 3 and 4. Border Terrier Judge: Mr T. Lawrence.

The Kennel Club's 50th Open Championship Show was held on Wednesday and Thursday of this week. Messrs Spratt's Patent Limited benched and fed the exhibits and Jeyes disinfected the show. *Our Dogs* judging books were used.

Border Terriers were a nice lot of puppies. Doony Vixen is quite a nice sort, good head, nice body, bone and coat. 2nd, Dot, nice head and good eye, typical mover. 3rd, Riccarton Betty, good body, nice head, sound mover. Open: 1st, Winnie, typical head, good eye, coat and body.

Mr S. Graham

Awards: Dogs: Puppies: 1. Mr E. C. Spencer, Doony Viper. Open 1. Miss Bell-Irving, Tinker; 2. W. Forster, Dan; 3. J. R. Carruthers, Flint; Res. J. Dodd, North Tyne Gyp. Bitches: Puppies: 1. E. C. Spencer, Doony Vixen; 2. W. Hurst, Flaxhead Fishwife; 3. Messrs Dodd, Riccarton Betty. Open: 1. K. C. Appleyard, Winnie; 2. Mrs Smith, Dot; 3. Messrs Dodd, Riccarton Meg; Res. D. Vixen.

The three championship shows had produced four CC winners with Tinker and Winnie each taking two and Liddesdale Bess and Teri each taking one. It was not until the following year that the breed's first champions were to emerge.

As far as championship shows were concerned, 1921 very quickly got into its stride with the National Terrier Club Show held at the Horticultural Hall, Westminster, on January 19, attracting a total of 1014 entries. The breed was judged by Mr J. J. Holgate who produced his own report.

'Border Terriers, with three classes, came up fairly well in the Mixed Novice Class. Ivo Roisterer won with something to spare, the desired size, with a typical head, nice neck and shoulders, very fair legs and feet, good body, set on of tail, and movement; he was shown a little too light and between his coats, but the texture is right. Mistress Jean, much the same type and pattern, needs improvement in legs and feet, nice size, good coat and movement. Clincher came 3rd, a well balanced correct-sized dog, failing in front, good body and coat, pleasing head. Ivo Rally, excellent head, good neck and shoulders, shade coarse in bone, good body, inclined to ring his tail, and not in very good coat, put down in good coat, should do much better. Doony Vixen, a shade long in loin and although I am in no ways in favour of a short-backed cloddy Border, a long loined dog of any variety is no favourite of mine; head is quite nice, eyes rather light, capital neck, shoulders, and legs and feet above average; dense coat of fair texture. Hadley Hussey, good make and shape, but not in very good coat. Open – Dogs: Tivi (*sic*) a most typical sound dog, excelling in coat and very sound, full up to size, but if his heart is good, size will never stop him; he had a slight pull in the loin, hindquarters and movement over the Novice winner, who gave him a close run for premier position. Clincher came 3rd and Hadley Hotspur, a grand bodied little dog with a capital head, good coat, failing a little in front. Dooney Viper's size told against him; reduce him a couple or three pounds and he would hold off many of the winners; his head is quite the correct otter type, capital front, good body with liberty and movement, lots of good dense coat, and sound behind. Open – Bitches: were repeats, Mistress Jean winning with something to spare. Dooney Vixen came 2nd and Hadley Hussey 3rd.'

On February 16 and 17 came the Birmingham National Show, which had attracted a total of 2183 entries, only 17 of which were from Border Terriers entered under Mr Ernest Bagley. The report was written by Sam Graham.

'Border Terriers were quite a small entry for two challenge certificates and the quality was really nothing to write home about. In puppies three turned up and Ivo Rally won; the best of a bad three, he was too full in coat and very soft at that; typical head and a good mover, bad tail carriage. 2nd Chimside Bounder, only a moderate one. 3rd Lawson shown rather poor and is long in body but has typical head and is a good mover. Novices: 1st Clincher a rattling good Border, with a good head, eyes, ears and a sound coat, good front, and ought without doubt to have won the challenge certificate; size and type and a worker by appearance, and we made him the best Border Terrier. Open: Dogs: 1st Ivo Roisterer, nice body and bone, fair coat, too wide and faulty in front, and rather full in eye; should have changed places with the 3rd. 2nd, Tinker, a good all-round hard-bitten Terrier with a good head, eyes, ears, bone, body and coat. 3rd, Clincher, ought to have headed the class. Res., Hadley Hotspur, moves rather badly. Open: Bitches: 1st, Liddesdale Bess, nice head, good body and ears, good coat and moves well. 2nd, Dooney Vixen, a typical Border, with nice head and body, and ought to breed a winner. Ivo Roisterer won the certificate for dogs and Liddesdale Bess that for bitches.'

The next show with championship status for the breed was the Ayr Show on April 26 and 27, which attracted a total of 895 entries though once more the entry in Borders was a poor one for judge Mr R. T. Raines. The report was written by Archie Mackinnon.

'Border terriers. A moderate entry as regards numbers. In puppies Chirnside Bounder won rightly, a smart little dog, with a head as near the approved type as we have seen, sound all round, good legs and feet, and game looking.

Mossknowe Ginger in many respects similar in type, and is equally good in points all round. Glenmuir Sage is also on really good lines and will, when matured, do better. In Novices Tib won, a handy size, good sound front, nice legs and feet, capital coat, rich colour and very sound. In Open Dogs, Teri an old favourite scored a popular win; now well known and in rare form. An old opponent in Tinker 2nd equally well known and in first class form. In Open Bitches Liddesdale Bess won, a capital Terrier, with a nicely balanced head, good eye and ears, shapely body and very sound. 3rd, Bunty is on the best lines and most typical throughout.'

In spite of its rather poor entry history was made at the 1921 Ayr Show for it was at that show that the breed's first two champions were made up. Tommy Lawrence's Teri here won his third Challenge Certificate, having taken his first under Jacob Robson at Edinburgh in the October of the previous year and his second at National Terrier in January under Mr J. J. Holgate. Willie Barton's Liddesdale Bess won her first CC at Carlisle, the breed's first championship show, under Simon Dodd but had had to wait until Birmingham under judge Mr Ernest Bagley for her second. Within a mere seven months of the first championship show for Border Terriers, the breed had its first two champions.

7 Recognition to the War

Although official recognition by the Kennel Club was a major event in the breed's history and opened the way to greater participation in Kennel Club shows and to championship status and, perhaps more importantly, gave access to a system of registration which would hence-forth remove most, if perhaps not all, the doubts about the pedigrees of Border Terriers, in many respects it made little difference to the attitudes and priorities of established breeders. We have already seen that Border Terriers were being carefully and systematically bred well before 1900, principally by people whose main, though by no means exclusive, interest was in producing working terriers. By continuing to breed terriers which could and did work and by showing the best of these they helped to prevent any suggestion that the breed should be glamorised in order to achieve greater success in the ring.

Such was the strength of their influence that even today, over sixty years after recognition, the breed remains firmly in contact with its real purpose in life.

John Dodd and John Carruthers seem to exemplify the prevalent attitude. John Dodd was Master of the Liddesdale, having succeeded to the joint mastership of the Border Hounds in 1876 when his father died, and his co-Master was John Robson of Byrness. In 1887, Mr Dodd went to Riccarton, later to be the home of Wattie Irving's famous kennel, and joined David Ballantyne as joint Master of the Liddesdale.

Mr Ballantyne resigned in 1899 and John Dodd carried on alone until 1920 when his son hunted the pack. The way in which these Border families were interlinked is perhaps best demonstrated by the fact that both John and Jacob Robson married sisters of John Dodd, whilst he maried a Miss Robson.

The Dodd/Carruthers partnership in 1930 produced Sir John Renwick's Ch Grakle but perhaps their major contribution to the breed's future was as owners of North Tyne Gyp's two sons, Ch Grip of Tynedale (1920) and Ch Dandy of Tynedale (1921). Ch Daphne and Ch Themis as well as the CC winners Allen Piper, Clincher Wisp

Willie Carruthers, of the very successful Dodd and Carruthers partnership, poses for a studio photograph with an otter killed by his three Border Terriers. Left to right they are Allan Piper ('21), his dam Jean of Tynefield ('20) and his son Tally-ho ('23).

of Frimley and Tinker were also sired by North Tyne Gyp who thus established himself as an important sire during the early days after recognition. He was originally called Gyp, and was bred by Norman Crozier in 1917 by Geoff out of Wannie of Tynedale. Geoff, also bred by Norman Crozier, was by Flint out of one of the many Wasps while Wannie, bred by Mr J. S. Pincher, was one of the North Tyne's terriers by Pincher out of Nettle.

None of these early breeders had kennel names and perhaps the first such to appear was that of Titlington, a name which though associated with only one champion, Ch Titlington Tatler, was to assume great significance exerted largely through Tatler's sire Titlington Jock. The Titlington affix was owned by Mr J. Field, who bred Titlington Rap out of his bitch Rags though no other which carried the prefix was bred by him. Titlington Jock sired three of the five Border Terriers which won Challenge Certificates during 1921. These three were Ch Titlington Tatler, Ch Teri and Hadley Hussey. Jock was whelped in 1909 by Weddells Rap out of a bitch variously called Tatters and Rosie. Rap was bred by John Smith by Ginger out of Newton Bessie and must have been born somewhere between 1900 and 1908. John Smith also bred two other dogs which appeared in early pedigrees. They were

George Sordy's Titlington kennel reviewed, by Fred Morris, in a 1922 issue of *Our Dogs*.

150   SUPPLEMENT TO "OUR DOGS."   DECEMBER 8, 1922.

THE CELEBRATED
Kennel of Border Terriers,

The Property of Mr. & Mrs. Geo. Sordy, Titlington, Glanton, Northumberland.

CH. TITLINGTON TATLER.

The "Titlingtons" need no introduction. That name is a household word wherever and whenever Border Terriers are mentioned. In reviewing this illustrious kennel it is difficult to know where to start and where to end. On the occasion of the writer's visit to Mr. Sordy's home, situated as it is in the very wilds of Northumberland, in a district where foxes, badgers, etc., are great and many, and where the Titlingtons "go to ground" without any hesitation, I can say without any fear of contradiction that at no time in my life have I ever seen so many Border Terriers owned by one kennel; and further I have never seen such a fine stud. They are all over the place—Ch. Titlington Tatler, Turk, Tartar Type, Twig, Tatters, etc.—like a swarm of bees. And this kennel is not of mushroom growth, for the Sordy family have for many years been closely identified with Border Terriers, and successfully too, for do they not hold the "blue ribands" of the Border Terrier fancy?

Space only prevents me giving full details of the great number of well-known winning dogs and bitches to be found in the kennels, but one characteristic struck me very forcibly—that all the inmates are of ONE type. They are not this type, that type, or the other type; not big, not little, but just "it"; and when they put their heads out of their kennels to take a look round, the visitor at once thinks of otters. The "king of the kennel," in fact, the king of the Border Terrier fancy, is Ch. Titlington Tatler. He is a great workman, and a great showman for he is the winner of all the best prizes at the best shows, and he is the holder of a "working certificate" and the Major Browne cup for best *working* Border Terrier. This valuable trophy he has won on two occasions—at Rothbury, 1921, and at Bellingham, 1922, the shows promoted by the Northumberland Border Terrier Club, at which the very elite of Border Terrierdom competed. He has also won the Hamilton Adams cup for the best Borderer with a working certificate; and to-day he is a fully fledged champion. He won another championship at Edinburgh the other day, where the representatives of this kennel won four 1st prizes, five specials, championship, and medal. His wins are great and many, and being still a young dog he will increase them. He is a great sire; Titlington Turk, T. Twig, Tweedside Red Type, etc., all big winners can call him "dad." By birth he is an aristocrat, for he is a descendant of the best Border Terrier strains. Stud dogs, brood bitches, and puppies are to be seen at Titlington. Breeders can find a great choice of stud dogs, and any fancier wishing to send bitches to Mr. Sordy's dogs should write him, or, better still, go and see him, his hunters, his dogs, and all that is his.   F. W. M.

Newton Rock (1911) and Newton Wasp (1913) but he appears to have relied exclusively on stock, which is now untraceable.

In 1922 two more Borders became champions. They were Ivo Rarebit, by Ch Teri and so a grandson of Titlington Jock, and Ch Themis, a daughter of North Tyne Gyp. A painting of Themis shows her as a very Irish Terrier looking creature but Miss Garnett Orme saw her very differently. 'Themis', she wrote, 'was a grand bitch with a very good head and she was bred by Mr Thompson on October 8 1920. She was by North Tyne Gyp from Lesbury Tatters and Tatters was by that grand old dog Branton Mick, who sired so many good Borders, out of a bitch called Betty. Themis has left many descendants to carry on her family with her daughter Ch Tertius, by Sniper (another son of Titlington Jock) out of Glanton Tatters. Themis' son Tantalus (by Blakadder) and Tornado (also by Blakadder) both go back to Newton Rock. Mated to Rattling Robert, who was a litter brother to North Tyne Gyp and whose name, incidentally, is often mistakenly given as Battling Robert in old pedigrees, Ch Themis produced Teri Trumpeter and Typhoon in 1922. Teri Trumpeter was a blue and tan grizzle and through him come many good Borders. He sired Compounder, the dam of Whaupland Mag and Jack of Larriston. Ch Teddy Boy was descended in direct female descent from him and from Tantalus comes Ch Finchdale Lass.'

Another name which recurs during this period is Tynedale, used most often as a prefix but again not associated with any particular breeder nor even always with terriers which could claim a legitimate connection with the Tynedale or North Tyne Hunts. The name was associated with two champions, Ch Grip of Tynedale, bred by Mrs E. Brown in 1920, and Ch Dandy of Tynedale, bred by Thomas Brydon in 1921. Both were by North Tyne Gyp. Grip was to sire Ch Barney Brindle who in turn sired Ch Kineton Koffey. He also sired Oxnam Pincher, the sire of Ch Jedworth Bunty from whom Sir John Renwick's Newminster kennel was largely bred. Oxnam Pincher also sired Ch Station Masher, whelped at Riccarton Junction when Wattie was Station Master. Interestingly enough, both these kennels, over sixty years later, remain influential in the breed through their owners' descendants. Lionel Hamilton Renwick is a respected championship show judge of the breed as well as of many others while Ronnie Irving is part of a family of breeders, exhibitors and judges who continue to exert their influence.

There appears to have been some doubt about Grip of Tynedale's pedigree which was finally resolved by Hester Garnett Orme and Adam Forster. Correspondence between the two illustrates the way in which they set about resolving such problems.

'We seem to have Grip of Tynedale ped. straight now. He was bred by Mrs E. Brown, Low House, Henshaw, Bardon Mill, his dam Nell shown at Bellingham 1921, for sale £20. She was bred by R. Waugh, West Gate, Haltwhistle whose owner G. D. Nellie in 1918 (date of Nell's birth 14/5/18). Nellie was bred by N. Crozier (address unknown) who bred Geoff, sire of North Tyne Gyp in 1913, Jock (sire of Ivo Roisterer) in 1912 and Nellie herself in 1909. Nellie was also the dam of Mrs Wood's Vic born 1910, a blue and tan. Mrs Wood got her from A. Forster but she said he did not breed her. In most pedigrees she comes as Nellie and her daughter as Nell, but in the Bellingham catalogue it is the other way round. The daughter Nell dam of Grip of Tynedale is also the dam of Honeycomb (dam of Scarside Bell) and as Honeycomb is bred by W. H. Downing she must have been sold to him at Bellingham. This is pretty well proved as though I haven't got Downing's address yet the W. Watson owner of Scarside Bell lived at West End, Haltwhistle and is different to A. S. Watson of Haslingden, Lancs, owner of

Cribden Comet. I expect they were related as Comet and Bell were mated. Anyway it seems that Nell went back where she was bred in Haltwhistle no doubt through her breeder R. Waugh. Now to go back to her dam Nellie who must have been bred about 1908 or 1909 as she had Vic in 1910. I have looked up all my bits and find that in the book *Reminiscences of Joe Bowman* several keen followers of the Ullswater were mentioned amongst which were the brothers N. and T. Crozier so I think it must be our Crozier and that he brought Wasp, bred by Joe which he probably owned and mated her to Robson's Flint or that he owned Flint himself and took him to work with the Ullswater. You remember Willie Barton told us that Flint was nice but had a soft coat, and that he would try and get in touch with the man "who had him" so it evidently did not belong to Jacob Robson. Wasp then was bred by Joe Bowman and owned by N. Crozier and bred Vic or Victor and Geoff and Jock to Flint.'

One kennel which had been in existence since well before recognition but which, like so many others of the period was never to have an affix, was that which belonged to the Forster family. Breeding Borders was very much a family affair. Mrs Forster was the daughter of John Carruthers and so bred to the task; sometimes it was she who was registered as breeder, sometimes her husband Adam, sometimes the two of them and sometimes their daughter Elizabeth. Their first litter appears to have been produced in 1916 out of an unregistered bitch bred by Mr A. Dagg and called Nailer II which, put to Barrow Jock, an unregistered dog bred by John Carruthers, produced Coquetdale Vic and Gippy, both bitches of considerable significance. Vic went on to a successful show career, particularly at the Northumberland Club's exclusive events and, mated to Titlington Jock, produced Little Midget, the dam of Coquetdale Reward, who was to produce Ch Ranter. Mated to Buittie Little Midget also produced Revenge and so must be regarded as one of the most influential bitches the breed has ever seen. Gippy, mated to Titlington Jock, produced Ch Titlington Tatler.

Well before recognition the Forster family had already established their kennel. Thirty-three years later, in 1949, they bred what were to be their last two champions in Ch First Footer and Ch Lucky Purchase, litter mates by Ch Future Fame out of Fully Fashioned each of whom carried lines back to their pre-recognition foundation stock.

We have now mentioned the dogs which were to exert the greatest influence during these early post-recognition years. Ch Grip of Tynedale became a champion in 1923 and was described by judges as a big, strong dog; qualities which in the absence of anything other than crude methods of worming coupled with often indifferent rearing were less prevalent than they are today when it might be said that the pendulum has swung too far towards methods which tend to emphasise size and strength rather than less easily attained qualities. Mated to Ch Liddesdale Bess in 1923 Grip produced Dubh Glass, which, owned by Miss Mary Rew, was described as a keen and clever worker. Unfortunately, he met an untimely end when he slipped and fell over a cliff at Lulworth Cove though not before he had sired the good bitch Hunt Law. Tweedside Red Tatters became a champion in 1923 and went on to win nine CCs under eight different judges and she was the dam of, amongst others, Ch Tweedside Red Topper, and was herself sister to Ch Tweedside Red Type and was closely related to Ch Ivo Roisterer as his dam Flossie, or Floss II, was also the dam of Chip, the dam of Ch Tweedside Red Tatters.

Ivo Roisterer, one of two unrelated dogs to carry the Ivo affix, the other being Rarebit, was whelped in 1915 and bred by Mr A. Drummond. He then passed into the ownership of John Carruthers and was shown at a number of pre-recognition shows until he was bought in 1919 for £25 by Mr Hamilton-Adams. The dog was killed in an accident on the road after being given to Capt. Silver when his owner went overseas in 1923. However, though Hamilton-Adams was soon to return to this country and again become involved with Kennel Club affairs, this seems to have been the end of his interest in Border Terriers.

In 1923 Tatters, a daughter of Titlington Tatler, became a champion. She was bred by Mr G. Hope on 11 December 1921 and later mated Ch Dandy of Tynedale and produced Tweedside Red Topper.

The Tweedside kennel was owned by Mrs David Black, a lady who had already established a reputation in Bulldogs but who, having made the unlikely change, was to find that this was quickly to be eclipsed by her Border Terriers. In all the Tweedside affix was to grace seven champions though, Red Type (20), Red Tatters (21) and Red Topper (23) apart, all were to belong to the post-war period and will be dealt with when we reach that time.

Revenge, another of the outstanding sires of this period, never became a champion, though he was to sire five. In a letter to Miss Garnett Orme, Adam Forster described how close he and the breed came to losing this important dog.

'Perhaps you didn't know how nearly he was never heard of. An old shepherd had asked me to give him a pup. Well my bitch, Little Midget, had a litter of two, one dog and one bitch. I gave the shepherd the pick and he took the dog. About six months after a neighbour's shepherd was at my house and saw the bitch puppy I had, and he bought it – an awfully good one. So he went to the shepherd who had picked the dog and told him he had made a bad pick as the bitch was so much better than his dog. The shepherd came straight with his dog to my house and asked me if I would change him as he would like a bitch. Well, when I saw his dog I did not need much persuading and he went off in high glee with the bitch. The usual dog show was held at Newcastle that year so I showed Revenge and he won 1st and a silver cup. When the shepherd got to know this, he landed back and wanted to change me again but of course there was nothing doing. Had he kept Revenge the first time, no one would ever have known he lived as he wanted him for hunting.'

Revenge's champions were Benton Biddy (25), Blister (29) and Bladnoch Raider (32) but it was the champion litter sisters, whelped in 1930, Todhunter and Happy Mood which were perhaps to have the greatest immediate influence over subsequent developments. They were out of a bitch called Causey Bridget, a grand-daughter of Titlington Jock, and were bred by Mr C. Renner, but were campaigned to their titles by John Renton, whose famous kennel was one of those which spanned the war years. Blister sired Ch Not So Dusty and through Stingo was grand-sire of both Ch Finchale Lass and Ch Share Pusher. Ch Bladnock Raider sired Ch What Fettle and Ch Gay Fine; both, like Not So Dusty, were bred by Mr J. Johnson.

Through Ch Benton Biddy, Revenge was grand-sire of Ch Brimball of Bridgesollers, a bitch which by winning 15 CCs was to establish a record which was not seriously to be threatened until the birth of Ch Dandyhow Shady Knight in 1966. Unfortunately, her duties in the ring kept her out of the nursery and so she was never given the opportunity to pass her qualities on to subsequent generations.

Benton Biddy's influence was to be of a different sort and was to extend through his grandson Ch Dinger to Ch Foxlair, described by some of the breed's sages as the best dog of the pre-war era. Ch Todhunter bred Ch Barb Wire for John Renton and so was the grand-dam of Ch Aldham Joker, another dog whose influence over the breed was to be profound.

In 1924, just two years after Revenge was born, Rival, another dog, who was to be influential, was whelped. He was bred by William Carruthers by Rab of Redesdale out of Tibby. Through Gem of Gold and Ch Dinger Rival he also appeared in both Aldham Joker's and Ch Brimball of Bridgesollers' pedigrees but it was through his son Ch Ranter that Rival's influence was felt most. Ranter was born in 1927 out of Coquetdale Reward, whose owner Adam Forster describes her in a letter to Miss Garnett Orme.

'Coquetdale Reward, the mother of Ch Ranter, was one of the nicest bitches I ever had. I think she was only once shown at a championship show, SKC at Edinburgh and she got the certificate and my other bitch Miss Tut was second to her.' What Adam Forster fails to mention here is that Miss Tut, who also went on to win a CC, was Reward's daughter. The letter continues – 'Coquetdale Reward was also a grand worker and one day I put her into a hole thinking it was a fox and it turned out to be a badger. She wasn't the sort to sit and bark behind the badger, she had to be over the dogs and at his throat so he gave her an awful punishing – tore all the flesh from her underjaw and when she came out she was in an awful mess. Reward went black fluid (and) could not see a thing and the day we went foxhunting and she followed after us following our footsteps – we were busy with a fox in a hole when she landed – she nosed around trying to find a hole, she had only her nose to go by and as soon as she found it, she went and tackled the fox. We were glad when she got out. She had some good dogs but Ch Ranter was the best, many people say he was the best Border ever shown in the North.'

Ranter sired Ch Grackle who in turn produced Ch Oakwood Pickle but another son, Furious Fighter, produced Ch Ranting Fury (37). Yet another grandson of Ch Ranter was Fearsome Fellow, whose double 'F' name denoted his origins in the Forsters' kennel. He sired Ch Deerstone Driver, the foundation of the Wharfholm kennel; he also sired Ch Dryburn Devilena and Ch Cravendale Chanter. However, it was as the sire of Ch Future Fame that Fearsome Fellow is best remembered.

Once more, however, we are in some danger of running too far ahead of our story and must retrace our steps to deal in greater detail with Oxnam Pincher's daugher Ch Station Masher, the first Border Terrier owned by Wattie Irving. Through Pincher, Station Masher went back to North Tyne Gyp while on her dam's side of the pedigree she carried lines back through Ch Teri to Titlington Jock. Mated to the North Tyne Gyp grandson, Ch Barney Bindle, she produced Ch Kineton Koffey (1928) which was given to Captain Pawson and did much to strengthen the breed's ranks in the south. In 1930, Masher was mated to Willie Barton's Whitrope Don to produce Ch Joyden. Surprisingly Koffey and Joyden were the only champions actually bred by Wattie Irving, though two other Borders, Hunty Gowk (1930) and Lady Pat (1935), bred by him each won two CCs. Wattie Irving's kennel, another which spurned the use of an affix, was based on the use of his stud dogs

SOME BORDER TERRIER KENNELS

exceptionally high degree of intelligence and loyalty, while they have their own very distinctive and attractive ways. One of their chief charms is that they are perfectly natural and unspoilt, with coats that are very easily kept in order.

CH. BLISTER, owned by **CAPT. M. C. HAMILTON, Forest Cottage, Forrest Hall, Northumberland,** still remains the outstanding Border Terrier dog of the day. He was bred by Mr. C. Renner, and was one of the famous litter which included Ch. Tod Hunter and Ch. Happy Mood. His sire was Revenge, and his dam Causey Bridget. Ch. Blister has won eight certificates, and is very game, and has been worked with both fox and otter hounds. He holds a M.F.H. working certificate. His sire, Revenge, was the sire of four champions, and Capt. Hamilton considers that he is largely responsible for the great improvement in the fronts of the present-day terrier. He has never seen a Revenge terrier with a bad front. Blister has sired quite a lot of winners, and looks like being as good as his sire in this respect. Capt. Hamilton keeps a select kennel of Borders, all of which are workers.

MISS DOBIE'S Border Kennels, Gifford, East Lothian.

Miss Dobie has only a small kennel, but her terriers are selected from the best working and winning strains. Amongst them BRANDY SNAP is outstanding; she is a full sister of Chs. Happy Mood and Tod Hunter. WHITTLE, whose puppies have done so well this past season, is a splendid working type. Her young daughter, Gala Red Hackle, by Ch. Blister, has a fine record. Though still not a year old, and shown only six times, she has won 17 firsts and special prizes, and both at Alnwick and the Scottish Kennel Club Show was awarded the trophy for best of breed. At the latter show she gained the challenge certificate. She was also successful at the Kennel Club Show in London, winning first, second, and third prizes in her classes. Gifford lies at the foot of the Lammermoor Hills, so that terriers are reared and exercised in the healthiest and most natural surroundings.

MR. WALTER IRVING, Station Border Terrier Kennels, Musselburgh.

This kennel was formerly at Riccarton Junction, amongst the Cheviot Hills, where the breed hunted regularly, and the strain is still kept with the local Foxhounds. Mr. Irving has sold many to fanciers in this country, and has exported quite a number to the United States of America, Canada, West Indies, and the Continent, where they have given entire satisfaction. The winning dog at the Scottish Kennel Club Show and the bitch at the Crystal Palace Kennel Club Show, both becoming champions, were bred by Mr. Irving; whilst another home-bred dog also holds the title. Many will remember that great bitch, Ch. Station Masher, who is still to the fore, and she played an important part in the founding of this kennel. Another great bitch in this kennel was the more recent Ch. Joyden. Her sire, Whitrope Don, and other winning dogs are at stud here. Mr. Irving has usually promising puppies and young stock for sale at reasonable prices.

MR. J. T. RENTON, Border Kennels, Langton, Duns.

Dogs here live under ideal conditions, having open fields to run in, in the very midst of a great hunting country. During the last three years just on 300 prizes have been won by these kennels. The best-known winners are perhaps that wonderful brace of bitches, CH. HAPPY MOOD and CH. TOD HUNTER, both of which are too well known to need comment. The stud dogs include DINGER and DANDY WARRIOR. Dinger is a well-known winner, including 1st and challenge certificate L.K.A., and reserve for the certificate at Cruft's Show. Dandy Warrior is a big winner, and one of the gamest dogs that ever went to earth. This dog has now been withdrawn from exhibition and work, having been badly mauled by a fox. He is being reserved for stud purposes. Mr. Renton has always puppies and adults for sale, and cordially invites inspection at any time.

JAMES GARROW.

Photo., Thos. Fall.
MR. J. T. RENTON'S CH. HAPPY MOOD.

THESE sporting little terriers have long been famed for their gameness in their native country—the borders of England and Scotland. The breed is an old one, and its points and characteristics have been carefully guarded and adhered to by breeders. In colour the terriers may be red (probably the most popular), wheaten, grizzle, or blue-and-tan. Though now so popular, and with large classes at all the principal shows, Border Terriers are still noted as "dead game" and hardy workers. They are used primarily for bolting foxes, otters, and badgers, but can also be gun trained, and are excellent with ferrets. They are ideal house dogs, being easy to train, and their close association with their sportsmen owners has developed an

Photo., Metcalfe, Barnard Castle.
CH. BLISTER. Owner, Capt. M. C. Hamilton.

A TYPICAL BORDER TERRIER BRED BY MR. IRVING.

Photo., Ralph Robinson, Redhill.
Miss Dobie's GALA RED HACKLE, C.C. and Gold Medal for Best of Breed at S.K.C. Show, 1933.

Cooperation between three influential kennels of the period produced this advert from a 1933 issue of *Our Dogs*. The world famous Scottish all-rounder, James Garrow, who wrote the generous appreciation.

and on Wattie's uncanny ability to spot promising puppies in the litters sired by them, a talent which was to keep the kennel well to the fore until the late 1950s.

Another kennel which operated in much the same way was that owned by John Renton who, with Adam Forster as Chairman, Wattie Irving as Secretary and himself as Treasurer, completed a triumvirate which was for many years to be influential in the Border Terrier Club. John Renton too was to achieve his greatest successes as a result of his ability to spot promising puppies in the nest. In the pre-war period he bred Ch Barb Wire (1934) by Ch Dinger out of his home bred Ch

The Famous Border Terriers

ONE of the best kennels of Border Terriers is that owned by Mrs. Ernest Twist, which contains two champions and other challenge prize winners. One is CH. FOX LAIR, an ideal specimen of his breed, excellent in body properties, straight and sound, and a real badger-headed fellow. He is the winner of eight challenge certificates at our premier shows, i.e., Kennel Club, Cruft's, Edinburgh, etc., and holds the unique record of having won three challenge certificates in succession at Cruft's. His fee is £3 3s., plus return carriage. He is proving his worth at stud and has some promising pups coming along — one, Hallbourne Pup, won at Brockenhurst, since when he has greatly improved. CH. WEDALE JOCK is another beautifully balanced Border of the correct type, full of character, keen in expression, and hard-coated. Of such is his quality that this year he has won challenge certificates

Photo., Thos. Fall.

CH. FOX LAIR.

**Belonging to
MRS. ERNEST TWIST,
OLD HALL, LITTLEBOURNE,
CANTERBURY, KENT**
Telephone : Littlebourne 22

at Cheltenham, Harrogate, and Edinburgh. He also is siring topping pups. Stud fee, £2 2s., plus return carriage. The young dog, ALDHAM JOKER, a very high-class terrier, that already has one challenge certificate to his name gained at the last Roundhay Ch. show, has fared particularly well at others, being only one point off securing his Junior Warrant. Only 17 months old, he is by Ch. Barb Wire ex Country Girl, litter sister to Ch. Bess of the Hall. A bitch that has done well is Winstonhall Bebe, which won the challenge certificate at the last Kensington Ch. show, and later was best of breed at Colchester. She is 15 months old, and is by Ch. Teddy Boy ex Ch. Bess of the Hall.

There are always some seven or eight bitches in the kennel, and some really promising pups, including two stormers by Ch. Fox Lair. Puppies and adults can generally be obtained at these kennels.

DECEMBER 16, 1938.   SUPPLEMENT TO "OUR DOGS."   93

Todhunter. Barb Wire was campaigned to his title by Mary Richmond. Also before the war, John Renton bred the CC winners Merriment (1932) and Epigram (1936) and was to own three champions in Happy Mood (1930), Ch Dinger (1931) and Ch Ranting Fury (1937) but it was after the war that his kennel was to reach its peak.

During his lifetime, and for some years after, Ch Foxlair ('34) was regarded by some of the breed's best breeders and judges as probably the best Border Terrier they had seen and certainly the best headed.

Sir John Renwick's involvement with Borders reflected a family interest which continues to this day through Lionel Hamilton Renwick. Ch Jedworth Bunty (28) was his first champion and was followed by Ch Grakle (30) and Ch Newminster Rose (35).

Another breeder of this period was Mr J. Johnson, whose early death robbed the breed of a valuable talent which in a three year period from 1932 to 1935 produced four champions. Ch Bladnoch Raider, by Revenge out of Red Gold, a Ch Ban of Tweeden grand-daughter, was the first but, also in 1932, from Hunty Gowk, a bitch bred by Wattie Irving by Whitrope Don, he bred, from a mating to Bh Blister, Ch Not So Dusty. Three years later using Ch Bladnoch Raider on Red Floss, a Hunty Gowk daughter, he produced the cleverly named champions Ch What Fettle and Ch Gay Fine.

All the breeders mentioned thus far in connection with the pre-war period came from northern England or from Scotland. However, the early progress and interest in the south had been maintained and there was a growing number of exhibitors who were beginning to achieve considerable success in the show ring. Foremost among these was Mrs Kally Twist whose first two champions were Ch Wedale Jock (1934) a son of Ch Heronslea and, more significantly, Ch Foxlair, a grandson through Rab O'Lammermoor of the Wattie Irving bred Knowe Roy. Foxlair is remembered by those who saw him as an outstanding dog with an exceptional head who had some claim to being the best Border Terrier produced to that time. Mrs Twist's third champion, however, was to have a greater influence over the breed as a whole and in particular the breed in the south than even Foxlair. He was Ch Aldham Joker (1937), a son of Ch Barb Wire out of Country Girl. However, his principal influence was to be felt after the war and so must wait until our next chapter.

Other kennels too were serving their apprenticeships during this period and were later to exert appreciable influence on the breed's subsequent development. The two decades between recognition and the outbreak of war can perhaps be regarded as a period of consolidation. Breeders whose initial interest had been in work were learning to come to terms with the demands of the show ring. Those who were principally attracted to the breed because of its potential as a show dog were learning of the importance of work to the breed's continued integrity and all were pulling together to ensure that a damaging dichotomy did not develop between show and working types. Geographically the breed was becoming more evenly distributed and as the influence of the best southern based dogs began to be felt, quality too began to even out though it would be some years before anything approaching equality between north and south was attained.

Some indication of the way in which the breed's popularity as a show dog has progressed since recognition is provided by show entries in 1938. At Crufts in February seventy-five Borders were paraded at the Royal Agriculture Hall in London while in the previous month the breed had produced, with nearly eleven Borders per class, the highest class average at the National Terrier Clubs Championship Show at Olympia, London. Even today, such a class average would be regarded as better than merely respectable though shows nowadays tend to be somewhat more generous with classification for the breed. At the National Terrier Club Show Share Pusher and Lady Pat won the CCs and the show's success made it seem that Crufts might be something of an anticlimax. This proved to be very far from the case as Tom Scott's report in *Our Dogs* showed:

'Border Terriers were a great entry under the popular Mr E. R. L. Hoskins. The puppy class contained no fewer than 22 youngsters. Barra of Bridgesollers, an exceptionally good bitch, good head, front and bone, well made up in body, harsh dense jacket, sound and free movement, keen expression. Ranting Fury, another smart one, scores in bone, front, legs well. Aldham Joker owns a typical headpiece, good front, cobby body, harsh jacket; moved freely. Verdict, sound, well balanced good looking youngster, head of nice quality, not quite as firm in shoulders and movement to (sic) those above him. Sandy of the Knoll scored in front, legs and feet; lost a shade in head to winner, pleasing body, harsh coat, good free mover, hard condition. Rumbold, handy, well balanced dog, good coat and body, shade loose in shoulders; shows nicely. Golden Rod, very promising, good looking terrier, classy head, keen expression, lovely body and coat; one who should do well; in good bloom. Share Pusher, attractive, well made dog, keen expression, good bone, front and shoulders, well bodied up, moves well; any amount of freedom; hard condition. Kineton Nici, a good shouldered, fronted, bodied terrier. Hard coat plenty of bone and substance, well coupled, quarters and movement very pleasing. Brownie O'Bladnoch did not pur all in at times but when he did he looked well, pleasing head, sound front, good bone, nice body and coat. Ch Foxlair, came, saw and conquered in a hot class; he was looking well and showed nicely, his virtues are known to all. Ch What Fettle gave the winner a close run, and he was well shown by his clever handler, another really good terrier, well worthy of his prefix, his condition was good. Ch Barb Wire made up a trio of grand terriers, he did his best and was not disgraced, a terrier every inch of him, showed well, condition good. Soor Ploom promising young bitch, head of nice quality, keen expression, sound front, bone and body pleasing. Winstonhall Phebe, nice type, body and quarters are good, coat is of good texture, head and expression are very typical, moved fairly well. Esksider scores in head, good body, moved a shade slack, good texture of coat. Rumwin Jane neat head, good bone and substance, well bodied, nice coat. Ch Brimball of Bridgesollers a great bitch, plenty of bone and substance, grand head; in superb form and proved a popular winner. Ch Gay Fine, another bitch whose quality is there for all to see, in good bloom. Lady Pat, good head, nicely bodied, good harsh coat, moves soundly.'

Crufts in 1938 must have been especially exciting with such a galaxy of talent on display and though most of the winners had travelled down from the north the entry suggests that the breed was well supported by southern exhibitors.

8 Post-war Years

The outbreak of war in 1939 was to result in the disappearance of a number of Border Terrier kennels which had been quietly establishing themselves during the immediate pre-war years. From 1920 the breed had steadily grown in popularity as a show dog, entries at shows all over the country were buoyant and registration figures were beginning to reach the mark at which breeders would have a sufficiently large pool of registered breeding stock to ensure a healthy future for the breed. Nor had popularity become so great that new difficulties and dangers had to be faced; progress had been steady rather than spectacular but with the outbreak of war a temporary halt was brought to this healthy state. In 1938 registrations, for the first time, had climbed above 300. In 1939 they were back in the mid-200s but in the following year had nosedived to a mere 69, declining further to 52 in 1941. The steady climb back to pre-war figures took until 1944 and then the climb continued until, in 1949, the breed reached 815 registrations. For some years registrations fluctuated about the 800 mark, in the early 1970s finally and confidently climbing above 1000. Unfortunately the Kennel Club twice in the 1970s changed the system of registration in such a way as to make it difficult, if not impossible, to make any meaningful comparisons with earlier figures.

In comparison with the popularity of other terrier breeds Border Terriers are about fifth in the group, measured by registration totals. They are about level with Airedales and behind Staffordshire Bull Terriers, West Highland White Terriers and Cairn Terriers and Bull Terriers. Registered numbers, however, are, in Border Terriers at least, an unreliable guide to popularity because a large reservoir of unregistered stock continues to exist. These dogs are bred primarily for work or as companions and though barred from competition at Kennel Club events are to be seen in large numbers at Working Terrier and Hunt Shows where they rub shoulders, as they do in the hunting field, with their registered brethren.

As we approach the present day writing a history of the breed becomes progressively more difficult. There is very much more detail available and time has not yet made its importance easier to assess. There are also a number of kennels whose major contribution to the breed is yet to come; time alone will allow the importance of each to be accurately assessed. Richard Baerlain, writing about racehorse trainers, encapsulated our problem when he wrote: 'Good horses make good trainers, and it is not unusual for a name to burn brightly for a while, only to fade when the horse, the talented member of the partnership, loses form or retires.' Precisely the same thing happens among breeders and exhibitors. A lucky purchase or mating may produce one champion or even two or three but to produce more, especially over a period of years, usually requires something more than good fortune.

A number of breeders have, since 1945, produced three champions; some of these will undoubtedly go on to produce more, others, sadly, have run their course.

Miss 'Jack' Eccles's Chalkcroft affix first appeared on Ch Fancy Girl of Chalkcroft (46) who produced Chalkcroft Duster, the sire of Ch Chalkcroft the Card (49) and Ch Chalkcroft Fancy (51).

Callum's son, Ch Girvanside Cruggleton Don (49), was one of three champions produced by George McConnell's Girvanside kennel, the other two being Ch Girvanside Tigress Mischief (48) and Don's son Ch Girvanside Sensation (55).

Captain Henry d'O. Vigne's Brookend affix graced just two champions, both by Brookend Vali out of Blackmorevale Fuzzy. They were Ch Brookend Baggins (58) and Ch Brookend Brandybuck (61) and were followed by Ch Makerston Foxlair (65), who was by Baggins as was Ch Wharfholm Wizardry (65).

That Maureen Wood's Derwood affix has not appeared on a champion should not obscure her connection with Ch Mr Tims (65) or with the outstanding stud dog Ch Wharfholm Warrant (68) both of which she bred. More recently her association with the Bannerdown kennel was developed when she made up Ch Bannerdown Capricorn (77). Warrant became the sire of six champions including Ch Mansergh Barn Owl, Ch Summer Belle, Ch Wharfholm Wonder Lad, Ch Bannerdown Viscount out of a Derwood bitch and in 1977, when he was eleven years old, Ch Rhozzum Tudor and Ch Bannerdown Capricorn.

Gilbert Walker's Workmore kennel relied on home-bred stock for its success with Ch Workmore Brackon (68), Ch Workmore Rascal (69) and her son Ch Workmore Waggoner (73) whose successes were achieved on both sides of the Atlantic. David and Joyce Fagan's first champions were the litter sisters Ch Lady Lucinda (68) and Ch Lucky Lucy (68), to be followed by the Ch Handy Andy son Ch Elandmead Ragamuffin (71). Edna Garnett's first success was with Ch Rhosmerholme Recuit (64); her daughter Ch Rhosmerholme Aristocrat (67) came next to be followed by Ch Duttonlea Sarah of Rhosmerholme (76).

Stewart Macpherson achieved something of a record in the breed when, with the help of Ted Hutchinson, his Brumberhill kennel made up its third champion just a few days before Stewart's 21st birthday. Ch. Brumberhill Blue Tansy (80), bred by Miss D. Lamb, was followed by the home-bred Ch Brumberhill Blue Maestro (83). Ch Brannigan of Brumberhill (84), bred by Mrs H. Deighton, then took the breed by storm and has been followed by the home-bred Ch Brumberhill Bittersweet (85) and Ch Blue Maverick of Brumberhill (85), bred by Mrs S. Clarke, and, like Brannigan, a Maestro son.

Betty Rumsam's Wilderscot affix was already well known before it appeared on her three home-bred champion bitches. These were Ch Wilderscot Beau Belle (74), Ch Wilderscot Silver Jubilee (77) and her daughter Ch Wilderscot Morning Star (78). Frances Wagstaff's three home-bred bitch champions are unusually all in tail female line from Ch Brehill Wayward Lass (77) through Ch Brehill March Belle (81) to Ch Brehill April Lass (84).

Only a handful of kennels have produced more than ten British champions and, though each will later be dealt with in detail, it is appropriate to mention Robert Hall's Deerstone kennel, Phyllis Leatt's kennel, Phyllis Mulcaster's Portholme's and Barbara Holmes's Wharfholme's, three of which had their homes in the Yorkshire Dales. Sadly none of these are now showing or breeding. Two other kennels which have also produced more than ten champions remain active; they are Anne Roslin Williams's Mansergh, now moved from Cumbria to Worcester, while Jean and Frank Jackson's Clipstones have travelled in the opposite direction from Sussex to Lancashire. However, in any balanced history of the breed one kennel is seen to stand away from the rest. Bertha Sullivan's Dandyhow affix, now shared with her daughter Kate Irving, is the only one to have been associated with more than twenty British champions and the score continues to increase.

Although breeding was severely curtailed during the war years a number of dogs were born which, as soon as it became possible once more to concentrate on more important matters, quickly became champions. Indeed 1944 has some claim to being regarded as a vintage year because born in that year were Ch Boxer Boy, of which more later, Ch

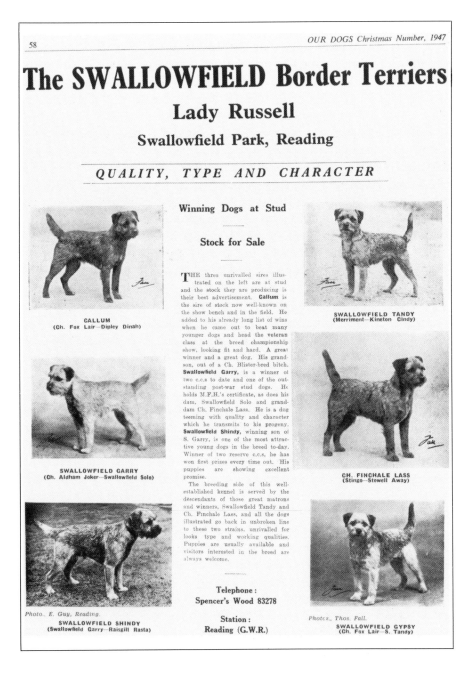

58   *OUR DOGS Christmas Number, 1947*

The SWALLOWFIELD Border Terriers

Lady Russell

Swallowfield Park, Reading

QUALITY, TYPE AND CHARACTER

CALLUM
(Ch. Fox Lair—Dipley Dinah)

SWALLOWFIELD GARRY
(Ch. Aldham Joker—Swallowfield Solo)

Photo., E. Guy, Reading.

SWALLOWFIELD SHINDY
(Swallowfield Garry—Raisgill Rasta)

Winning Dogs at Stud

Stock for Sale

THE three unrivalled sires illustrated on the left are at stud and the stock they are producing is their best advertisement. **Callum** is the sire of stock now well-known on the show bench and in the field. He added to his already long list of wins when he came out to beat many younger dogs and head the veteran class at the breed championship show, looking fit and hard. A great winner and a great dog. His grandson, out of a Ch. Blister-bred bitch, **Swallowfield Garry**, is a winner of two c.c.s to date and one of the outstanding post-war stud dogs. He holds M.F.H.'s certificate, as does his dam, Swallowfield Solo and granddam Ch. Finchale Lass. He is a dog teeming with quality and character which he transmits to his progeny. **Swallowfield Shindy**, winning son of S. Garry, is one of the most attractive young dogs in the breed to-day. Winner of two reserve c.c.s, he has won first prizes every time out. His puppies are showing excellent promise.

The breeding side of this well-established kennel is served by the descendants of those great matrons and winners, Swallowfield Tandy and Ch. Finchale Lass, and all the dogs illustrated go back in unbroken line to these two strains, unrivalled for looks type and working qualities. Puppies are usually available and visitors interested in the breed are always welcome.

Telephone :
Spencer's Wood 83278

Station :
Reading (G.W.R.)

SWALLOWFIELD TANDY
(Merriment—Kineton Cindy)

CH. FINCHALE LASS
(Stingo—Stowell Away)

Photos., Thos. Fall.

SWALLOWFIELD GYPSY
(Ch. Fox Lair—S. Tandy)

Rona Rye, which became John Renton's first post-war champion, and Ch Swallowfield Garry.

The Swallowfield affix belonged to Lady Russell who had served notice of things to come when she made up Ch Finchdale Lass (37) but it was a son of Ch Aldham Joker, Ch Swallowfield Garry (44), who was to push her kennel into the front rank. Garry was out of Swallowfield Solo, a daughter of Callum, Ch Foxlair's illustrious son. He sired Ch Swallowfield Shindy (46) out of Raisgill Rasta, an Aldham Joker daughter, bred by Miss Hester Garnett Orme. Then two more Swallowfield champions, Coromaine (47) and Nutmeg (47), both sired by Callum, were produced before Garry sired Ch Swallowfield Fergus (50) out of S. Chloe, yet another daughter of Callum. Sadly Fergus was the last champion to carry the Swallowfield affix but Lady Russell's continued enthusiasm was demonstrated when she made up Ch Dandyhow Sandpiper (68). During the immediate post-war period Lady Russell had made extensive use of two dogs, Ch Aldham Joker and Callum, both of which had a considerable influence on the breed. Callum, Latin for thick skinned, would get our vote as the best named Border Terrier.

Though Aldham Joker was ultimately to prove to be an outstanding stud dog it is difficult to decide whether he should be regarded as a late developer or as a dog whose early success was restricted by the war. Whatever the reason it was not until 1944, when he was already a veteran, that Joker sired his first two champions, Ch Swallowfield Garry and Ch Boxer Boy. Two years later he produced, for Phyllis Mulcaster, Ch Portholme Marthe of Deerstone, which became the first of Mr Robert Hall's champions. Also in 1946 he produced Mrs David Black's Ch Tweedside Red Biddy to get a well known pre-war kennel back into winning ways. After another interval of two years he then produced Ch Hallbourne Bracket for his owner, Mrs Twist, and then, in the following year, now a venerable thirteen-year-old, he produced Ch Hallbourne Badger, arguably the most significant of his offspring.

Callum never became a champion but must be included among the very short list of dogs which, though they did not achieve great success in the ring, nevertheless proved to be outstanding stud dogs; he was bred by Mr J. J. Pawson by Ch Foxlair out of Dipley Dinah, a daughter of Ch Heronslea. In addition to his two Swallowfield champions Callum also sired Ch Dronfield Berry (47), Ch Lucy Gray (48), and Ch Girvanside Cruggleton Don (48) and, most important of all, Ch Billy Boy (48).

Prior to the war John Renton had produced three champions but it was from 1944 onwards that his greatest impact on the breed was made. This second series of champions began with Ch Rona Rye (44); then came Ch Vic Mery (48) followed by Ch First Choice (50), a bitch by

John Renton with Ch
Happy Day (59) taken in
1967.

Tweedside Red Silvo. Ch Scotch Mist (54) was next and her daughter by Ch Future Fame, Ch Ranting Roving (57). Then it was the turn of the litter brothers by Ch Tweedside Red Kingpin, Ch Barnikin (59) and Ch Happy Day (59). Two offspring of Ch Hawkesburn Beaver and Border Queen, Ch Handy Andy (65) and Ch Hawkesburn Happy Returns (66), then brought John Renton's long and illustrious career to a close thirty-six years after he had produced his first champion.

Wattie Irving had also established a pre-eminent position in the breed by producing four champions prior to the war. His success continued after it with Ch Rising Light (45) and Ch Alexander (54). Then came three champions all by Ch Tweedside Red Kingpin. These were Ch Rab Roy (58) and the litter sisters, Ch Brieryhill Gertrude (59) and Ch Bright Light (59). Wattie's career, between Ch Station Master and Ch Bright Light, had spanned almost forty years. During

Until the 1970s Phyllis Mulcaster's Portholme kennel had produced more British champions than any other.

The PORTHOLME Border Terriers

OUR DOGS Christmas Number, 1951

Left to right : CH. PORTHOLME MAIRE, CH. PORTHOLME MAGIC, CH. PORTHOLME MAMIE and CH. PORTHOLME MANLY BOY

At Stud:—Ch. Portholme Manly Boy and Ribblesdale Roger (Sire of Ch. Portholme Maire and Ch. Portholme Mamie) . . . Puppies by these dogs usually for sale

Mrs. STANLEY MULCASTER, Great Stukeley, Huntingdon. Tel.: Huntingdon 359

117

this time he had, apart from producing, though not always breeding, a string of champions, he had also founded what amounts to a dynasty of Border Terrier breeders and judges. In addition, as Secretary of the Border Terrier Club, with John Renton as an able Treasurer and Adam Forster in the Chair, he had worked for the breed during a crucial stage in its development and had, after the war, helped to set it on a firm footing.

One of, if not the, most successful show kennels prior to the 1960s was that which belonged to Phyllis Mulcaster. Her Portholme affix graced no less than thirteen champions, a score which, though eventually to be eclipsed by the Dandyhow affix, has, as yet, been equalled by no other.

The first of her champions was Ch Portholme Magic (46). Two years later came Ch Portholme Manly Boy (48), bred by Mrs G. Edwards by Deerstone Dauntless, a son of Callum, and out of Skirden Serens, a grand-daughter through her dam, Deerstone Mischief, of Callum's blood. Manly Boy too was to prove to be an outstanding stud dog. In the following year the litter sisters Ch Portholme Maire (49) and Ch Portholme Mamie (49) were bred by Mr E. Lee by Mr Arthur Duxbury's Ribbleside Roger, a son of Deerstone Defender out of Portholme Gayless. The dam was Nettle Tip, bred by Miss Garnett Orme by Portholme Rob out of Raisgill Ribbon, a daughter of Callum.

In 1952 Manly Boy sired Ch Portholme Merryman and in the following year Ch Portholme Mirth. Then in 1958 came Ch Portholme My Fair Lady out of a Manly Boy grand-daughter. In 1960 came the last four Portholme champions with Ch Portholme Macsleap out of Mirth, Ch March Belle, Ch Portholme Mr Moses out of My Fair Lady and Ch Portholme My Duskie Lady of Merryman. Three of the four, therefore, had Manly Boy as their grandfather. However, it was not just within the Portholme kennel that Manly Boy's influence was felt. He also sired Mr Donald Goodsir's Ch Carahall Cornet (50) as well as Ch Deerstone Destiny (55) and Ch Deerstone Desirable (58) for Mr Robert Hall and in so doing brought his stud career to a successful close at the ripe old age of ten.

The fact that Manly Boy sired two Deerstone champions serves to introduce Mr Robert Hall's successful kennel which produced twelve champions, six of them home-bred. The first was Ch Portholme Marthe of Deerstone (46), an Aldham Joker daughter out of Portholme Ruby who carried a lot of Dr Lilico's Bladnoch blood. Then came Ch Deerstone Driver (47), a son of Adam Forster's Fearsome Fellow who was to become Mrs Barbara Holmes's first champion. It was not until

The DEERSTONE Border Terriers

Owned by: Mr. R. HALL, The Lodge, Gledstone, Nr. Skipton, Yorks

Telephone : Earby 2126   -   -   -   Station : Skipton (L.M.S.)

DURING 1947 the following awards were won :—

Deerstone Defender.—S.B.T.C. open show, 1 first, 1 second, reserve best dog; S.B.T.C. ch. show, 2 firsts, **challange cert.** and **best of breed;** Peterborough ch., third open dog. Report : "Much improved since last I saw him, nice size, sound coat, strong loin, good quarters, moved well." He came third in open at Altrincham ch. show.

Bladnoch Brock of Deerstone.—S.B.T.C. open, 1 first, 2 seconds; London ch., 3rd graduate, 3rd sp. open; Edinburgh ch., **reserve challenge cert.** in a record entry. Report : "Very sound and upstanding, good quality head, grand legs and feet, harsh coat; looks like his job; later won special for most workmanlike dog." Brock was reserve for the c.c. at Silsden ch. show.

Brock is litter brother to Ch. B. Spaewife, and has now developed into a grand dog. He shows signs of being even a greater success as a stud dog, and this is not surprising considering his breeding. His first puppies are outstanding in head, and inherit his correct size and balance.

Defender's first puppy to be shown was 2nd in puppy class at London ch. although only six months old, and many more winners are expected to be out shortly.

A feature of these two dogs is that breeders who have used them are again sending bitches —proof of the high standard of their progeny. Both are at stud at a fee of 4 gns.

In bitches, **B. Tinker Bell** (also litter sister to Spaewife) is a ch. show winner, and should prove her worth as a matron. The young bitch **Portholme Marthe of Deerstone** won puppy dog or bitch at Blackpool ch., also puppy and maiden bitch, National Terrier ch., and is predicted by a number of judges as a certain champion. She was reserve for the c.c. at both Silsden and Altrincham ch. shows. Deerstone Dauntless was sold to Mrs. Mulcaster at 11 months of age, and has won every time exhibited, including four ch. shows. Mr. Hall has a high opinion of this dog.

The dogs live an outdoor life, and as Mr. Hall is agent on an estate of 6,000 acres, the dogs get plenty of freedom.

Photo., Hedges, Lytham.
DEERSTONE DEFENDER

OUR DOGS Christmas Number, 1947   123

Robert Hall's Deerstone kennel was one of a number from the Yorkshire dales and one of the most successful during the immediate post-war period. This advert dates from 1947.

1955 that the next Deerstone champion came; this was Ch Deerstone Destiny (55) and he was followed by Ch Deerstone Desirable (58). Destiny's son Ch Deerstone Realization (59) was born in the following year and in 1962 Ch Deerstone Douglas, a grandson through Ch Portholme Mirth of Manly Boy, was born. The last of the home-bred champions was Ch Deerstone Dugmore (66), yet another Manly Boy grandson. Then came Ch Deerstone Busybody Madam (64) with Ch Deerstone Larkbarrow Rainbow (67), bred by Mrs L. Farthing, and Ch Deerstone Falcliff Ramona (67), bred by Ellis Mawson, completing the dozen Deerstone champions.

Mr and Mrs David Black's Tweedside Red affix had made its mark with Ch Titlington Tattler's Tweedside Red Tatters (21) and Ch Tweedside Red Type (27). Tatters, mated to Ch Dandy of Tynedale had produced Ch Tweedside Red Topper (23). Borders then seem to have taken something of a back seat in the Blacks' household until after the war came the Ch Aldham Joker daughter, Ch Tweedside Red Biddy (46), to be closely followed by Ch Tweedside Red Salvo (47) and Ch Tweedside Red Gloria (48), a daughter of Tweedside Red Playboy. Then, by Salvo, came Ch Tweedside Red Glamorous (49) and finally the Glamorous son of Ch Girvanside Cruggleton Don, Ch Tweedside Red Dandy (53), just 32 years after the kennel had produced its first Border Terrier champion. However, a review of the kennel's champions would omit what was arguably the most significant product.

The Noted "Tweedside" Border Terriers,

The Property of Mrs. David Black, at No. 14, Tweed Street, Berwick-on-Tweed.

WHEN this lady decided to have a sport and hobby on her own—apart from her husband's celebrated kennel of Tweedside Bulldogs—I really wonder if she ever anticipated she would, with such lightning-like rapidity, strike the peak height of affairs in showing and breeding? One never can tell, yet I know she was well fortified with knowledge of the breed type and where the blood to answer her purpose could be obtained.

The chief show and stud dog the roost is TWEEDSIDE RED TYPE, a son of Ch. Titlington Tatler. Type has

TWEEDSIDE RED TYPE.

put up a brilliant sequence of premier wins, having not less than six reserve championships to his credit, and over seventy 1sts and other prizes. His recent wins are :—1st Limit and 1st Open and the silver cup for the best Border Terrier in the show at Sandy; 1st Limit and 1st Open, Dundee; 1st Open Liverpool, and 2nd Limit; 2nd Open and reserve championship at Birmingham last month. A dog in his prime, he owns a beautiful short, characteristic head and foreface, with a dark muzzle, neat-hung dark ears, just the size in body, rare front and legs of bone, a sandy red, harsh coat, with well-carried tail. A jaunty, showy, game little dog He is an outstanding stud dog, and gets quality puppies of large numbers. His fee is £4 4s.

It is given to few to make a bitch a full champion in record time, yet this is what happened with TWEEDSIDE RED TATTERS (Ch Titlington Tatler ex Chip), a bitch whose head is a marvellous picture study, rare ears and outstanding body, dark eyes. She won her spurs under such judges as Mr. Calvert Butler at the National Terrier Club's show, Mr. Sam Graham at Cruft's, Mr. T. Wallace at the Great Joint Terrier Show, and at Leeds under Mr. J. J. Holgate, the above highly important shows being practically the only times this wonderful specimen has been out, and that is sufficient answer as to her qualities.

T. RED BETTY is a later litter sister to Type. A class-moulded bitch in body and head, very well-carried ears, and gives the wanted head, expression, and dark eyes. The latest additions to her wins were three 1sts at Dundee Show. She is in addition a valuable stamp of a brood bitch. But we come to a litter of six puppies that would gladden the hearts of the oldest connoisseurs. They are by Dandie of Tynedale ex Ch. T. R. Tatters. A glorious lot of all reds with black points—heads, ears, and bodies are here. There is another litter of five by T Red Type ex T. R. Molly (Tug ex Fawdon Ginger), another valuable lot of short-backed reds, with promising heads and ears.

In young stock as well as matured Mrs. Black is strongly fortified, and it seems to me she is trying to

eclipse the performances of her husband in Bulldogs. She has a big task in front of her. Mrs. Black is very keen on this variety, and has made it a study for many years, and the mere fact that she has sprung right away into the forefront in the variety is an ample certificate to her knowledge of what a proper Border ought to be.

F. G.

MRS. AND MR. DAVID R. BLACK WITH A TEAM OF WINNING BORDER TERRIERS.
Left to right: Ch. Tweedside Red Tatters, Tweedside Red Molly, and Tweedside Red Type.

Tweedside Red Kingpin, a son of Ch Girvanside Cruggleton Don, never became a champion but sired Ch Rabroy and then in one incredible year Ch Barnikin, Ch Brieryhill Gertrude, Ch Bright Light and Ch Happy Day.

In 1947 the first of the eleven Leatty champions was born. This kennel, owned by Phyllis Leatt, wife of the famous all-round judge George Leatt, produced champions in a number of breeds. The first of the Leatty champions was Ch Leatty Lace (47). Then came Ch Leatty Druridge Dazzler (49), followed by a daughter of Dazzler, Ch Leatty Lucky (51). Ch Leatty Billy Bunter (54) was a son of Ch Billy Boy as was the home-bred Ch Leatty Loyal Lass who was out of Lace. Ch Leatty Juliet of Law (55) was a daughter of Ch Wharfholm Wizard and was to provide the foundation on which the Mansergh kennel was to be built. Ch Leatty Joy Boy (55) was bred by Bertha Sullivan in the days before her affix had been registered. Another son of Ch Billy Boy was Ch Leatty Plough Boy (59) and he was followed by Ch Leatty Emblewest Betsy (62), Ch Leatty Felldyke Badger (62) and finally Ch

Mrs David Black's Tweedside kennel had a well established reputation in Bulldogs before turning, with outstanding success, to Border Terriers. This advert dates from 1923 but the kennel was to produce winners for over thirty more years.

OUR DOGS Christmas Number, 1951 249

The LEATTY Kennels

Mr. GEORGE LEATT, Middle Row, Skipton, Yorks.
Telephone 883

GEORGE and Phyllis Leatt have in their time kept Bulldogs, Schipperkes, Wire Fox Terriers, Scotties, Poms, Whippets and Cockers (their first breed) before making the Leatty prefix so well known in Border Terriers and Smooth Fox Terriers. With this varied experience it is not surprising that Mr. George Leatt is becoming increasingly popular as an all-round judge, in addition to his appointments to judge a variety of terriers at championship shows; or that Mrs. Leatt judged her first championship show of Border Terriers at Kensington this December. She has been judging

LEATTY DRURIDGE DAZZLER

Bulldogs for quite a time at open and members' shows.

Ch. Leatty Lace was Mrs. Leatt's first Border Terrier champion, and after this came **Ch. Lily of the Valley**, who is at the moment nursing a litter by **Leatty Druridge Dazzler**, which has the enviable distinction of holding the Wedale Jock cup for most points won by a Border Terrier in variety classes during 1950 and offered by the Southern Border Terrier Club. He has already won one c.c. and two reserve c.c.s, and should soon make up the trio of champion Borders in one kennel. He is siring

good winners, including the well-known reserve c.c. winner, Happy Laddie, and is at stud at four guineas.

Leatty stock has always commanded a ready sale and in addition to home business Mr. and Mrs. Leatt have exported Borders to the U.S.A., and Bulldogs, Smooth Fox Terriers and Scottish Terriers to many other parts of the world. They are always very ready to help beginners with sound advice. All inquiries for stock, of which they always have some for sale, or for stud work receive their immediate attention.

A. Jean Hopwood.

Photos, Hedges, Lytham.
CH. LEATTY LACE

CH. LILY OF THE VALLEY

The Leatty kennel produced no less than eleven champions in Britain and by exporting stock, often as the agent for other kennels, also exerted an international influence on the breed's post-war development.

Leatty Felldyke Gorse (65), both the last two having been bred by John Harrison.

Two dogs recur as the sires of Leatty champions. One was Callum and the other his son Ch Billy Boy (48). Billy Boy was bred and owned by Larry Waters out of Misty Dawn, a daughter of Boxer Boy and therefore a grand-daughter of Ch Aldham Joker. Billy Boy sired no less than ten champions to establish a record which was to remain undisturbed for over thirty years. His first champion was Ch Redbor Revojet (52), then came Ch Braw Boy (53) to be followed with almost monotonous regularity by Ch Leatty Billy Bunter (54), Ch Dipley Dighy (55), bred by Hugh Pybus out of Ch Bumble Bee, a home-bred daughter of Boxer Boy, and so yet another champion grandchild of Ch Aldham Joker, Ch Full Toss (57) and Ch Silver Sal (58), bred by Larry Waters but campaigned to her title by her owner Jim Short. In 1959 Billy Boy's final crop of champions were born; they were Ch Coundon Trudy and Ch Wintonhall Coundon Tim, both bred by Miss Nancy

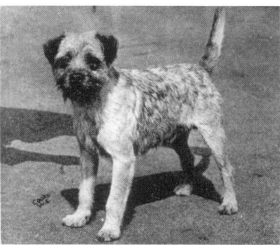

Turrall out of her Ravensdowne Roxana, and finally came Ch Leatty Plough Boy.

The first Border Terrier champion owned by Barbara Holmes was Ch Deerstone Driver (47) and only some time afterwards was the Wharfholm affix, which was to become so well known, registered. Ch Wharfholm Winnie (51) was a daughter of Driver out of Ch Portholme Marthe of Deerstone and she, like most of the Wharfholm champions, was home-bred. Marthe also produced, to Ribbleside Rocket, Ch Wharfholm Wench (52) and Ch Wharfholm Wizard (52) and then Wizard, mated to Winnie, produced Ch Wharfholm Wink (54). Ch Mansergh Wharfholm Wistful (58), also by Wizard, came next. Ch Wharfholm Blue Moon (60) out of Ch Richies Dream brought new blood into the kennel as did Ch Wharfholm Wayward Wind (63) out of the same bitch. Ch Wharfholm Wizardry (65) was a son of Mansergh Wharfholm Wistful and Ch Mr Tims (65) who was out of Wistielass. Then came Ch Wharfholm Warrant (66), also out of Wistielass. Warrant put to Wayward Wind produced Ch Wharfholm Wonder Lad (67) and finally came Ch Wharfholm Mansergh Tinkerblue (72).

Mr and Mrs Adam Forster conformed to the Border tradition by not having an affix, though their stock can often be recognised by the double 'F' initials. Foremost among these is the outstanding sire Ch Future Fame (48). His daughters Ch Lucky Purchase (49) and Ch First Footer (49) were followed by Ch Hugill Sweep (56) who brought to a close a career which had begun in 1927 with Ch Ranter. In all Future Fame sired six champions, the last two Ch Ranting Roving (57) and Ch Rayndale Ramone (57) when he was nine years old, but it was

ABOVE LEFT Ch Future Fame ('48), a dog who has had a very considerable influence on the breed's post-war development.

ABOVE RIGHT Ch Golden Imperialist ('52), owned in Britain by Phyllis Leatt and exported to Europe to become the breed's first continental international champion.

probably through his subsequent descendants in a number of the breed's most successful kennels that he made his greatest impact.

Mary Vaux's first champion was Ch Oakwood Pickle (32) by Ch Grakle. After the war came Ch Vic Merry (48) and, out of a Newminster bitch, Ch Newsholme Modesty (67). Finally came Ch Easingwood Rascal (70).

In 1949 the first of Kally Twist's five Hallbourne champions was whelped. Mrs Twist's kennel was Ch Aldham Joker's home and it was he who sired Ch Hallbourne Bracket (49) and Ch Hallbourne Badger (50). In his turn Badger sired the litter brothers Ch Hallbourne Blu Val (52) and Ch Hallbourne Brick (52). Val later sired Ch Hallbourne Constancy (54). The kennel's outstanding stud dogs had a profound effect on the breed, particularly in the south.

One of the Scottish kennels to achieve success was Carahall, owned by Donald Goodsir, the first of whose four champions was Ch Carahall Cornet (50), a son of Manly Boy. It was almost a decade later before Ch Carahall Coffee (61) was born. Coffee then sired Ch Carahall Cicely (62) and her little brother Ch Gay Gordon (62) owned by Grace Gaddes, one of the extensive Irving clan whose father Mervyn had made up Ch Hornpiece Salvia (50) over ten years earlier.

Mr and Mrs Bobby Benson's Daletyne kennel at Hexham, in the heart of Border country, was at the height of its success in the early 1960s. The kennel's first champion was Ch Joytime (53), the second, Ch Eignwye Daletyne Santara (62), a grandson of Joytime, came nine years later. Then Daletyne Rory, one of the handful of dogs which failed to get their title but which nevertheless proved to be outstanding stud dogs, produced Ch Daletyne Batchelor (64), Ch Daletyne Dundrum (64) and, for Mrs Howdon, Ch Highland Gyp (64). Then a repeat of the mating which had produced Batchelor produced Ch Daletyne Decora (65). Decora was the last of the Daletyne champions but was not the end of the kennel's influence. Ch Leatty Felldyke Badger and Ch Wharfholm Wayward Wind were both out of Daletyne bitches, and Batchelor also sired Ch Rossut Motcombe Barnbrack (67), bred by Jack Cobby, the South and West Wilts huntsman, but made up by Catherine Sutton. Jack Price's Ch Oxcroft Vixen (66) was also out of a Daletyne bitch as were David Fagan's litter sisters Ch Lady Lucinda (68) and Ch Lucky Lucy (68). It was not until 1975 that the last champion directly by or out of Daletyne stock was born. This was Int Ch Bombax Xavier, bred in Sweden by Gunnar and Carl Gunnar Stafberg. Xavier was by Int Ch Daletyne Danny Boy out of Swed Ch Clipstone Clover. After a very successful show career in Scandinavia

Xavier was brought to England where, owned by Jean Jackson and Carl Gunnar Stafberg, he became the first, and thus far the only, foreign-bred Border Terrier to become a British champion.

Walter Gardner's Maxton affix came to the fore with Ch Maxton Mannequin (54), a grand-daughter of Ch Future Fame. She bred Ch Maxton Miss Mink (56) and Future Fame mated to one of his own daughters produced Ch Maxton Matchless. Matchless then sired Ch Marrburn Morag (59) who, mated to him, produced Ch Maxton Monarch (59). The same mating produced Maxton Mhairi who, mated to Millbank Tarka, a son of Matchless, produced Ch Maxton Makrino (67) and Ch Maxton Marla (67). The intensity of inbreeding used in the Maxton kennel is unique in Border Terriers. The tool is a sharp one which, used wisely, can achieve outstanding results but which, used unwisely, can fail to produce either short- or long-term benefits.

Then came a kennel which should, perhaps, have a chapter to itself. Bertha Sullivan's Dandyhow kennel has produced twice as many champions as any other. It produced a dog which equalled Billy Boy's stud record and then one which surpassed it. It produced the first bitch to

Dandyhow Brussel Sprout ('59) taken when he had reached an advanced age and had produced his ten champions.

breed four British champions and has provided the foundation stock for some of the most successful kennels. The Dandyhow story is not at an end for, though now very much reduced in numbers, it continues to produce winners.

The foundations of Dandyhow's success were laid in 1950 when Mrs Sullivan bought a daughter of Ch Swallowfield Gary, Bint Superior, and a daughter of Ch Tweedside Red Playboy, Brin's Selection, but it was not until 1957 that the kennel bred its first champion. This was Phyllis Leatt's Ch Leatty Joy Boy (57). Then came the first of the champions to carry the Dandyhow affix. They were Ch Dandyhow Bitter Shandy (58), Ch Dandyhow Sultana (61) and Ch Dandyhow Suntan (61), Suntan being owned by Arthur Beardwood. Ch Dandyhow Soraya (62) was the first bitch to have bred four British champions, three of these being to an equally remarkable dog, Dandyhow Brussel Sprout (59). They were Ch Dandyhow Shady Lady (66), Ch Dandyhow Seashell (66) and Kitty Welch's Ch Thrushgill Dandyhow Silhouette (68).

Dandyhow Brussel Sprout, known as Veg, was by Fighting Fettle out of Beautiful Spy. He produced his first champion in 1961. This was Ch Mansergh Dandyhow Bracken (61). Another five years were to pass before his next champions came these were Ch Dandyhow Shady Lady (66) and Ch Dandyhow Seashell (66). Eva Heslop's Ch Corburn Ottercap Farm Lassie (67) and Ch Dandyhow Sweet Biscuit (67) came next to be followed by Ch Thrushgill Dandyhow Silhouette (68) and the litter brothers Ch Dandyhow Sandpiper (68), who became Lady Russell's last champion, and Ch Dandyhow Shady Knight (68), who was destined to make an even bigger mark on the breed than his remarkable sire. Harold Roper's Ch Borderbrae Candy (69) and Jean and 'Harry' Singh's Ch Vandameres Band of Gold (70) completed the ten champions which set Veg alongside Billy Boy as the breed's leading sire.

In the early 1970s one of Veg's sons began to emerge as a star in his own right, this was Ch Dandyhow Shady Knight (68), who by winning 24 CCs, all under different judges, was to beat the record which Ch Brimball of Bridgesollers had established over thirty years earlier. He sired twelve champions whose names read like a Who's Who of Border Terrier kennels. The list begins in style with four champions born in the same year, Ch Llanishen Illse of Clipstone (70), Ch Dandyhow Burnished Silver (70), Ch Hawkesburg Nutmeg (70) and Ch Foxhill Foenix (70). These were followed by Ch Dandyhow Quality Street (71), Ch Foxhill Fidelity (72), Ch Oxcroft Pearl of Mansergh (73), Ch

Vandameres Burnished Gold (73), Ch Dandyhow Spectator (74), Ch Dandyhow Nightcap (75), Ch Dandyhow Silver Ring (76) and Ch Dandyhow Humbug (76).

In addition to those already mentioned Dandyhow has also produced Ch Dandyhow Margery Daw (72) by Ch Cravendale Copper, and Ch Dandyhow Forget-me-not (78), Ch Dandyhow Scotsman (80) and Ch Dandyhow Marchioness (80), all by Ch South Box. There have also been Ch Duttonlea Suntan of Dandyhow Grenadier, his son Ch Uncle Walter of Dandyhow (81) and his grandson by Uncle Walter, Ch Dandyhow Crofter (82), and Ch Dandyhow April Fool (85) owned by Dave and Track Fryer. During a thirty year period there have been no less than 27 Dandyhow champions plus another 48 champions in other kennels which were by or out of Dandyhow terriers. The record is one which is unlikely to be equalled, let alone beaten.

The old established west country affix, Eignwye, belongs to Bob Williams whose first champion was the home-bred Ch Eignwye Enchantress (57), followed by Ch Eignwye Daletyne Santara (62). Then came two home-bred champions, both by Solway Cawfields Duke. They were Ch Eignwye Tweed (70) and Ch Eignwye Wheatear (75). Another kennel which has been appearing on good Border Terriers for a number of years is Madelene Aspinwall's Farmway affix. Her first champions were Ch Covington Dove (57) and Donald Goodsir's Ch Carahall Cornet but it was not until Ch Farmway Red Robin (62) that a champion carrying the Farmway affix was to appear. After Red Robin came Ch Farmway Fine Feathers (73), a grandson of Ch Deerstone Douglas. Then came Ch Farmway Moneybird (77) out of Dandyhow parents, Ch Farmway Snow Kestrel (77) and Ch Farmway M'Lady Robin (81).

The Mansergh affix began as the sole property of Mary Roslin-Williams and was principally associated with her black Labrador Retrievers. However, a close association with hunting inevitably led to the affix being shared with her daughter, Anne, and becoming increasingly associated with Border Terriers who, from 1958 onwards, have produced a steady flow of champions. The first was Ch Mansergh Wharfholm Wistful (58), followed by Ch Mansergh Dandyhow Bracken (61). Ch Mansergh April Mist (61), bred by Seth Tripcony, followed and then came Ch Mansergh Rhosmerholme Amethyst (66), a bitch bred by Edna Garnett which presented younger Jacksons with pronunciation problems as a result of which she became widely known as Hammersmith. Then Ch Mansergh Barn Owl (68) was bred by Ted Hutchison by Ch Wharfholm Warrant and was followed by Ch

Wharfholm Mansergh Tinkerblue (72). The Shady Knight son, Ch Oxcroft Pearl of Mansergh (73), bred by Jack Price, came next and then followed a string of home-bred champions including Ch Mansergh Cushy Butterfield (75), Ch Mansergh Sergeant Pepper (75) and his son Ch Mansergh General Post (76). Then came General Post's son Ch Mansergh Pearl Diver (78), Pearl Diver's daughter Ch Froswick Button of Mansergh (81), bred by Roger Westmoreland, and, out of Button, Ch Mansergh Toggle (84).

Ellis Mawson's Falcliff kennel was another which had its home in the Yorkshire Dales. Its first champion was Ch Falcliff Tantaliser (66) and, out of Deerstone Daybreak, the litter brother and sister, Ch Ribbleside Falcliff Trident (67) and Ch Deerstone Ramona (67).

Ch Hawkesburn Beaver (63) was not only the first champion owned by Felicity Marchant but was also her first Border Terrier and her first show dog. Others have repeated this achievement but most must acquire patience before acquiring their first champion. Bred by Mervyn Gaddes, Beaver was by Ch Gay Gordon and in his turn produced Ch Hawkesburn Happy Returns (66), bred by John Renton. Happy Returns then produced Ch Hawkesburn Nutmeg (70) by Shady Knight and Ch Hawkesburn Spindle (73) by Knight's little brother Ch Dandyhow Sandpiper.

Dorothy Miller's Foxhill kennel's first champion was Ch Foxhill Fusilier (65) who was followed by the Ch Happy Day daughter, Ch Foxhill Firm Favourite (66), and by Fusilier's son, Ch Foxhill Fulbert (69). Then came two Shady Knight daughters, Ch Foxhil Feonix (70) and Ch Foxhill Fidelity (72), the latter owned by Ruth Urie who also made up Ch Hobbykirk Destiny, a son of Ch Deerstone Dugmore. Ch Step Ahead sired the other two Foxhill champions, Ch Foxhill Ferelith (75) and Ch Foxhill Firefly (76). The kennel's beneficial influence over the breed has extended well beyond its Peebles home.

One of the kennels which, until overtaken by events, maintained what might almost be regarded as a traditional reluctance in the breed to use an affix is that of Ronnie Irving. Grandson of Wattie, son of Andrew, his first champion was Ch Bounty Tanner (65) who sired Ch Arnton Fell (69) out of Station Masha, a litter sister of Ch Gay Gordon who belonged to Ronnie's cousin Grace Gaddes, and Ch Carahall Cicely. Then came Ch Llanishen Penelope (73) who, put to Dandyhow Napoleon, bred Ch May Isle Misty (73). The litter brother and sister, Ch South Box (76) and Ch Din Merry (76), came next. Marriage to Kate Sullivan has meant that subsequent Borders shown by Ronnie have all carried the Dandyhow affix.

Jack Price's Oxcroft affix came to the fore with Ch Oxcroft Vixen (66) by Oxcroft Rocket, who also sired the prolific sire and winner Ch Oxcroft Moonmagic (69). Ch Oxcroft Pearl of Mansergh (73) came next and Ch Oxcroft Rocker (78), a son of Rocky, then sired Ch Oxcroft Tally (80) and, out of Dandyhow Blue Stilton, Ch Ragsdale Blueberry (81). Blueberry was made up by Frank Wildman and John Bainbridge whose Ragdale kennel has since made up Ch Ragsdale Blue Covert (84), also out of an Oxcroft bitch.

Harold Jenner's Ch Maid of Honour (66) was followed by the litter mates, Ch Final Honour (71) and Ch Summer Belle (71). Then came Ch Step Ahead (73), a son of Ch Maid of Honour and a grandson of Ch Knavesmire Kopper and Ch Wharfholm Warrant, all of which, like a number of others beginning with Miss Vaux's Ch Dryburn Devilena (50), were handled in the ring by Ted Hutchinson. By winning 26 CCs Ch Step Ahead became the most successful show dog within the breed and exerted further influence, especially over two kennels, by siring eight champions. For Dorothy Miller's Foxhill kennel he produced Ch Foxhill Fantastic (76), Ch Foxhill Ferelith (75) and Ch Foxhill Firefly (76) and for Pete and Maureen Thompson's Thoraldby kennel he sired Ch Thoraldby Yorkshire Lass (74), Ch Thoraldby Star Quality (75), Ch Thoraldby North Star and Ch Thoraldby Star Appeal of Lairdarch (75). Finally Ch Step Ahead produced, for Bob Owen, Ch Grenze Skylight (77).

Arthur Duxbury's first two champions illustrate the way in which the use of prefixes used to confuse rather than reveal a dog's breeding. The first was Ch Ribbleside Falcliff Trident (67), bred by Ellis Mawson. The second, bred by Arthur, was Ch Duttonlea Lilian (69) and finally came the outstanding sire Ch Ribbleside Ridgeman (70).

Ch Duttonlea Mr Softy (68) was Wilf Wrigley's first champion and was followed by Ch Duttonlea Lilian (69), Ch Duttonlea Sue (76) was next and then Mr Softy sired Ch Duttonlea Ambassador (77). The litter mates, Ch Duttonlea Steel Blue (80), who has come so close to breaking Ch Brimball of Bridgesoller's long established record, and Ch Duttonlea Suntan of Dandyhow (80), both by Dandyhow Grenadier, came next.

Jean and Frank Jackson's first champion, Ch Clipstone Hanley-Castle Bramble (69) was bred by Roger Clements. Then came the litter brother and sister Ch Clipstone Carrots (70) and Ch Clipstone Guardsman (70). In 1970 Dennis Wiseman mated a Henleycastle bitch to Shady Knight to produce Ch Llanishen Illse of Clipstone (70). Carrots mated to Dandyhow Napoleon produced Ch Clipstone

Meg, who started it all for us.

Cetchup (73) who won three CCs while still a puppy and proved to be an outstanding, if somewhat accident-prone, worker. Guardsman mated to Illse produced Ch Clipstone Comma (73). The kennel then acquired Int and Nordic Ch Bombax Xavier (75) who produced Ch Clipstone Clicquot (78). Clicquot mated to Ch Llanishen Reynard (77), who got his title while in the Clipstone kennel, produced Ch Clipstone Chasse (81) who established something of an unenviable record when 25 championship show judges recognised her championship worth but fourteen did so by awarding reserve CCs. Ch Clipstone Cumin (82) mated to Ch Dandyhow Marchioness produced Ch Bannerdown Boomerang (83) and Ch Bannerdown Cavalier (83) in the same litter, to a Cetchup daughter Ch Clipstone Chit Chat (83). Cumin's sire, Clipstone Dash (80), produced Ken and Tracey Thomas's Ch Clipstone Tea Rose of Stonekite (84).

Mr and Mrs John Bradley's career as breeders got off to a flying start with the Ridgeman litter mates, Ch Napoleon Brandy (73) and Ch Gaelic Coffee (73). Ch Road to Mandalay (80) followed and then, by Ch Mansergh Pearl Diver, came Ch Linne of Duthill (80).

Sylvia Clarkson's West Country kennel and its Sprignell affix produced their first champion in Ch Sprigness Selina (74) by Sprignell Sceptre whose breeding demonstrates the kennel's firm foundations. Mated to Hawkesburn Little John Selina produced Ch Sprignell Spice (79) while Selina's dam put to Ch Dandyhow Silver Ring produced Ch Sprignell Crystal Bell (79).

The first champion to carry Gordon Knight's Sundalgo affix was Ch Sundalgo Salvador (74), a son of his first champion, bred by Jack Price, Ch Oxcroft Moonmagic (69). Then came another Moonmagic son, Ch Sundalgo Serenade (75), to be followed by Ch Duttonlea Sue (76). Gordon Knight then campaigned Ch Savinroyd President (76) after the death of his owner, Jack Lindley. Then came the third of the home-bred champions, Ch Sundalgo Slate Blue (83), a son of President.

Like Gordon Knight's kennel Dennis Wiseman's is another which has its roots in terrier work. Dennis's Llanishen affix was first seen on a champion in the Shady Knight daughter, Ch Llanishen Illse of Clipstone (70). She was closely followed by Ch Llanishen Penelope (71), by Llanishen Ivanhoe, a litter brother of Illse, who made such a mark in Sweden. Then came Ch Llanishen Rosemary of Coundon (73) and Ch Llanishen Reynard (77) before Ch Llanishen Red Eagle (79), handled by Dennis and his daughter Denise, was campaigned to his title.

Jean and 'Harry' Singh's first champions were Ch Vandameres Band of Gold (70), by Brussell Sprout, and Ch Vandameres Burnished Gold (79), by Shady Knight. They were followed by Ch Vandameres Daybreak (74) and then by the Ridgeman daughter, Ch Vandameres Daylight (80).

Ch Thoraldby Miss Mandy (72) was the first champion produced by Pete and Maureen Thompson. Mated to Ch Step Ahead she produced Ch Thoraldby North Star (75), Ch Thoraldby Star Quality (75), Ch Thoraldby Yorkshire Lass (74) and Ch Thoraldby Star Appeal of Lairdiarch (75), thus becoming only the second bitch to breed four British champions and the first to do so all to the same dog. This same mating also produced Thoraldby Miss Magic who, mated first to Ashbrae Aurora, produced Ch Thoraldby Trillion (79) and, mated to Mr Chips of Thoraldby, then produced Ch Thoraldby Traveller (73). Maureen and Pete Thompson also owned and campaigned Ch Loiriston Amber (81).

Ch Wharfholm Warrant produced Ch Bannerdown Viscount (73), the first of Pam Creed's Bannerdown champions. He also sired Ch Bannerdown Capricorn (77) who was campaigned to her title by Maureen Woods. The kennel also produced Ch Dandyhow Silver Ring (75) and Ch Dandyhow Marchioness (80) and bred the Cumin sons out of Marchioness, Ch Bannerdown Boomerang (83) and Ch Bannerdown Cavalier (83).

Ch Thoraldby Yorkshire Lass (74) was the first Border Terrier campaigned to its title by Ron and Kath Hodgson. She was followed by Ch Foxtor Blue Jester (75) before their Foxwyn affix appeared on Ch Foxwyn Shoot a Line (81). Then, bred by Lynn Briggs and owned in partnership with her, came the Shoot a Line son, Ch Lynsett Trouble Shooter (82).

The breed, unlike some others, is in a healthy state. There are no known problems of hereditary disease, it has not been subjected to thoughtless and callous commercial exploitation, the threat to the standard has receded and the breed, alone among the recognised terrier breeds, remains in close contact with its original purpose in life. Its popularity has grown steadily rather than spectacularly or dangerously. Club shows which even ten years ago might have been content with 200 entries now expect over 300 and there are six rather than three clubs serving the breed's interests. Although there are now more opportunities to win CCs there are far more entries at championship shows than in the past. Twenty years ago forty or fifty would have been regarded as quite respectable whereas nowadays the most popular shows are looking towards 200 entries.

The breed is in a fortunate position and will remain so providing that functional considerations remain of paramount importance, providing that commercial exploitation is kept at bay and providing that exhibitors can continue to seek the opinion of interested and knowledgeable judges, can accept their decisions with good grace and can continue to enjoy their association with Border Terriers and with their fellow enthusiasts.

9 Borders Overseas

To have written a book about Border Terriers without mention of the breed's development overseas would have been to have left it in a very incomplete state. Clearly, however, it would have been both presumptuous and dangerous for anyone whose experience of the breed has largely, though not entirely, been gained in one country to have attempted to do so. We have been fortunate to have judged the breed in Scandinavia and America as well as in Britain but our experience of the breed outside Britain is insufficient to provide a reliable guide to what has happened overseas. We are, therefore, particularly indebted to friends from overseas who have contributed the material for this chapter.

Holland by Erica Bons-de Wever

After Sweden, Holland is the European country where the Border Terrier is most popular, and the numbers in Holland have been rising rapidly. The breed was first introduced into Holland at the end of the 1920s. The original imports were Sandyman of Kandahar bred by Wattie Irving, Southboro' Stanzo and Lady Ruby but none were bred from and so after the Second World War there were no Border Terriers in Holland.

In 1951, Mrs Langhour-Stein imported River Lad bred by John Renton and during the following years four more Border Terriers were imported. A number of puppies were bred and a number of matings between Glenluffin and Raisgill Rego produced no less than 32 puppies. In 1957 Mrs de Raad imported Ch Golden Imperialist and later imported Ch Braw Boy and Winstonhall Dunkey. In 1968, Mr and Mrs Bons-de Waver imported the bitch Deerstone Destina and two years later brought the first blue and tan into Holland. He was Wharfholm Wickersworld. From about 1970 the breed began to increase steadily both in numbers and quality, and, for several years, there was no need to import more dogs into Holland. This situation was helped because Ch Deerstone Dugmore was in Germany and Deerstone Decisive in Belgium. Both were used at stud.

In those years, the outstanding dog was Ch Roughdune's Estate Agent, a son of Dugmore. He really put his mark on the breed and especially his wonderful temperament, happy, quiet and never aggressive. He was a very sound dog whose movement was widely admired.

Miss Crucq's Half House kennel was started with a daughter of Wickersworld but later she bought Dandyhow Knight Errant, and then she imported Ch Mansergh Pearl Diver. Both Knight Errant and Pearl Diver were extensively used and had a great influence on the breed in Holland.

During this period, Mrs de Rad imported several dogs including Gar Thistle, Llanishen Argosy and American Ch Woodsmokes Douglas. More recently, Ch Brumberhill Blue Maestro came from England.

The first Champion to be made up in Holland was Harm's Southboro Stanzo in 1933. The next was in 1958 and was de Raad's Ch Golden Imperialist. Since then, fifteen of the forty-seven Dutch champions have been imported, the rest bred in Holland.

Germany by Erica Bons-de Wever

Without doubt, Miss Wiebke Steen has been the leading person in the breed for many years. She started with a Portholme bitch and then got Ch Deerstone Dugmore and more recently she bought Bugs Billy, a dog with mainly Dandyhow blood. The breed has recently become more popular in Germany with a number of dogs having been imported from England.

Some people in Germany use Border Terriers for boar hunting. They used to use German Hunt Terriers, which are something like a black and tan old-fashioned Fox-terrier. The breed is very hardy and this meant that a lot were killed by boars. Border Terriers use their brains and keep the boar busy without coming within his reach until the man with the gun arrives. Both British and Dutch bred Border Terriers have been used with good results.

New Zealand by Jim Graham

In 1949, Pat Gilchrist imported the bitch, Tweedside Red Soda by Tweedside Red Playboy out of Lady Toto, recorded as bred by Mrs

J. J. Scot, England. Soda was imported in whelp to Tweedside Red Silvo. She produced three dogs and two bitches. A dog from this litter, Glendare Tyne, mated back to Tweedside Soda gave a litter registered as made up 4/ in 1951. In 1953 a repeat mating resulted in a litter of three dogs.

It was in the second half of 1973 that Rosemary Williamson commenced exhibiting in New Zealand. A bitch, Farnway Swinging Chick, was imported from Mrs Madeleine Aspinwall. Chico, as she was known, was by Farmway Black Hawk out of Hobbykirk Barsac.

Mr and Mrs Jim Graham brought in a dog and a bitch to establish their Otterhead kennels in 1974. The dog was Wilderscot Guardsman, bred by Miss Daphne Rumsam by English Ch Clipstone Guardsman out of Farmway Blue Dove, and the bitch Farmway Swansdown, bred by Madeleine Aspinwall by Deerstone Despot Duty out of Farmway Red Puffin, one litter of which produced Ch Otterhead of Southdean.

There has been a renaissance of Border Terriers in New Zealand and it is to be hoped that there will not be a repetition of what occurred after previous introductions when the life of the breed was solely dependent on short-lived enthusiasm from isolated breeders.

A number of new exhibitors, some of them already famous in other breeds, have taken to the Border Terrier and so the situation augurs well for the future in New Zealand. It will be seen that, in the forty or so years since Border Terriers first came to New Zealand, there have been at least three attempts to establish the breed. It is to be hoped that the impetus and continued thrust given and maintained by the enthusiasm of dedicated owners will be more successful than those of their predecessors in this aim. The links established between New Zealand and Australia, by their exports and their success in that country, should do much to assist in this confident expectation.

Australia by Jim Graham

It is thought that Border Terriers first arrived in Australia in the 1930s. The first recorded Border Terrier was owned by a Mrs Russell of Victoria.

Next, in the early 1960s, Mr George Sheanis of Sydney, New South Wales, imported a brace of Borders of the Solway prefix. Unfortunately, shortly after arriving in Australia, the bitch died. The dog, handled by a well known terrier personality in New South Wales, Mr John Ellsin, was made up to Champion and awarded a Group Win.

Australian Champion Barambah Goliath, a very stylish Australian bred champion owned by R. & S. Godwin and bred by Jim Graham.

There is little doubt that this was the first Border Terrier to gain this recognition in Australia.

'The Border Terrier Club of New South Wales,' writes John Caldwell, 'the only Club of the breed in Australia, started as an idea.' John Caldwell, who had been in the Show and Obedience Worlds for nearly forty years, wrote a letter in May 1981 addressed to all the exhibitors of Border Terriers at the Royal Show held in Melbourne in 1980. This suggested that a Border Terrier Club be formed. He received a few replies which gave the names of other prospective members. Since that time, membership has grown from the original core of nine founder members to almost a hundred, being represented in New Zealand and in the UK as well as Australia.

The Club's first Parade was held at the Queenbeyan Showgrounds in February 1983. At this show, which was judged by Mrs Francis Sefton, editor of the *National Dog Newspaper* of Australia, Robert Bartrum's Rhozzum Venture (Imp UK) was judged Best Exhibit and Dick Emery's dog Aust Ch Foxjoy Berberis was runner-up. The New South Wales controlling body, the Royal Agricultural Society Kennel Contrao (RASKC), granted the club affiliation in 1985.

Sweden by Carl Gunnar Stafberg

The story of Border Terriers in Sweden began in about 1935 when Mrs Anna Bergman bought two Border Terriers from John Renton.

They were Happy Thought and Sacey Queen. Happy Thought became an International Champion and Sacey Queen, who only started her show career when she was eleven years old, became a Swedish Champion. Mrs Bergman bred some litters but the breed did not immediately become established in Sweden. However, a link with the future was forged when Miss Julia Geiger bought Burrens Two Pence from Mrs Bergman in the early 1940s.

Mr Leijonhufvud, who lived in the very south of Sweden, next imported Tweedside Red Joker, Cramaden Twig, Raisgill Risky and Portholme Mab. The kennel produced three champions, Ch Mellby Marvellous, Ch M Micki and Ch M Blissy, but after some time the line ceased to exist.

Miss Brita Donner got her first Border Terrier from the Mellby kennel; this was Mellby Monkey, born in 1950. In 1957 she imported four dogs from England and it was then that the breed began to gain in popularity in Sweden. They were Leatty Linkup by Ch Leatty Druridge Dazzler out of Queens Beaty, and Leatty Golden Randy out of Int Ch Golden Imperialist out of Fancy Free, both of which easily became champions in Sweden. They were followed by Jessica of Tharhill by Ch Wharfholme Wizard and a blue and tan dog Todearth Blue Jacket by Ch Ilfracombe Dandy; he also became a Swedish champion.

From Linkup and Randy came Int Ch Monkans Tico-Tico, a Best in Show winner when he was seven years old, Ch Monkans Trapper, and Monkans Ylva. Tico-Tico and Ylva were kept in Miss Donner's kennel. Linkup and Jessica produced Monkans Uarda. Trapper and Uarda produced Monkans Olly who went to Karin Haglund's Hagmarkens kennel. Uarda was later mated to Blue Jacket to produce the famous three litter sisters, Monkans My, Mymlan and Mikron. My was kept in the kennel, Mymlan went to Julia Geijer's Juniper kennel and Mikron to Bombax kennel, owned by Gunnar and Carl-Gunnar Stafberg. All three became champions.

Blue Jacket and M Ylva produced Ch M Ikke and Ch M Inka and in a later litter Ch M Beetle. Ylva together with Int Ch Bombax Ericus Rex produced Ch M Hanne.

Brita Donner did very little showing and breeding from the mid-sixties but has kept her line going. Recently, now living in Finland, she has taken up showing again and there are more Border Terrier champions with the Monkans prefix.

Karig Haglund got Monkans Olly in 1960. She then bought Bombax Diana and from England got Ludside Treacle. From Diana she bred

Ch Hagmarkens Bimba. Bimba mated to Int Ch Toinis Mikko produced the very nice bitch Ch Hagmarkens Minka. Minka mated to Int Ch Llanishen Ivanhoe produced the well known show and hunting dog Int Ch Harmarkens Into, owned, as was Ivanhoe, by Krister Giselsson.

Julia Geijer, Juniper kennel, started in 1961 with a bitch puppy from Brita Donner. This was Monkans Mymlam who later became a champion. She also bought a daughter from Mymlam's litter sister called Bombax Erica, who also became a champion. Mymlam was first mated to Ch M Trapper and produced the champion litter sisters Juniper Mynta and J Myrra. She was then mated to Int and Nordic Ch Bombax Despot to produce Ch Juniper Mysen Angstrom. Erika was mated to B Despot and so bred Ch Juniper Justus and Int Nord Ch Juniper Juniper.

In 1965 Miss Geijer imported Wharfholme Warrentop from Mrs Holmes. He quickly got his title and among some very nice offspring were Ch Juniper Jimbo and Int Nord Ch Juniper Jerrantop. In 1969 Eng Ch Manergh Rhosmerholm Amethyst came from England to Juniper kennel. She had been mated in England to Ribbleside Robert the Bruce and in a litter of six produced Juniper Klarobert, Klarissa and Klabbette, all three of which became Int and Nord champions. Julia Geijer kept Klarobert and Klarissa. Klabbette was sold to Julia's cousin Margaretha Carlsson who was already the owner of Juniper Jerrantop. Amethyst was next mated to Int Nord Ch Juniper Juniper and produced Juniper Klettermus and, in a later litter, Juniper Klorophyll both became Int champions. Klettermus went to Aune and Anja Luoso, Kletters kennel in Finland, and became one of the top winning Border Terriers in that country. Amethyst also had a litter by Int Nord Ch Daletyne Danny Boy, imported by Carl Gunner Stafberg from Bobby Benson in England. This mating produced Int Nord Ch Juniper Lissandra who was mated, in 1975, to Int Nord Ch Hagmarkens Into to produce Juniper Kanak who sired many champions. Later Klissandra produced Int Nord Ch Juniper Kampe and Ch J Kara Barn by Int Ch Bannerdown Monarch.

During the early 1970s Julia Geijer bought two litter sisters from Dandyhow. They were Dandyhow Sweet Pickle and Dandyhow Sweet Polly, by Dandyhow Brussel Sprout out of Dandyhow Solitaire and so bred the same as the famous Ch Dandyhow Shady Knight. Together they did a lot of good to the breed in Sweden. Pickle was mated to Int Nord Ch Bombax Ericus Rex to breed Blue Peter and Blue Perericus and then, mated to Juniper Kanak, produced Juniper Pyssimanda,

Ch Bombax Xavier ('75), bred in Sweden by Gunnar and Carl Gunnar Stafberg and, after a very successful show career in Scandinavia, brought to Britain where, owned jointly by Jean Jackson and Carl Gunnar Stafberg, he became the first, and remains the only, Border Terrier born outside Britain to become a champion under Kennel Club rules.

Juniper Pyts and Juniper Pysen, all of which became champions. Mated to Ch Hanleycastle Rebel Polly produced Juniper Pollyanna and Juniper Polka, both champions. Pollyanna also became an obedience champion. Then, mated to Juniper Kanak, Pollyanna produced Juniper Purjo, Juniper Puella and Juniper Puttifar, all champions. Polly was later mated to Int Nord Ch Bombax Desperado and from this litter came Juniper Pampe and Juniper Palinette. More recently Ch Juniper Kara Barn, mated to Pampe, produced Ch Juniper Jubeppo and Juniper Jubepsi. The most recent winner from Juniper is Ch Juniper Jonses Daga by Ch Grenadier out of Juniper Palinette.

Bombax kennel, owned by Gunnar and Carl-Gunnar Stafberg, a father and son partnership, started in 1961 with a bitch puppy named Monkans Mikron. Later Monkans Trapper was also bought from Britta Donner. Both became champions. The first Bombax litter was born in 1963 from Ch Leatty Panaga Tess, imported from George Leatt. She had been mated in England to Smokey Cinder and from the litter came Int Nord Ch Bombax Despot, a well known winner in

those days. The next litter was by Trapper out of Mikron and contained
Ch Bombax Joker. Joker mated to Tess daughters gave Int Nord Ch
Toinis Mikko and Ch Bombax Xantippa. At the end of the 1960s the
Stafbergs imported Daletyne Danny Boy and Felldyke Bonnie Hinnie,
both by Daletyne Rory. Danny Boy quickly got his international and
Nordic titles and became the top Border Terrier stud dog in Scandinavia by siring at least twenty-one champions. Bonnie Hinnie became
a Swedish champion and, mated to Despot, bred Nord Ch Bombax
Dolloy and Bombax Despotic Girl who, in her turn, was the mother
of Int Nord Ch Bombax Nickname, by Toinis Mikko, who became the
foundation bitch of Mona Hadman's Tallernas kennel.

Ch Bombax Xantippa became the mother of seven champions, five
by Danny Boy, Bombax Gunfighter, B Gossip, B Gutterperka, B
Lurifax and B Leonine, and two by a Danny Boy son, Int Nord Ch
Bombax Ante. These were Bombax Josefine and B Jehu. Gossip was
kept at Bombax. Jesefine became one of the corner stones in Kletters
kennel in Finland and Leonine was then foundation bitch of Kristina
Gunnardontter's Urax kennel.

In the beginning of the 1970s the Stafbergs imported first Eng Ch
Foxhill Fulbert, who after getting his Int and Nordic titles went to
Norway, and, a little later, Clipstone Clover and Eng Ch Clipstone
Guardsman. Clover was mated to Int Nord Ch Bombax Lurifax to
produce the two champions Bombax Tallyho and Bombax Titbit. In
her next litter, this time to Danny Boy, she produced Bombax Xavier
who became an International and Nordic champion before going to
England where, campaigned by Jean Jackson, he got his English title.
Titbit mated to Toinis Mikko sired Int and Nordic Ch Bombax Blizzard.

Gossip had a number of champion offspring but the most important
were Bombax Vice Versa, by Clipstone Guardsman, Int Nord Ch
Bombax Hunter, by Danny Boy, and Bombax Eliza, by Bombax Xavier.
Vice Versa produced two of the top winning dogs in Sweden; they
were Bombax Desperado by Bombax Xavier and Bombax Mastermind
by Blizzard. Both became International and Nordic champions. B Eliza
mated to Blizzard produced Bombax Label and Bombax Lollipop, both
champions. Then Dandyhow Creme Caramel of Clipstone, a Shady
Knight daughter, came from the Clipstone kennel to Bombax. She was
mated to Desperado to give the litter sisters Bombax Peebles and
Bombax Popcorn, both Int and Nord champions, and both produced
champion offspring. Peebles went to Margareta Grafstrom, Redrob
kennel. A Desperado daughter out of Bombax Cinderella produced, to

Int Nord Ch Bombax Hunter, Ch Bombax Unika. Mastermind mated to Popcorn then produced Ch Bombax Yatsy.

Mona Hedman's Tallarnas kennel started in 1972 with a bitch puppy from Bombax which quickly became an International and Nordic champion. Her name was Bombax Nickname. She really was a goose which laid golden eggs and became the mother of twelve champions. Int Nord Ch Tallarnas Nej Da, by Danny Boy, was kept, while Int Nord Ch Tallarnas Nypon Flinga went to Inger Morgren, Trientalis kennel. A daughter from Nypon Flinga by Danny Boy went back to Mona and became Int Nord Ch Tallarnas Dans Flinga. Mona then imported Dandyhow Observer who, mated to Tallarnas bitches, produced T Tallarnas Lycko Par, Lille Orkan, Nickodemus and Fantomen, all International and Nordic champions, winning a lot and siring nice puppies. The next dog to come to Mona Hadman was Dandyhow Grenadier; he too has sired some good puppies.

Margaretha Carlsson, Quisin kennel, started with Juniper Jerrantop and Juniper Klabbette. She then imported Dandyhow Sherry Brandy and Int Nord Ch Bannerdown Monarch. Margaretha also got a very nice bitch by Dandyhow Nightcap out of Ch Bannerdown Butterscotch. This was Ch Redrobs Vessalina. The best known of the Quisin

Int and Nord Ch Llanishen Ivanhoe ('70), bred in Britain by Dennis Wiseman but exported to Sweden where, owned by Krister Giselsson, he proved to be an outstanding show dog and sire as well as a first class worker. Ivanhoe's litter sister was Ch Llanishen Illse of Clipstone.

Border Terriers are Int Nord Ch Quisin Yipayk, Int Nord Ch Quisin Yempella and Quisin Yonja.

Kristina Gunnarsdotter, Urax kennel, started with Bombax Leonine who gave Ch Urax Fjalar when mated to Foxhill Fulbert, and Int Nord Ch Urax Garm and Int Nord Ch Urax Grima when mated to Clipstone Guardsman. Grima, mated to Juniper Kanjak, then produced Int Nord Ch Urax Katla and, mated to Bombax Desperado, gave Urax Debora. Then Debora, mated to Tallarnas Lille Orkan, produced Int Nord Ch Urax Lif.

Redrob kennel, owned by Margareta Grafstrom, started with a daughter of Bombax Xavier and Whispering Hekate called Int Nord Ch Redrob Viktoria. Int Nord Ch Bannerdown Butterscotch was then imported and became the mother of five champions. One of the best known dogs from this kennel was Int Nord Ch Redrob Titus, who was by Llanishen Ivanhoe out of Redrob Viktoria.

There are many other breeders in Sweden and throughout Scandinavia who maintain small kennels which regularly produce winners; unfortunately space does not allow all to be mentioned.

Although the Swedish Border Terrier Club Show is not a championship show wins are very highly prized. The number of dogs entered is often far higher than at any other Scandinavian show. Many, as at all club shows, are pets which might never do well in the show ring but sometimes outstanding dogs emerge from homes which have never before had a show dog. All the major kennels too are represented and all are trying to win. As often as possible the club invites judges from Britain and then competition is especially keen and a win very highly prized.

America by Robert and Ruth Ann Naun

There is no record of exactly when the Border Terrier was first recognised by the American Kennel Club, but we can assume that the recognition of the breed took place before 1927, when the first Border Terrier was registered in the American Kennel Club Stud Book.

A review of the *Kennel Club Gazette* in the years before 1930 shows that 19 Borders were exported to the United States. Only three, however, were registered in the American Stud Book. The first was Barney Boy (Ch Dandy of Tynedale × Queen o' the Hunt) bred by Messrs Dodd and Carruthers, and imported by Mr H. S. Cram. The second, Nessy (Arnton Billy × Nessey), bred by Miss E. Hardy, was imported by Mr G. D. Thayer. The third was Blacklyne Lady (Ch Ben of Tweeden × Blacklyne Wasp), bred by Mrs Armstrong, and also imported by Mr Thayer.

The first British champion imported to the United States was Rustic Rattle (Crosedale Jock × Crosedale Judy), bred by Mrs J. A. Simpson, and brought to the United States by Percy Roberts.

The 1930s saw few Border Terriers registered with the American Kennel Club. The decade did produce, however, the first American bred Borders to be registered. They were from two litters bred by Mr C. Gordon Massey of Trappe, Maryland. The first litter was whelped in Aiken, North Carolina, on April 1, 1931, and was by Mullach (Arnton Billy × Arthorn Lady) out of Always There (Hunting Boy × June of Twinmstead). The second litter was whelped on July 28, 1931, at Trappe, Maryland, also sired by Mullach out of Dryffe Judy (Whitrope Don × Ch Station Masher). Mr Massey had a number of Borders and, while he did not exhibit his dogs very often, he would exhibit at his home show. At the Talbot County Kennel Club near Easton, Maryland, in 1935, he entered eleven Borders including a number of important ones – i.e. Knowe Roy, Baiter and Red Twister, all out of Ch Todhunter bred by John Renton.

A second prominent name that appears in 1930s Border registrations is Mr William MacBain. In 1937, Mr MacBain imported Pyxie L'Bladnoch in whelp to Ch Foxlair. From this mating came Diehard Sandy, the sire of Am Ch Diehard Dandy. Pyxie, the first recorded American champion, was mated in her next season to Mr Massey's Red Twister and produced Am Ch Diehard Dandy's dam, Diehard Betta. From Betta came Borders who would have important positions in the pedigree of the Philabeg and Dalquest Border kennels of following decades.

The Border Terrier made some significant gains in the 1940s, due in large part to the efforts of Dr Merritt Pope (Philbeg kennels). Dr Pope was the moving force in the promotion of the Border Terrier in the years 1941–1946. He was a key figure in the founding of the Border Terrier Club of America. In December 1946, Captain John C. Nicholson wrote to Dr Pope suggesting that a Border Terrier club be formed to aid the advance of the breed. Captain Nicholson and his wife had emigrated to the United States at the end of World War II and had brought with them Swallowfield Say When and Dronfield Reckless.

By mid-January 1947, William MacBain, of Diehard kennels, wrote Dr Pope agreeing to the need for a club. Soon Emerson Latting, who owned Diehard Dandy, the second recorded American Border champion, joined the group.

Captain Nicholson and Dr Pope met for the first time at the

Westminster Kennel Club Show in New York City in February 1947. They decided that a descriptive standard for the breed was needed. Their goal was to develop a standard acceptable to both Border breeders and the American Kennel Club. They decided to use the British standard as a guide, and to enlarge and, they hoped, clarify it for an American audience. Dr Pope was elected chairman of the standard committee and Mrs Nicholson was designated its Secretary/Treasurer. The embryo of 'The American Border Terrier Club' was formed.

The first task that Dr Pope and Mrs Nicholson undertook was to canvass American and British breeders for comments and suggestions regarding the proposed standard. From the efforts of this duo, countless suggestions and comments were tabulated and the tentative standard was presented at a meeting of the American Border Terrier Club on August 28, 1948, at Pittsfield, Massachusetts. This important meeting was attended by Dr Pope, Captain and Mrs Nicholson, and Miss Margery Harvey. Mr MacBain was absent but sent his written approval.

The American Border Terrier Club now had a written standard and a membership of ten: Dr and Mrs Merritt N. Pope (Philabeg), William MacBain (Diehard), Emerson Latting (Balquhain), Mr and Mrs Charles Schindler, General Edgar E. Humer, Miss Gertrude B. Dunbar, and two new members from Dalquest kennels, Miss Margery Harvey and Miss Marjory Van Der Veer, the latter two being invited by Dr Pope when they purchased a bitch puppy from the Popes.

The standard was approved by the American Kennel Club on March 14, 1950. Shortly after the Border Terrier Club of America was formed as a permanent organisation. Dr Pope was elected President, Captain Nicholson was elected Vice-President, Mrs Clara Nicholson was elected Treasurer and Miss Marjory Van der Veer was elected Secretary, a post she held until 1982.

In 1964, after a disappointing 1963 Specialty, the BTCA held its Specialty in conjunction with the Greenwich Kennel Club in Connecticut. It was at the Greenwich show in 1969 that the Specialty presented its first English breeder-judge, Mrs Barbara Holmes of Wharfholm kennels. In 1972 the Border Terrier Specialty moved to Woodstock, Vermont, its present location.

With the move the Border Terrier as a breed showed growth both in numbers and in visibility in the show ring. As one might expect, there was also a marked increase in membership in the BTCA. The year 1972 saw the first group win by a Border, Am Ch DG's Wattie Irving of Dalquest, and the first Utility Dog and Tracking Dog obedience titles earned by a Border, Am Ch Chief of Lothian, UDT, CG. Group wins and placements became more common until the historic day in 1977 when Br Am Ch Workmore Waggoner went Best in Show. The next year, 1978, saw the Border become the first terrier to become an Obedience Trial Champion (OU Ch Pete, UD).

In 1972 came the first Border to earn an American Working Terrier Association Certificate of Gameness, American bred Am Ch Bandersnatch Snake, CD, CG. The seventies also saw the establishment of the first regional Border Terrier Clubs – the Border Terrier Fanciers in the West (1976) and the Midwest Border Terrier Club (1977).

The 1980s have seen a spectacular growth of interest in Borders in the United States. After several years of discussion and negotiations, the American Kennel Club accepted the Border Terrier Club of America as a member club in 1980. Membership of the BTCA grew to over 300 members in this decade, and several new breeder judges were added to the AKC approved judges list, which for so many years held only the name of one breeder-judge, Miss Van Der Veer.

1986 saw the first Specialty of the BTCA to be held on the West Coast. Supported and organised by the Border Fanciers of the West, it was held in conjunction with the Kern County Kennel Club Show. 1986 thus becomes the first year to see two Border Specialties held in one year. Clearly, the BTCA has made marked advances in the forty years since its inception at the benches of the Westminster Club Show in New York City in 1946.

Of the kennels of the early days in the US, William MacBain's Diehard kennels, Emerson Latting's Balquhain kennels, Captain and Mrs Jack C. Nicholson's Dronfield kennels, and George Beckett's Dour kennels, only the Philabeg kennels of Dr and Mrs Merritt Pope were still active in the late forties, finishing Am Ch Philabeg Red Mill, Am Ch Raisgill Romper of Philabeg, and then in the early fifties finishing Am Ch Philabeg Accent, Am Ch Philabeg Actress, and Am Ch Ribbleside Racketeer of Philabeg.

With the phasing out of the older kennels which had started the Border Terrier in the United States, there appeared on the scene three new kennels, which remained active almost to the present day and which have had a tremendous impact upon the breed. These were Dalquest, Shelburne, and the kennels of Mrs Marion Dupont Scott, which never had a prefix. Perhaps the most productive of the three kennels has been the Dalquest kennels of Miss Marjory Van Der Veer and Miss Margery Harvey. The impact of these dedicated Border breeders on the Border Terrier in America has been enormous. Originally breeders and exhibitors of Dalmatians (hence the name Dalquest), Miss Harvey and Miss Van Der Veer procured their first Border, Am Ch Philabeg Red Bet, from Dr and Mrs Pope. Since that time, Dalquest has owned, or bred, over 44 champions before retirement from the Border ring in 1983. A number of dogs were imported by Dalquest. Am Ch Portholme Matilda (Ch Portholme Manly Boy × Ch Portholme Mamie) arrived in 1953 and was soon followed by Am Ch Portholme Max Factor (Ch Carahall Cornet × Portholme Marcorine). Max Factor, or Geordie as he was called, sired ten champions – three with Am Ch Dour Dare, four with Am Ch Golden Fancy, two each with Am Ch Carahall Cindylou and Am Ch Dalquest Smokey Tigress. With Geordie came Am Ch Portholme Meroe, who with her companion Geordie was made up within a year, no easy task when you had to travel far and wide to find enough Borders to make the necessary major wins for a championship.

Two years later came Am Ch Portholme Mhor of Dalquest (Portholme Mustard × Ch Portholme Mirth). A real showman, Mhor was Best Border at the first Border Specialty in 1959. He sired 13 champions, to earn his Gold Register of Merit. Among the champions out of Am Ch Portholme Meroe was the Silver ROM winner Am Ch Dalquest Dauntless.

The next and most famous Portholme Border to come to Dalquest was one which Miss Van Der Veer and Miss Harvey purchased themselves, Br Am Ch Portholme Macsleap of Dalquest (Portholme Mask and Brusth × Ch Portholme Mirth). Having already sired three champions in England he came to the United States at the age of four and a half and went on to sire 10 more in this country. In addition he won the 1965 Specialty, arriving in the US only two days beforehand, and finishing his American championship in four shows within four months. Mhor sired the first Border group winner Am Ch DG's Wattie Irving of Dalquest, as well as Mex Am Ch Bandersnatch Brillig, CD, and Am Ch Rose Bud of Lothian, later to join the Town Hill kennels of Mr and Mrs Henry Mosle.

Another very productive kennel, one which has never had a prefix but one which produced a number of outstanding ROM winners, was Mrs Marion Dupont Scott. Mrs Scott died in 1984 but the Borders of her kennels continue under the able direction of Damara Bolte, who, with the help of others interested in maintaining this line, continues to show and breed Borders, developing this famous kennel. Mrs Scott, along with Carroll Bassett, had a number of champion Borders in the fifties and sixties. Her first ROM winner was Am Ch Carahall Cindylou

(Ch Carahall Cornet × Carahall Charm), bred by Mr Goodsir in Britain. However, Mrs Scott's most outstanding ROM Borders were the famous duo of Am Ch Rob Roy Buckler and Am Ch Shuttle, both Gold ROM winners. Buckler was sired by Mrs Scott's British import Am Ch Farmway Dandyhow Likely Lad out of Tweed's Easter, daughter of Falcliff Target. Am Ch Shuttle was sired by Mrs Scott's Am Ch Bull Run out of Katie, a daughter of Br Am Ch Falcliff Tantalizer.

Together with Buckler she produced American Champions Nonstop, Delta, Scooter, Buckshot, Concorde, Express, Razzle, Dazzle, Ransom, Contrail, Supersaver, Standby and Piper Cub. The champions from this potent pair have continued their parents' tradition of producing many champions.

The third important kennel with marked influence in the post-Second World War period is the Shelburne kennel of the Webb family. Shelburne and the Webb family have been associated over the years with the Shelburne Hunt, organised in 1903 by J. Watson Webb. This earliest recognised private hunt in the USA remained active until 1953.

The Shelburne prefix is continued to this day by Mrs Kate Seeman, who was a member of the Webb family. Upon joining the family, Kate quickly became fascinated by the versatility of these little brown Border Terriers, who were great with kids, sturdy, good house pets, and also readily adapted to the hunt, to retrieving, and to hunting woodchucks or even lizards when something more appropriate was not available.

The first Shelburne champion was Am Ch Shelburne Slipper, a Bottles daughter, out of Ch Golden Fancy who was herself a British import bred by Mrs Ormston. She finished her championship with three five-point major wins. The second important Shelburne champion was Br Am Ch Lucky Purchase (Ch Future Fame × Fully Fashioned) bought from Adam Forster. The list of imported Borders in this kennel over the years is remarkable in quality and extent and includes: Am Ch Chalkcroft Blue Peter, Am Ch Golden Fancy, Br Am Ch Dandyhow Bitter Shandy, Br Am Ch Brieryhill Gertrude, Br Am Ch Jonty Lad, Am Ch Covington Eagle, Am Ch Dandyhow Sarah, Am Ch Deerstone Tylview Dusty, Br Am Ch Deerstone Debrett, Am Ch Deerstone Decorum, Br Am Ch Dandyhow Shady Lady, Am Ch Monty of Essenhigh, Am Ch Redridge Ramona, Am Ch Elandmead Psalm, Br Am Ch Workmore Waggoner, WC, Am Ch Redridge Russet, Br Am Ch Cannybuff Cloud, Am Ch Workmore Tristar, and Am Ch Starcyl March On.

Ch Workmore Waggoner ('73) bred by Mary Walker, after gaining his title in Britain, took the breed in America by storm.

The most famous of the impressive group of Shelburne Borders was Br Am Ch Workmore Waggoner, WC, who was Best of Breed in the first BTCA Specialty in which he participated, and in the subsequent four Specialties as well. He won his first Specialty coming from the Veterans Class. A Gold ROM winner, Workmore Waggoner has achieved the distinction of having sired the most champion get of any dog in this country to date. Although not used a great deal by breeders outside of Shelburne until his later years, he has at the time of this writing produced 23 American champions. Wags was especially productive with ROM winner Am Ch Redbridge Russet, imported by Shelburne from J. R. Goodfellow, and, additionally, with Silver ROM Am Ch Highdyke Alpha (Am Ch Dandyhow Bertie Bassett × Clipstone Cider Rose) owned by Oldstone, and her niece Bronze ROM Am Ch Highdyke Tish of Cymri Hill (Am Ch Brockett Hurdle × Am Ch Highdyke Twiglet) owned by Cymri Hill kennels. It is interesting that in pedigree all three of these bitches are strongly influenced by Dandyhow breeding and Ch Dandyhow Shady Knight in particular.

A kennel well known for its outstanding imports is the Trails End kennel of Mrs Nancy Hughes. The three best known of these imports are Br Am Ch Workmore Brackon, imported in 1972 and co-owned with Nancy Kloskowski; Br Am Ch Final Honour, imported in 1973, co-owned with David Kline; and Ch Duttonlea Autocrat of Dandyhow imported in 1982.

Final Honour's daughter, Gold ROM winner, Am Ch Trails End Peacefull Bree, the foundation bitch of Lothlorien kennels, has produced 12 champions. His son, gold ROM winner, Am Ch Little Fir Gremlin of Ariel, owned by Kenneth Klothen and David Kline, has produced 11 champions.

Duttonlea Autocrat of Dandyhow (Ch Dandyhow Grenider × Ribbleside Morning Dew) has produced 18 champion get up to this time. Five of these champions were out of another British import, Ch Dandyhow Forget-Me-Not.

David Kline, besides co-owning Br Am Ch Final Honour and Am Ch Little Fir Gremlin of Ariel, bred three ROM winners in his own kennel, Little Fir. In addition to Little Fir Gremlin of Ariel, there was the Gold ROM winner Am Ch Little Fir Kirksman (Am Ch Llanishen Senator × Am Ch Little Fir Autumngold) who produced 10 champions for Mrs Finley's Woodland kennels, and Am Ch Little Fir Autumngold (Am Ch Falcliff Target × Am Ch Rhosmerholme Belinda), who produced four champion get.

Two other Midwestern kennels making an impact upon the breed in recent years are the Woodlawn kennels of Mrs Betsy Finley and the Ketka kennels of Miss Carol Sowders. A prolific breeder, Mrs Finley's kennels have been the home of a number of ROM winners. The most outstanding in terms of number of champions produced are Gold ROM Am Ch Little Fir Kirksman (Am Ch Llanishen Senator × Am Ch Little Fir Autumngold) with 10 champions, bred by David Kline; Am Ch Edebrea Dusky Maiden (Elandmead Prospect × Tarka May Princess) bred by Miss M. Edgar, co-owned with Mary C. Pickford, with nine champions; Am Ch Dalquest Rebecca of Woodlawn (Deerstone Ryak of Dalquest × Dalquest Teri), bred by Dalquest kennels, with nine champions.

The second Midwestern kennel making an impact on the breed in recent years is Carol Sowders' Ketka kennels. Ketka is unique in that it is one of the few American kennels which has not imported Borders. Miss Sowders has produced several Gold ROM winners: Am Ch Ketka Swashbuckler (Am Ch Rob Roy Buckler × Am Ch Little Fir Rob Roy's Robin, CG), owned by Miss Sowders, produced 15 champions; and Am Ch Ketka Gopher Broke (Am Ch Beaverwood's Bold Blaze, CD, CG × Dalquest Ketka Critter), co-owned by Miss Sowders with David Tinker, has nine champions.

The Eastern seaboard of the USA has been the historic stronghold of the Border Terrier in the United States. Here were found the early kennels of Diehard, Balquhain, Dour and Philabeg, and then the later kennels of Dalquest, Shelburne, and of Mrs Dupont Scott already discussed. It is here that we find the several remaining kennels with multiple ROM winners.

Camilla Moon's Highdyke kennel has been very successful despite its small size. Breeding her foundation bitch Clipstone Cider Rose (Int Br Ch Clipstone Guardsman × Br Ch Llanishen Ilse of Clipstone) to a Ch Dandyhow Shady Knight son from Oldstone kennels (Am Ch Dandyhow Bertie Bassett), Cider Rose had her only litter, which included ROM winners Am Ch Highdyke Alpha and Highdyke Twiglet. Twiglet in turn bred to Am Ch Brockett Hurdle (a son of Ch Step Ahead, and himself a ROM winner) and produced Am Ch Highdyke's Tish of Cymri Hill, the foundation bitch of Kate Murphy's Cymri Hill kennels. Tish herself is also a ROM winner.

The Bandersnatch kennels of Margaret and Harvey Pough have had a relatively long history in breeding Borders in the United States. Also a small kennel, Bandersnatch produced the ROM winning bitches Mex Am Ch Bandersnatch Brillig, CD (Am Ch Portholme Macsleap of Dalquest × Dalquest Jody of Town Hill, CD); Bandersnatch Beamish, full sister of Brillig, owned by Louanne Hammett; and Ch Bandersnatch Jubjub Bird, CDX (Am Ch Bandersnatch Snark, CD × Am Ch Bandersnatch Border in Blue, CD), owned by Grizella Sqilagyi.

Another small kennel new to Borders, but well known for Sealyhams and Airedales, is the Seabrook kennels of Barbara and Lesley Anthony which has had strong success in both exhibition and breeding. Am Ch Concorde (Am Ch Rob Roy Bucker x Am Ch Shuttle), a Bronze ROM winner, has produced Am Ch Seabrook Spriggan, himself a Bronze ROM winner. Concorde was the first owner-handled, American-bred Border Terrier to win a Best in Show. Concorde's daughter, Am Ch Seabrook Galadiel, has also the distinction of having won a Best in Show.

Lothlorien Border Terriers have been closely associated with the obedience ring and the working trials of the American Working Terrier Association. Lothlorien's foundation bitch Am Ch Trails End Bree, UD, was acquired by Joann Frier-Murza from Nancy Hughes. A daughter of Br Am Ch Final Honour out of Br Am Ch Workmore Brackon, Bree produced 12 champions by several different stud dogs. Included among these champions was Am Ch Lothlorien Jollymuff Tickle, herself a Bronze ROM winner, owned by Diane Jones's Jollymuff kennels. Tickle herself produced Am Ch Jollymuff Crisply

Critter, another ROM winner, owned by Kendall Herr. Over half of Bree's offspring went on to get obedience degrees with one, Am Ch Lothlorien Easy Strider, UD, owned by Nancy Hiscock, going on to get his utility degree as did Bree herself.

The Oldstone kennels of Robert and Ruth Ann Naun began with the acquisition of a bitch puppy, Am Ch Borderseal Bessie (Int Br Ch Clipstone Guardsman × Chuch Wuca) in 1972 while on holiday in Britain. However, it was not until another puppy, Am Ch Dandyhow Bertie Bassett (Ch Dandyhow Shady Knight × Polo Mint), was acquired on a second trip to Britain in 1975 that Oldstone began to show some progress in a breeding programme. Bertie, a Bronze ROM winner, bred to Borderseal Bessie, produced the Gold ROM winner Am Ch Oldstone Ragrug. With Clipstone Cider Rose he produced two ROM winners, Am Ch Highdyke Alpha and Highdyke Twiglet. Am Ch Highdyke Alpha, a Silver ROM winner, lives at Oldstone. However, it was only late in her breeding career, when bred to Br Am Ch Workmore Waggoner, that she produced her champion get. She had two litters with Wags, a total of eight puppies with seven becoming champions. Am Ch Oldstone Ragrug has to date produced 12 champion get to six different bitches. Three were produced when bred to Am Ch Bandersnatch Jubjub Bird, CDX, and four when bred to Am Ch Jollymuff Crispy Critter. Another Bronze ROM winner, Farmway Bella L'Oiseau, bred by Betty Rumson and co-owned with Jean Clark of Stonecroft kennels, has produced four champions, two by Am Ch Oldstone Hadrian, an Am Ch Highdyke Alpha son, and one by Am Ch Oldstone Leatherneck, an Am Ch Dandyhow Bertie Bassett son.

In relation to the history of pure bred dogs in the United States, the history of the Border Terrier is a brief one. Both the breed's beginnings and its recent growth demonstrate that a numerically small breed is completely dependent upon breeders. The future of the Border Terrier in America lies directly in their hands. The Register of Merit Award has been emphasised here since these sires and dams have very literally shaped the Border Terrier in America. Continuing to breed Borders of proper type, temperament and quality, and with the subtle distinctiveness of the breed represents our major undertaking of the future.

10 Good Companions and More

It would be wrong to assume that the stress placed on the breed's roles as a working terrier and as a show dog means that these are its only important roles or in any way denigrates the breed as a companion. Those who are unfamiliar with the demands made on a working terrier or a show dog might assume that success in either activity demands qualities which are incompatible with those required in a companion. Nothing could be further from the truth. Both working and show dogs need to have equable temperaments, to be capable of mixing amicably with other animals and being handled by strange people, and they need to be reasonably obedient and physically sound and resilient. Those who suggest that show dogs are nervous, highly strung creatures lacking physical soundness cannot have given any thought to the demands which a successful career in the ring imposes on a dog. Equally those who regard working dogs as pathologically aggressive cannot have any idea of the way in which a working terrier is expected to perform.

Both working and show dogs, particularly Border Terriers, are usually also cherished companions. Most, after a hard day in the field or at a show, return to their accustomed place by their owner's hearth or under their duvet. For thousands of years, during which our present physical and psychological needs have been created, man has lived in close contact with other animals. Only since the beginning of the Industrial Revolution has this contact been threatened. For many people the contact is now broken though the needs remain. We may try to satisfy them vicariously through Sooty and Sweep, Basil Brush, Rupert Bear, Mickey Mouse, Top Cat, Kermit and Miss Piggy or, as spectators, share the adventures of Attenborough, Bellamy, Durrell and Morris. Or we may turn into one of those unhappy people whose unrecognised and unfulfilled need turns into antagonism to all animals and often to their own species.

In recent years this need has begun to receive renewed recognition from the medical profession. People who own pets, particularly dogs, have been found to be less prone to illness and, should they become ill, to recover more quickly than those who do not own dogs. As a consequence 'ɔgs have found a place in all sorts of institutions where their presence helps the sick, bewildered, deprived, violent and angry people of our society. It is sometimes argued that dogs are a threat to health and so they might be if they are not properly cared for.

Anyone who has decided that home would be a happier, more secure and more interesting place for the presence of a dog and has also decided that the dog should be a Border Terrier has already avoided a number of problems which might have been encountered had some other breed been chosen. Border Terriers do not suffer from the sort of hereditary and congenital problems with which some other breeds seem beset. This, of course, is not to say that problems, sometimes probably inherited, do not occur in Border Terriers just as they do in our own species. Even in machines, where a uniform standard of perfection is theoretically possible, perfection is not always attained. Animals are not machines and perfection is not even theoretically possible; problems are bound to occur.

The breeds which appear to have the greatest problems tend, on the whole, to be those which have long been separated from their original purpose in life or in which their breeders have lost sight of the import-ance of that purpose. Those which are numerically too small to sustain a healthy breeding population may also have problems just as the very popular breeds, having attracted breeders more concerned with quantity than quality, will have more than their fair share of difficulties. Breeds which sell readily for high prices also tend to have problems as the irresponsible cash crop puppy farmers and the supermarket dealers use the opportunity to take a quick profit. Border Terriers are fortunate to avoid the worst of all these problems though it has to be said that often breeders may not always maintain the high standards which are necessary if the breed is to avoid problems in the future.

It has been said that those who wed in haste will repent at leisure. Much the same might be said about buying a dog, though deciding what breed most appeals to you is at least as much a matter for the heart as for the head. Obviously you will consider whether your home is the sort of place which can accommodate a dog and you will decide whether you are prepared to give a dog the daily attention that it will need throughout its life. If there are doubts on either score you would be best advised to postpone getting a dog until the doubts have been resolved.

Most Border Terrier breeders aim for quality rather than quantity. Even many of the best known kennels may produce no more than a couple of litters each year. They will seldom advertise, except perhaps in the breed club publications, they are unlikely to be on the books of agencies which put potential buyers in touch with available puppies and they may well have a waiting list for their stock. Unless you are very fortunate you may well need patience during your search for a suitable puppy. There are, however, a number of ways in which you might surmount the difficulties. Through the breed note writers of the weekly dog magazines or from the national kennel club you will be able to get the name and address of breed club secretaries who, in their turn, will be able to put you in touch with breeders in your area. Alternatively you could, again from the dog magazines or the breed club secretaries, find out when shows which offer classes for Border Terriers are to be held in your area. At club events and all the major championship shows you will be able to see a number of Border Terriers from different kennels. You will be able to talk to their owners and, often, their breeders and it is likely that you will find someone who has or will soon be having a litter. If, however, a few visits to shows do not produce the information you need all has not been lost. You will have met a number of fellow enthusiasts, and you will probably have joined a breed club. You will have had some enjoyable days among the breed which you admire and, perhaps most important of all, you will have gathered a great deal of information which will help you when the time comes to choose a puppy.

By this time you should have decided precisely what you are looking for. Do you want a young puppy or might an older dog suit your purpose better? Do you want a dog or a bitch? Are you looking just for a companion or will you want to work or show your dog as well? It's as well to get our own mind clear about all these points before you begin to approach breeders in earnest. A young puppy will give you the opportunity to watch and enjoy its development but will also demand from you far more initial care and attention than would an older dog. It's for you to decide which best suits your particular circumstances. If you are buying a young puppy you will never, never, never buy it from anyone but its breeder. The early weeks of any puppy's life are vitally important. It should be protected, as much as possible, from the stress which is necessarily involved in changing homes, changing diet and being introduced to new surroundings with threats, by way of infection, for which it is unprepared. Any breeder who sells puppies to a dealer cannot have the sort of concern for their

A typical crowded ringside during judging at the Southern Border Terrier Club's 1987 championship show at Cheltenham racecourse. This show and other popular club shows can now confidently expect entries in excess of 300.

future which is part and parcel of any responsible breeder's attitude. The chances are that puppies bought from dealers will not have been as carefully bred or as well reared as puppies which have been cared for only by their breeder.

All Border Terriers are, or should be, companions. Some are also worked or shown and some combine all three roles. If you have decided that you are not interested in show or work this does not mean that you need be or should be satisfied with second best. You will want a dog of which you can be proud. You would not be wise to accept second best. Many people have done so and then later discovered an ambition to show their dog only to be frustrated by owning a dog which was not good enough. Furthermore second best is unlikely to cost less than a really good puppy, especially when all the costs of keeping a dog are taken into account.

Whether you want a dog or a bitch is a matter for personal preferences. Dogs tend to be bigger, stronger and perhaps more independent than bitches. Bitches come into season twice a year and unless carefully confined will contrive to find themselves a mate. Dogs, however, are sexually aware throughout the year and at any time may go 'in search of love and beauty'. Some vets and welfare organisations recommend that pet animals should be neutered. The unavoidable fact, however, is that unwanted puppies are not produced by well cared for dogs. If an in-season bitch escapes there are perfectly safe non-surgical ways

Ch Bounty Tanner (65), Ronnie Irving's first champion and a wonderful character.

of terminating her pregnancy as well as ways of postponing seasons until they are convenient. Surgery is too often resorted to as a means to avoid the consequences of a lack of proper care. You, it is to be hoped, will be a caring and responsible owner.

What you want then, if only to satisfy your own pride, is a quality Border Terrier which has been thoughtfully bred and carefully reared. This you are most likely to find in a kennel which has, over a number of years, demonstrated an ability to produce top class Border Terriers which have proved their worth in the show ring or in the field. Eventually you will find a breeder, perhaps in your area, though you must also face the possibility that you may have to travel to find a suitable puppy, who has or who will shortly have puppies available. Let us assume that you have found a reputable breeder who expects to have a litter in the near future. You will be able to find out who the parents of the prospective pups are and, if you have done your homework properly, the information will be of value. You may have seen the parents, their offspring or their near relations and can go some way towards assessing what the pups might be like. You will also be able to tell the breeder precisely what your requirements are, having made your interest known, and must wait until the litter is born.

A few days after the puppies were due to be born contact the breeder to find out what might be available. At this stage the breeder should be able to say whether or not a puppy is available which might suit your needs. You might even go so far as to make an appointment to see the puppies, and even to confirm your desire to have one. Don't, however, expect to be allowed to see the puppies until they are at least a month old. Good breeders will not expose very young puppies to the stress and risk of infection which an inspection might involve. They will put the welfare of the puppies before your understandable impatience. In any case it is only after the pups have become active, more robust, more independent beings with individual characteristics that a visit will be of value to you. You may be able to see the sire, (useful if you are looking for a dog) and the dam, but don't expect her to be looking her best after rearing a litter.

You may be shown the whole litter or just those from which your choice is to be made. Most breeders have learned that all buyers invariably want the same puppy and so, to avoid problems, keep those which are not available out of sight. When you look at the litter remember that you are seeing individuals which have never been outside the group and which will respond to your attention not as individuals but according to their place within the group's complex relationships. It is surprising how much puppies change as the dominant sibling leaves the group or when they are removed from the group. If the pups are active, fat, clean, glossy, bright eyed and vigorous you can be fairly sure that they are healthy. If any seem unhealthy you would be wise to leave all the puppies alone. Ill health spreads rapidly through a litter. If all seems well you might then proceed to finalise your choice though if this can be deferred until the puppies are older then so much the better. You can, to some extent, rely for guidance on the breeder, who will, from long previous experience, have a very shrewd idea of how each puppy is likely to develop. But the final decision and responsibility for that decision are entirely yours. You may seek advice, though you must remember that the advice of those who know nothing, as well as of those who appear to know everything, should be treated with very great caution.

Make further good use of your visit to find out what diet the pups are having, what bedding they are accustomed to, what worming regime

Ch Clipstone Chasse (81), taken when she was still a puppy but already a firm favourite in the Jackson household.

the breeder uses, whether their inoculations will have begun before they go to their new homes, whether or not the breeder is covered by a transferable insurance system and, of course, when your choice will finally be yours. In this way you can make whatever arrangements are necessary to ensure that the puppy has a troublefree transfer to your home and that all is in readiness to receive it. Young puppies have a lot of growing to do and the less stress they are subjected to the better for them. It is amazing how well, at little more than eight weeks old, they adapt to a new home and a new regime away, for the first time in their lives, from their litter mates. Border Terriers, even as adults, are well able to adapt to new lives and homes. The breed's philosophy enables them to make the best of whatever situation they may find themselves in but that is no reason why they, particularly as puppies, should be exposed to unnecessary stress.

Eventually the interminable few weeks will pass and the time will come, when the puppy is at least eight weeks old, for you to collect your new charge. Try to do so at a time when you can devote all your attention to the puppy's needs, when your home is quiet and calm. When you collect the puppy the breeder will give you, if they have not already done so, a pedigree, a diet sheet, registration papers, inoculation papers if these are appropriate, and more than likely some promotional material distributed by pet food firms. You will also receive a receipt

Ch Hanleycastle Judy (63), with Hanleycastle Vicki and a venerable Hanleycastle Russ at a meet of the Ledbury Foxhounds.

which confirms the terms of your transaction. These should be simple. You will have bought the puppy and paid for it outright. Think very carefully before you enter into any sort of agreement which does not give you complete ownership and total control of your puppy. A reduced price in exchange for a puppy or puppies when you breed from your puppy not only often leads to trouble but forces you into a course which you may, subsequently, not find attractive. What is more it means that the puppy will be more expensive than an outright purchase.

Once you have got your puppy home, introduced it to its bed and given it a feed, it can be allowed, though not forced, to explore its new surroundings. Its curiosity, however, is likely to come second to a desire to sleep. Young puppies need a lot of sleep; even adult dogs need far more sleep than we do. Puppies will play vigorously for a short time and then, quite suddenly, collapse into sleep. A puppy which feels secure in its bed will seek this out; it should be encouraged to do so and its privacy respected, especially by children who may be inclined to put their wishes before the puppy's needs.

The bed to which your puppy will be able to retire at will should provide, as well as privacy, warmth and comfort. A strong cardboard box, cosily lined, though perhaps les grand than you think your puppy deserves, is ideal. A puppy deprived of the company of its litter mates, perhaps living a solitary existence and going through the trauma of

Ch Coundon Trudy (59), owned and bred by Nancy Turrall, and her litter brother Ch Winstonhall Coundon Tim (59), owned by May Long, did the double at Leeds in 1962.

teething may, for play or comfort, chew. It is better if it chews a renewable cardboard box than an expensive bed, and especially an expensive plastic bed which may shed indigestible fragments. Furthermore, though a healthy puppy will go to some lengths not to soil its bed, accidents can happen and it is far easier to replace a cardboard box than to clean a bed which is not disposable. The puppy should be given every opportunity to keep its bed clean. Many breeders train puppies to soil on newspaper which, though usually convenient, can sometimes lead to misunderstanding with unread copies which somehow find themselves on the floor. If a puppy is provided with a newspaper during the night or when it is to be left alone for any appreciable period it will, more often than not, make use of this facility. The puppy should also be put outside immediately after it has fed. Like babies, puppies will invariably soil immediately after they have fed. Housetraining is simply a matter of instilling in the puppy's mind the correct association. Put it outside frequently and praise it when it performs. Make your displeasure clear when it soils indoors but only if you catch it in the act. Dogs cannot associate past events with present punishment, just as they have no concept of the future. They live entirely in the present, or so the experts tell us.

An eight-week-old puppy will need four feeds a day. These should be spread evenly through the day with the interval between the last feed of one day and the first feed of the next being reduced to the most convenient minimum. As adults Border Terriers tend to have voracious and catholic appetites. Not to put too fine a point on it they are greedy. In fact they are very greedy. If an adult Border Terrier refuses its food you should consider the possibility that it is in love or dead. Puppies may at times, particular when they are teething, be slightly more capricious but, even so, a loss of appetite should never be treated lightly. Neither should a Border Terrier's greed be pandered to. Give a Border Terrier all the food it wants and you will end up with an unhealthy, obese and pathetic creature, the very antithesis of all that is to be admired about the breed. A fat Border wheezing along on sluggish legs is a sad sight, the product of an over indulgent owner who would probably be shocked to learn of the cruelty involved in such treatment.

Feeding a Border Terrier can be as simple or as complex an operation as you care to make it. Some owners adhere to old fashioned methods which involve frequent trips to the abattoir, succulent stews bubbling in large pans and secret additives. Anyone with the necessary knowledge of a dog's nutritional requirements can adopt this course but for those who lack the knowledge or inclination there are, fortunately, far easier ways. There are, on the market, a wide range of proprietary foods, either complete diets or tinned foods which are intended to be supplemented with an appropriate biscuit. Some are quite excellent, others less so. The best are produced by expert nutritionists and supported by the resources of a large company, the worst are knocked up in back street sheds from whatever materials are most readily available. Choose a well known brand recommended by satisfied users and you are unlikely to go far wrong. It is, perhaps, prudent to avoid foods which are based on or which contain milk because Border Terriers appear often to have an inability to cope with too much lactose. Milk and milk products tend to give them diarrhoea. Most of the best proprietary foods produce a range of products suitable for different circumstances. Puppies, working dogs, pregnant and lactating bitches, sick or injured dogs and older dogs all benefit from an appropriate diet and it is as well to choose one which offers at last some of this variety. Once you have found a diet which is satisfactory, stick to it. Dogs don't need and don't appreciate variety and a change invariably leads to stomach upsets. Remember that dogs are basically carnivores intended to thrive on a diet which we would find monotonous. Vets are accustomed to dealing with problems which result from dogs being fed unsuitable food at Christmas and other public holidays.

As the puppy grows the number of feeds will be progressively reduced until, by the time it is eight or nine months old, it is one or perhaps two meals a day. Some owners prefer a regime based on two feeds, others give only one. It's a matter of personal choice but do remember that the total amount of food in two feeds should not be more than is given in one. Give your puppy its own dish; in this way it is easier to assess and adjust the amount of food you give. Dog dishes come in a variety of shapes and sizes. Choose one which is easily cleaned and big enough for an adult, a seven-inch bowl is about right. As far as materials are concerned, enamel tends to chip, glass and crockery may break, aluminium is easily chewed and plastic may splinter if it is chewed. A good quality stainless steel dish may seem expensive but a good one will last a very long time.

Once your puppy has settled into its new home you will need to make arrangements to have its course of protective inoculations started, if the breeder has not done so, or completed, if they have. Before you bought the puppy you should have found a local vet who has a particular interest in dogs. Local dog breeders will be able to recommend a good one. Vets, like dog breeders, vary in quality. When they are good they are very, very good but when they are bad they are often expensive as well. Your vet will use one of a number of different available vaccines chosen against his knowledge of the particular needs of the locality and of your puppy. The vaccine will offer protection against parvovirus, distemper, hardpad, and the two forms of leptospirosis. Outside Britain and a few other countries, there may also be a need for a protective rabies vaccine.

On your first visit to the vet your puppy will probably be given a thorough examination. You will probably be inundated with advisory and promotional literature some of which may duplicate what you have got from the breeder but all of which will be worthy of at least a cursory glance and some will be well worth studying very much more closely. The examination should confirm that you have chosen your puppy wisely and that it is healthy. In order to keep it so you will need to worm it. Worming preparations are far better got from your vet than over a chemist or pet shop counter.

Your puppy should have been wormed by the breeder at fortnightly intervals from about the age of three weeks. This regime should be continued until the puppy is about twelve weeks old and then at six-monthly intervals for the rest of its life. All animals from time to time play host to a large and for the most part unpleasant collection of parasites; dogs are no exception but because we live in such close

The job for which Border Terriers are intended demands that they are resourceful and active, formal tests of these qualities tend, therefore, to be treated with contemptuous ease.

proximity with dogs their parasites seem to impinge more sharply on our consciousness than do those of other animals which cause us much more harm. In fact most canine parasites pose no threat at all to our species; those which do are less likely to cause harm than are some of the vaccines with which we routinely protect our children. Furthermore the threat posed by these parasites can be entirely eliminated by proper care and routine worming. In the last few years the efficiency of worming preparations has improved enormously; the best now not only kills worms and their eggs in the stomach, but may also kill those which have migrated to muscle tissue. The next step will be to make their effect longer lasting.

There are, in fact, two basic sorts of parasites: endoparasites which live within their host, and ectoparasites which live on it. The various types of parasitic worm are in the first category. Fleas, lice and ticks are in the second. These latter almost seem to occur spontaneously and often go unnoticed. A walk through the countryside is sometimes enough to collect a tick or two. Familiarity with a flea-infested dog or contact with the places in which it has rested may produce an infestation of fleas. Unpleasant though these things are, they will cause us no harm and are easily destroyed by means of the immense and effective arsenal available to us from the vet's surgery. Precautionary routine inspections and deterrent sprays are the best methods of defence.

The veterinary profession has not yet devised an appointments system that works. You are likely to spend some time waiting to see your vet and might usefully employ the time by examining his notice board which, along with all manner of things both interesting and sad, will probably contain information about local training classes and the activities of local canine societies. You might make a note of these for future use.

Only when inoculations have provided your puppy with protection against the fatal and crippling diseases to which dogs are prone will you begin to consider taking it among other dogs or to places where other dogs have been. Prior to this time its breeder and yourself will respectively have started and continued a period of socialisation which is intended to accustom the puppy to all the sights and sounds, all the experiences which it is likely to meet during its adult life. Puppies reared in isolation up to the age of about twelve weeks, protected during that period from the normal life of a busy household, may subsequently be unable to adjust to new situations. They will be shy, nervous and fearful for the rest of their lives. Socialisation is therefore of great importance and it is somewhat ironic that those who don't understand breeding seem continually to be trying to produce rules which would make socialisation very much more difficult. During this important but vulnerable period your puppy should be exposed to as many new experiences as possible without also exposing it to infection or unnecessary stress. Once the course of inoculations is complete the range of experience can carefully and gradually be extended. One way in which this can be achieved is by taking a puppy to training classes. These offer a variety of courses ranging from basic training such as will be necessary for any well behaved companion, to ring training intended to fit a dog for the show ring, obedience aimed at competitions and agility training again aimed at competitions. All have one thing in common: they are great fun and help people to get more fun out of their dogs. Whether your ambitions point in one direction or another these classes can help.

One of the many nice things about Border Terriers is that they allow their owners to take part in any one of these activities as well as others. They are ideal companions, they can be shown both in Kennel Club events and at hunt and working terrier shows, and though they are not the ideal obedience dog Border Terriers have done well in the obedience ring and have done exceptionally well in the emergent agility tests which, if we may be allowed a modest prophecy, will in a few years' time probably be rivalling show jumping as a popular entertainment. Or if you would like to share the fun you get from your Border Terrier you might consider joining one of the schemes which introduce dogs to hospitals, old people's homes and other, similar, institutions where their presence, on regular visits, provides interest, comfort, solace and understanding for those who are deprived of the companionship of a dog of their own. There are so many different ways in which you can derive enjoyment from your Border Terrier.

Before your puppy came to you the breeder will have made quite sure that its coat was clean and glossy, its nails short, its ears clean and that it was, in every way, spick and span. You will, of course want to keep it in this pristine condition. Doing so is very much your job. Take a Border Terrier to the average canine beauty parlour and you will probably return to find an expensively clippered caricature of what the breed should look like which will take months to restore to some semblance of normality. In order to do a very much better and very much cheaper job yourself you will need some basic equipment. A fairly stiff brush, perhaps a terrier pad or a comb, scissors, your finger and thumb, patience and a clear idea of what a Border Terrier should look like. Some cotton wool or cotton buds for cleaning ears, a good pair of nail clippers and a dentist's scaler and you have all that is needed to keep a Border Terrier looking immaculate.

Put your dog on a table for a few minutes each day, give it a quick but thorough inspection to check for parasites, injuries and other blemishes. Check eyes, ears, teeth, nails and coat. Remove any straggly hairs, a few removed each day will obviate the need for major and tedious stripping required to remove a mass of dead coat. Most dead hair can be removed by brushing, the rest, in ears, down the neck, on the tail and on the undersides will need to be carefully removed by finger and thumb. Doing so needs practice but by making sure you take too little rather than too much and with a good picture in your mind of what the end result should look like you are unlikely to go far wrong.

If your Border is exercised along hard roads its nails will seldom need trimming; if it gets most of its exercise on grass the job will need to be done more often. You will need a good pair of nail clippers, a firm hand and a steady eye. If the job is done often little will need to be removed and the dog will not resent the operation. If you leave it until the nails are longer you may find that, having removed more, you have cut into the quick. The result will be an alarming quantity of blood, a resentful dog and a very much more difficult task next time. Teeth too need regular inspection. Some dogs seem to accumulate tartar at an alarming rate, others hardly at all. A scaler, used regularly, will keep teeth in good order and inspection will forewarn of any serious problems which will need veterinary treatment. Anal glands too should

Ch Hawkesburn Beaver
(63) was not only Felicity
Marchants first champion
he was also her first
Border Terrier.

be inspected regularly. These are below the anus and, in some dogs, particularly those which get a diet deficient in roughage and which receive only sedate exercise, can become filled with excreta. Cleaning them out is not pleasant but is easy. Hold the tail with one hand, with the finger and thumb of the other press, from about one inch below, upwards towards the anus. The contents of the glands will be projected from the anus and the task is complete. There are times when Border terriers need to be bathed, if only for the comfort of their owners. Routine bathing is seldom necessary for other reasons if only because dogs do not have sweat glands all over their skin.

So much then for the basics of routine maintenance. There is of course much more to be learned and much more that you will learn, or be taught by your Border Terrier. Each and every subject to which we have, necessarily briefly, referred, rearing, training, feeding and the rest, could itself form the subject matter for a book far bigger than this one. There are already a number of such books; some of the best are companions to this one, and you will want to read at least some of them. Remember, however, that dogs have been living with man for many thousands of years. They are resilient and adaptable creatures, and perhaps none of them more so than Border Terriers. Given a caring and thoughtful owner they will not be at all troublesome to keep in health and they will repay all the attention you give them in ways of which you may not have even dreamt.

Having a fit and healthy Border Terrier as a companion is, in itself, a source of sufficient enjoyment and pride to satisfy many owners but in reality they are missing a great deal by being so easily satisfied. By owning a Border Terrier you have the means to gain access to a wide variety of activities from which you could derive even more fun. Don't dismiss any until you have at least thought about what they might do for you, what through them you might do for the breed in which you have such interest and, perhaps most importantly, what you might do for others. As a new owner you will join one or more of the breed clubs. These you will find run a wide variety of activities which vary from the purely social, at which people who share an interest in Border Terriers can gather together to share their common interests, to the championship show, at which all are striving for the successes which will make their dog a champion. In between are a whole range of activities sufficiently varied to cater for every taste and every level of ambition and which cater also for every age and every part of society. There are very few, if any, other competitive activities which provide for such a wide range and which can be enjoyed for so long.

Showing dogs is too often presented by the ill informed sections of the press as a cut-throat, unscrupulous and somewhat disreputable activity. In our experience it is nothing of the kind. Competitors themselves choose, according to their ambitions, what level they wish to operate at, and fellow competitors are usually helpful and friendly, ready to give advice and assistance and ready, above all, to ensure that everyone enjoys themselves. Border Terriers are a friendly and sporting breed and their owners, on the whole, are jealous of a reputation for being every bit as friendly and sporting. By joining a breed club and by taking part in its activities you will be introduced to the world of dog shows in the pleasantest way possible. You may wish to restrict your involvement to the small match meeting which clubs hold or you may wish to fly far higher. The choice will be yours and yours alone but don't be at all surprised if, as in our case, an ambition which you didn't suspect existed ignites and takes you into new places and introduces you to new activities and to many new friends.

If showing does not appeal to you, you might enjoy training your Border Terrier for obedience. It's not the ideal breed but some owners have achieved great success in obedience trials. Or, if you are every bit as fit and active as your dog, you might like to try your hand at the agility game, newly arrived on the scene but which has already achieved remarkable popularity. Your vet's notice board might well give you the whereabouts of local clubs, and these you will find every bit as friendly and helpful as the breed clubs. If your vet's notice board is devoid of information then try your national kennel club.

Of course you may not relish competition at all but may still want,

in some way, to share and extend the enjoyment you get from owning a Border Terrier. You may well find that joining one of the schemes which provides visitors, with their dogs, for hospitals, homes and other institutions will not only extend your interest but will do so in a way which will benefit others less fortunate than yourself. You need only to see what effect a happy and friendly dog has on a room full of withdrawn, depressed and perhaps sick people to realise not only how worthwhile these schemes are but also how important is the place which dogs occupy in our society and our homes.

Ch Ragsdale Blueberry (81) was bred by Jack Price by his Ch Oxcroft Rocker out of Dandyhow Blue Stilton. She is owned by Frank Wildman and was shown by John Bainbridge.

The important thing to remember in whatever activity you choose is that everyone started with as little or less experience and knowledge as you will. Some may be regarded as experts but they too will still have much to learn. All will be united in a regard for and an interest in the breed which has claimed your affection. They too will want to learn and enjoy themselves among friends. There is nothing to fear and much to hope for.

11 Breeding and All That

One of the likely consequences of owning one Border Terrier is that, sooner or later, you will want another. Two dogs which live and play together are often more content than a single, lonely individual. They retain an air of independence which, if it is not taken too far, is somehow more appropriate to the character of a Border Terrier than is a more servile and dependent attitude. In order to get your second Border Terrier, you might go out and buy another. In which case, having already met and overcome the pitfalls once, you will be well equipped to do so again. You might, however, decide that you will breed your second Border Terrier yourself.

That you will need a bitch in order to do so is something which we, in this sexually explicit age, might be expected to realise but it is surprising how often breeders are approached by the owner of a pet dog to provide a 'wife' for it. In practice, dogs which are used at stud are invariably those which have demonstrated, either in the field or in the show ring, that they are far better than average. Unless a dog has a good pedigree, has proved his worth and has already produced quality puppies he is unlikely to be attractive to other breeders as a stud dog. If you are going to breed, you will need a bitch. In the previous chapter, we stressed the importance of not being satisfied with second best. If you have not taken this advice or if you have been unfortunate and found yourself with a bitch which has serious faults, you should not breed from her. There is no point in perpetuating second best. The only sound reason for breeding a litter is in order to try to produce really good, and hopefully outstandingly good, puppies. In any case, if your regard for the breed is genuine, you will not want to do other than produce puppies which are a credit to the breed and which will be a credit to you, their breeder.

As a breed, Border Terriers are fertile, prolific and easy whelpers. The bitches make good, if robust rather than solicitous, mothers and puppies are reared with a minimum of fuss and problems. Which is not to say that problems do not occur. Any livestock breeder must expect problems and be prepared to overcome them. The more animals are bred, the longer breeding continues the more problems will be met and the greater will be their range. Indeed, it may be that the challenges provided by these difficulties and by the pursuit of what may well be an unattainable standard of excellence motivate the very best breeders.

Breeding is very much a cyclical process. Puppies are born, reared, grow into adults, are mated and themselves produce puppies. It is very difficult to decide at which point a description should break into the cycle. It is not even easy to decide just where the process of producing and rearing a litter of puppies begins. Certainly the process does not begin only with their birth because by that time they will have been individual, if parasitic, beings for almost nine weeks and will have flourished according, among other things, to how well or how indifferently their dam has been cared for. Before they are even conceived, the well-being of the puppies will have been, to an extent, affected by the health and vigour of their dam which will itself, at least partly, be a product of how well she was reared. There is an impressive body of research work, mostly carried out on farm or laboratory animals, but nevertheless broadly applicable to dogs, which shows that animals with lower than average birth weight for their species, those which are part of litters which contain more individuals than the average, and those which have low antibody levels, perhaps as a result of being deprived of mother's milk while it contains the necessary amount of colostrum, have a reduced expectation of survival. Here are several good reasons why litter sizes should be kept within the bounds of what a bitch can be expected to rear satisfactorily.

In our experience, litter size has varied from one to nine, though our dogs have on two occasions sired litters of ten to other people's bitches and we know of one well authenticated report of a litter of eleven. The average litter size is just a little under five. Litter size, however, is dependent on a number of factors: the age and condition of the bitch, whether she was mated at the optimum time during her season, and the care she received during her nine weeks of pregnancy. The number of puppies in a litter is also influenced by hereditary factors. Some lines are undoubtably more prolific than others and it is even likely that a sustained attempt to breed for this factor could further increase litter size though with what consequence to the quality of individual puppies it is impossible to predict.

It is sometimes claimed that litter size is also affected by a dog's

Ch Oxcroft Rocker (78) bred by Jack Price, illustrates the way in which a good Border Terrier will last, this photograph was taken when Rocker was in his tenth year.

fertility. It is true, of course, that like bitches dogs may be more or less fertile or even totally infertile but we doubt if a dog's relative fertility has any great effect on litter size. We heard the story of a breeder whose kennel housed two or three good dogs of varying ages. A fellow breeder arranged to bring a bitch to be mated and suggested that it would be best to use the oldest dog because his bitch was a maiden and he didn't want her to have a big litter. She was mated to the old dog and eventually produced a litter of ten puppies. The stud dog's owner was not slow to point out how fortunate it was that a younger dog had not been used!

If you have chosen your bitch wisely, and your efforts have been blessed by no more than average good fortune, you will be the owner of a healthy bitch, without any glaring faults and typical of her breed. There is then no reason why she should not be bred from. However, in order to produce quality puppies she must be mated to a quality dog, preferably to one which has already demonstrated an ability to produce top class puppies out of bitches which are closely related to your own bitch. You may have to travel some distance in order to use such a dog, but even the longest journey is very much to be preferred to making do with second best.

During the process of selecting your preferred dog, you may receive all sorts of advice. If your bitch is particularly well bred or of outstanding quality, she may well have a queue of suitors, not all of which will be at all suitable. Remember that none of the advice you receive will be infallible, that all breeders, no matter how experienced, make mistakes. It is best that you make your own decisions and accept the consequences of your own mistakes because only then will you have fair claim to your own successes.

Undoubtedly, you will receive all sorts of advice about the value or evils of inbreeding, which is simply the mating of animals which have a blood relationship. In fact, it is impossible, in a breed as numerically small as Border Terriers, to avoid some degree of inbreeding. It is for you to decide what degree is desirable.

Much of our perceived and received attitudes towards inbreeding stem, not from careful thought based on soundly analysed scientific principles, but, directly or indirectly, from the sentiments expressed in verses 6 to 17 in chapter 18 of the Old Testament Book of Leviticus. What often masquerades as a scientific attitude is in fact a moral one neither intended for nor relevant to the breeding of livestock. It is true that inbreeding is a sharp tool capable of causing great harm if used unwisely but it is also a valuable tool which can produce, indeed has produced, enormous improvement to the quality of livestock. In fact, when one considers that only about ten per cent of the Border Terriers which are born are at all likely to be bred from and that the total population in Britain is probably no more than ten thousand it becomes apparent that it is practically impossible to avoid some degree of inbreeding. The clever breeder uses this to advantage, the bad one tries to ignore it.

We have already said that the development of an individual puppy is influenced by the way in which its dam was reared and by the state of her health when conception takes place. Its development is also affected by the way in which the bitch is treated during her pregnancy. Its individual needs begin, if not actually during the act of mating, then not more than three weeks later when the fertilised egg has become implanted on the uterus wall and is continuing the miraculous transformation which will change it from a small group of cells to a complex being. During the first few weeks the puppy and its litter mates are still sufficiently small to be adequately sustained from the bitch's normal diet and there is, during this period, merit in protecting the bitch from even the minimal stress which a change of diet might produce. During the next two weeks, the puppies will achieve a weight equal to about one quarter of their birth weight and will continue to grow at an accelerating rate, achieving about half their birth weight by the eighth week and doubling it in the last week. It is, therefore, only during the last weeks of pregnancy that the bitch has need of a significantly increased nutritional intake, a need which is reduced by the increased efficiency with which she converts her food during this period. Even so the pre-natal development of a litter imposes a need for additional food during the last two or three weeks of pregnancy which must be satisfied for obvious reasons with more nutritious food given in more frequent small meals rather than by an increased bulk given in one or two meals.

The process of being born is, for any puppy, a gruelling experience from which it emerges wet, tired, sore and, for the first time, with a need to search for both food and warmth. It will, unless kept warm, rapidly lose essential body heat, will then become moribund and unable to get the nutrition it needs in order to restore body heat. All carnivores have relatively numerous offspring in order to compensate for a high death rate. Severov's studies of wolves show that almost half the young of wolves die in their first year. If we, as dog breeders, want to avoid this natural wastage we must ensure that puppies are warm and well fed.

By the time you decide to breed from your bitch, she will have had two or three seasons, a pattern will have been established which will allow you to predict, with some degree of accuracy when her next season is due. Bitches are only fertile for a few days, in some breeds only a few hours during their season, it is during this period that they must be taken to the dog. If you are using a good dog he will have other bitches waiting for his services and because seasons tend to occur during spring and autumn you may need to stake your claim in good time. Once you have decided on a particular dog, let its owner know of your interest and tell them when you expect your bitch to be in season. When your bitch next shows signs of coming in season, signs which you will by now know well, the swollen vulva, the discoloured discharge followed by a colourless discharge, then the overt sexual behaviour, you should again let the dog's owner know the situation.

Ch Farmway M'Lady Robin (81) bred by Mrs Marnham, by Lesley Gosling's Akenside Robin Hood out of Farmway Warbler, a daughter of Ch Workmore Waggoner.

About twelve days after the discoloured discharge has given way to a colourless one the bitch should be taken to the dog, because it is at about this time that she will be ovulating. To mate her before this stage is reached will mean that only the first of her eggs will be fertilised, to mate her later will mean that only the last will be fertilised and either course could mean that no pups are born because not all fertilised eggs survive to full term. It may well be that the right day for mating is not the most convenient day for you. You must then decide whether you want your bitch to have puppies or just to have sex. If it's the first you will take her to the dog on the right day, if it's the latter you will take her when it is most convenient to you. Beware though of the latter course. A good dog will very quickly show whether or not you have chosen the right day; its owner is unlikely to be best pleased if you have not arrived at the optimum time.

Some bitches, and particularly those which from a very early age have lived solitary lives, may be difficult to mate. You should allow plenty of time for the exercise and should expect not to have the exercise rushed by the owner of the stud dog. You should expect to witness the mating. How else will you know whether the selected dog has been used or the bitch been mated? You should be prepared to help though should not demand to do so. The stud dog's owner will be at pains to ensure a quick and successful mating and will call on whatever assistance is necessary to achieve the desired result. Once a

Ch Dykeside Gordon Ranger (85) cleverly bred and owned by Marjory Stavely. Ranger has several lines back to the legendary Shady Knight.

mating has been achieved, the dog and bitch may tie for as long as an hour. In our experience, the longest ties tend to take place out of doors in weather which is either wet or cold, or more likely, both. However, you need not be unduly alarmed if the classic tie is not achieved. Some very succcessful stud dogs never tie, some bitches refuse to hold the dog in a tie. As in all aspects of dogdom, it is as well to remember that nothing happens invariably.

After the mating and a welcome cup of coffee – or, among Border Terrier breeders, very probably something stronger! – you will be required to pay the stud fee. In Britain, this is usually about half to two-thirds the price of a puppy. In Scandinavia, it is often divided into two components, the first a charge for the service and the second dependent on the number of puppies born. Whatever the system do not, without very careful thought, enter into any agreements which give the owner of the stud dog a right to any puppies. You may find that only one is born and that, after all your plans, all your expense and all your care, you are left with nothing. If you have a particularly good bitch or if the mating particularly appeals to the stud dog's owner, you may find that they express an interest in seeing the litter after you have made your choice. You should be pleased and might well find that such an arrangement yields all sorts of benefits.

Once the bitch has been mated, she should be protected from any stress, from anything with which she is unfamiliar, for about a week. During this vulnerable period the embryos will implant on the uterus wall after which they are, within limits, very resilient little beings. The bitch should also be protected from the attentions of any other dogs. This may not be at all easy, because she may well not only encourage these attentions but might also go to some lengths to search them out. If by some mischance the bitch does get mated by another dog, several choices face the owner. The pregnancy may be terminated by a vet, the pups can be left until full term and then either destroyed or passed to new owners as pedigree unknown. If the second dog was also a Border Terrier, the litter can, in some countries, be registered as having two sires or can now be blood tested, along with the sires, in order to ascertain which pups are by which sire. The newly developed tests are conclusive and will in future resolve any possible doubts about any puppy's true parentage.

What is regarded as the normal gestation period for dogs is 93 days. In our experience with Border Terriers, litters can be expected to arrive about two days before this time has elapsed. During the gestation period, they undergo a truly miraculous transformation from a few cells to a very complex being capable of living an independent existence. During the first few weeks of their existence, these tiny creatures impose little strain on the bitch. The increased efficiency with which she converts her food is sufficient to supply their very small additional nutritional needs. Not until the pregnancy is half complete will the puppies achieve even one quarter of their birth weight and from that point on, will grow at an accelerating rate to achieve about half their birth weight after about eight weeks, doubling this in the final week. Only during the last two or three weeks does the bitch need a significantly enhanced nutritional intake. This should be provided as more nutritious food; if you have selected your normal food well you will find that within the range is an appropriate product which will not involve a dramatic change in her diet. The food should be given in the form of an increased number of small meals rather than as one or two larger ones which the bitch, with her growing load, might find uncomfortable to digest.

Among all breeders, novice or vastly experienced, there is an understandable curiosity to know whether or not a bitch is in whelp. The information has little or no practical value but there is a strong temptation to ask a vet for his opinion. Unless he has access to an ultrasonic scanner, which is very unlikely, his diagnosis will rely on more or less skilled palpation, best carried out when the bitch is about three weeks in whelp. It might then be possible to tell whether a bitch is in whelp but if no embryos can be felt this does not mean that she is not in whelp. It might only mean that the bitch is too tense or muscular to make palpation easy or that the pups are tucked well up under the ribs. In any case a positive diagnosis is not a positive indication that, perhaps due to the sort of stress involved in a visit to the vet or to some infection picked up in the waiting room, the embryos will not subsequently be reabsorbed. It's best to leave well alone and to curb curiosity until the signs become obvious.

Before the bitch is due to give birth, suitable whelping quarters must be prepared for her. Once more the ubiquitous cardboard box is ideal, if not quite so grand as many might think suitable. If the box is placed within a small pen – about 4′ × 2′ is big enough – the bitch will be given some extra privacy and the puppies will be confined to a place of safety. We use a whelping box which has a wire front and solid lid which gives increased protection and warmth. Warmth, for newly born puppies, is important. They emerge, wet, sore and tired, from an environment in which nourishment is constantly supplied and which has a constant temperature of 37°C. An isolated puppy will very quickly become hypothermic in a temperature even as high as 26°C. Warmth is, therefore, essential to their survival. Contact with the bitch, of course, supplies much warmth but even so there is often a need for supplementary heat and protection against draughts.

When the birth is imminent, the bitch will become restless and begin to prepare her 'nest'. If she is bedded on paper, which is easily disposed of and is sterile, she will tear it into small shreds. This first stage of the birth process, which might last for as long as twenty-four hours without reason for alarm, ends as the bitch begins to have the contractions. These will progressively become more frequent and stronger and, all being well, will result in the first puppy being born within not more than an hour or two after regular contractions have begun. You should become increasingly concerned if this stage is prolonged and should not delay in seeking veterinary advice.

Puppies normally emerge into the world head first, though in fact a great many do so feet first without, it seems, causing any great problems to their dam. They are wrapped in a tough membrane which the bitch will normally tear open, after which she will begin licking the puppy to stimulate breathing and circulation. She will also bite through the umbilical cord which attaches the puppy to the placenta. Having done so she will proceed to eat the membrane, cord and placenta. Allow her to do so because the placenta contains a substance which stimulates milk production.

However, a bitch whelping for the first time and particularly one which has been rather over humanised by the sort of solitary existence to which we earlier referred may find the whole business very bewildering. In which case, it is for the breeder to take a hand. You must, using well sterilised scissors, open the membrane in which the puppy is enclosed, and, with a clean towel, dry it and clean it, at the same time, stimulating its breathing and circulation. You will need also, to cut the umbilical cord. Do so about half an inch from the puppy having first gently massaged any residual contents of the cord towards the puppy. At this stage the puppy can be returned to the bitch or kept, well and warmly wrapped in a warm, clean towel, while other puppies are born. However, as each puppy is born, allow the bitch an opportunity to carry out her duties herself. Most bitches learn very quickly what is expected of them and can then be allowed, under careful supervision, to carry on unaided.

Once all the puppies have been born ensure that each is suckling. A puppy which does not suck quite soon after it is born has a very much reduced chance of survival and an increased chance of infection. When this has been achieved and the bitch has settled down to a well earned rest comfortably curled round her new family you may celebrate the arrival of your first litter. Most likely you will feel like doing so by going to bed. It's surprising how many litters are born at night! The bitch will appreciate a drink; water or glucose and water is all that is needed for her; you may need something stronger.

During the next few days the bitch should be encouraged to leave the nest from time to time, though she may be reluctant to do so. Examine each puppy, weigh them if you like, check on their sexes and see whether any are blemished in any way. While the bitch is away from her family, she should be fed, small and nutritious meals and at least for the first twenty-four hours rather bland ones. After this, the increasing demands of a growing litter will increase her need for food to three or even four times her normal need. Do not stint her because through her you are feeding her pups.

Before the puppies' eyes open, at about ten days, you must decide whether or not you intend to remove their dew claws. This is one of the very many subjects about which Border Terrier breeders are not unanimous. Some argue for leaving dew claws alone, others believe

Ch Butterscotch, owned
and bred by Jimmy
Stewart. Sadly
circumstances have
prevented her passing her
quality onto another
generation.

that they are a nuisance, an eyesore and a source of trouble. The decision is yours. If you decide to remove them, you will need a pair of sharp, sterilised scissors, keen eyes, a steady hand and some determination. Take the bitch well out of earshot, take each puppy and with a firm clean cut, remove the dew claws. Place it back with its litter mates and, when the job is done, allow the bitch to return to her family. Within minutes, her concern will have vanished and the litter will be suckling as though nothing untoward had taken place.

Very soon, after the puppies' eyes have opened, they should be wormed for the first time, the time and subsequent regime being dependent on the particular vermicide you are using. Do follow the manufacturer's instructions precisely. Vermicides are far safer than was once the case but overdosing still does more harm than good. At this stage too the puppies can be introduced to food other than mother's milk. You will read, perhaps, of all sorts of complicated ways to encourage puppies to eat. In our experience, Border Terriers, even at this very early stage in their lives, need little tuition. Put some canned puppy food or some well soaked complete puppy food through a liquidiser and present it to the puppies. At first, they will do more paddling than eating and the bitch will have an enjoyable time cleaning up the ensuing mess. They will soon learn and will from then on be demanding food four or even six times a day. Once this stage has been reached and the bitch has decided that her duties are coming to an end, she should be allowed to visit them only when she feels like it. By the time the pups are about a month old, they will be almost independent and the bitch will be taking no more than a polite interest in their well-being.

The puppies will be growing at a prodigious rate and must be fed accordingly so that by the time they are eight weeks old they will be independent enough, strong enough and experienced enough to go to their new homes without the attentions of well meaning but often very inexperienced owners causing any great problems.

Appendix

British Border Terrier Champions: 1920 to 1987

Name of Dog		Sire	Dam	Breeder	Owner
Acanthius Nacarat (79)	D	Ch Foxhill Fantastic	Acanthius Honour Bright	Mrs C. M. T. Lindsay	Breeder
Aldham Joker (37)	D	Ch Barb Wire	Country Girl	Miss V. Smither	Mrs E. Twist
Alexander (54)	D	Moidore	Dewar Pride	Mrs A. S. Crowe	W. Irving
Alverton Fury (45)	B	Hunter's Boy	Lady Venture	W. Welton	W. Hancock
Alvertune Martin (50)	D	Ch Future Fame	Chartreuse	W. Turnbull	Breeder
Arnton Fell (69)	D	Ch Bounty Tanner	Station Masha	W. R. Irving	W. Hancock
Ashbrae Anouska (76)	B	Ch Ribbleside Ridgeman	Suki Suzette of Ashbrae	Mrs E. Cuthbertson	Breeder
Ashbrae Jaffa (81)	D	Ch Dutonlea Suntan of Dandyhow	Thoraldby Tipoline	Mr & Mrs A. Cuthbertson	Breeder
Bannerdown Boomerang (83)	D	Ch Clipstone Cumin	Ch Dandyhow Marchioness	Mrs P. M. Creed˜	Mrs W. Griffiths
Bannerdown Capricorn (77)	B	Ch Wharfholm Warrant	Bannerdown Honeysuckle	Mrs P. M. Creed	Mrs M. Wood
Bannerdown Cavalier (83)	D	Ch Clipstone Cumin	Ch Dandyhow Marchioness	Mrs P. M. Creed	Breeder
Bannerdown Viscount (73)	D	Ch Wharfholm Warrant	Derwood Tia Maria	Mrs P. M. Creed	Breeder
Barb Wire (34)	D	Ch Dinger	Ch Todhunter	J. Renton	Miss M. Richmond
Bargower Silver Dollar (53)	D	Ginger	Dusty Maid	Miss J. Machray	R. Drummond
Barney Bindle (23)	D	Ch Grip of Tynedale	Brigend Beauty	Miss J. D. Potts	Breeder
Barnikin (59)	D	Tweedside Red Kingpin	Betty's Dream	J. Renton	Breeder & T. Harper
Beenaben Brock (76)	D	Forest Samson	Bluemink of Beenaben	J. B. Baxter	Breeder
Benthor Garry (66)	D	Pride of Pothouse	Benthor Bran	F. Bennett	Breeder
Benton Biddy (25)	B	Revenge	Mollyway	Dr S. Fullerton	Breeder
Billy Boy (49)	D	Callum	Misty Dawn	A. L. Waters	Breeder
Bladnoch Raider (32)	D	Revenge	Red Gold	N. A. McEwan	J. Johnson
Bladnoch Spaewife (45)	B	Dipley Dusty	Bladnoch Jinty	Dr W. Lillico	Breeder
Blister (29)	D	Revenge	Causey Bridget	A. Stewart	Capt M. C. Hamilton
Blue Doctor (82)	D	Ch Dandyhow Scotsman	Dandyhow Hot Chocolate	Mrs M. Staveley	Breeder
Blue Rock (84)	B	Ch Oxcroft Rocker	Padevisor Raft	Mrs P. Bamforth	Breeder
Blunstan Kestrel (78)	B	Oxcroft Rocky	Corburn Nala	F. Stanton	Mrs L. A. Gosling
Bombax Xavier (75)	D	Int Ch Daletyne Danny Boy	Swed, Fin Ch Clipstone Clover	C. & C. G. Stafberg	Mrs J. Jackson & C. G. Stafberg
Borderbrae Candy (69)	B	Dandyhow Brussel Sprout	Dandyhow Siani	H. Roper	Breeder
Borderbrae Commodore (66)	D	Dandyhow Saracen	Dandyhow Siani	H. Roper	Breeder & Mrs B. Sullivan
Bounty Tanner (65)	D	Dandyhow Samaritan	Deerstone Deborah	T. Newall	W. R. Irving

Name of Dog	Sire		Dam	Breeder	Owner
Boxer Boy (44)	Ch Aldham Joker	D	Daphne's Dream	Mr & Mrs W. J. Eccles	D. Jackson
Braestone Brushwood (76)	Ch Breastone Voyager	D	Rhosmerholme Bunty	Mrs E. Marsden	Mrs M. McAfee
Braw Boy (53)	Ch Billy Boy	D	Lassiebelle	J. S. Bell	Breeder
Brehill April Lass (84)	Ch Oxcroft Rocker	B	Ch Brehill March Belle	Mrs F. E. Wagstaff	Breeder
Brehill March Belle (81)	Ch Mansergh Pearl Diver	B	Ch Brehill Wayward Lass	Mrs F. E. Wagstaff	Breeder
Brehill Wayward Lass (77)	Ch Dandyhow Nightcap	B	Ragus Dark Secret	Mrs F. E. Wagstaff	Breeder
Bridgesollers, Brimball of (33)	Ch Dinger	B	Bunty of Bridgesollers	Miss M. Richmond	Breeder
Brieryhill Gertrude (59)	Tweedside Red Kingpin	B	Jean's Wendy	Miss J. Galbraith	W. Irving
Bright Light (59)	Tweedside Red Kingpin	B	Jean's Wendy	Miss J. Galbraith	W. Irving
Brookend Baggins (58)	Brookend Vali	D	Blackmorevale Fuzzy	Capt H. D'O. Vigne	Breeder
Brookend Brandybuck (61)	Brookend Vali	D	Blackmorevale Fuzzy	Capt H. D'O. Vigne	Breeder
Brumberhill Bittersweet (85)	Ch Mansergh General Post	B	Brumberhill Blue Mist	S. McPherson	Breeder
Brumberhill Blue Maestro (83)	Brumberhill Blue Minstrel	D	Blue Minx of Brumberhill	S. A. McPherson	Breeder
Brumberhill, Blue Maverick of (85)	Ch Brumberhill Blue Maestro	D	Timbertops Inkie Dollar	Mrs S. P. Clark	S. McPherson & E. Hutchinson
Brumberhill Blue Tansy (80)	Chevinor Ribro	B	Blue Rose	Miss D. J. Lamb	S. A. McPherson
Brumberhill, Brannigan of (84)	Ch Brumberhill Blue Maestro	D	Fine Lady	Mrs H. Deighton	S. A. McPherson & E. Hutchinson
Bumble Bee (49)	Ch Boxer Boy	B	Bracken Biddy	H. Pybus	Breeder
Butterscotch (83)	Ch Dutonlea Suntan of Dandyhow	B	Nippy Sweetie	J. Stewart	Breeder
Cannybuff Cloud (78)	Ch Napoleon Brandy	B	Ciggie of Cannybuff	Mrs Crowther Davies	Mrs C. M. Walker
Carahall Cicely (62)	Ch Carahall Coffee	B	Carahall Coralyn	D. Goodsir	Breeder
Carahall Coffee (61)	Winstonhall Wiseman	D	Kergil's Karen	W. Jacklin	D. Goodsir
Carahall Cornet (50)	Ch Portholme Manly Boy	D	Carahall Crystal	D. Goodsir	Breeder
Chalkcroft Fancy (51)	Chalkcroft Duster	B	Chalkcroft Tui	Miss B. M. Eccles	Breeder

Name of Dog		Sire	Dam	Breeder	Owner
Chalkcroft, Fancy Girl of (46)	B	Devonside Diversion	Portholme Gypsy	B. McLelland	Miss B. M. Eccles
Chalkcroft the Card (49)	D	Chalkcroft Duster	Dronfield Merrylegs	Miss B. M. Eccles	Breeder
Cherisette (45)	B	Sandy of Dhibban	Fortune	Dr & Mrs G. M. Martin	Breeder
Chevinor Rasamat (70)	D	Chevinor Rogue	Chevinor Dandyhow Sunsprite	A. H. Beardwood	Breeder
Chevinor Ripple (74)	B	Ch Duttonlea Mr Softy	Chevinor Remarvic	A. H. Beardwood	Breeder
Chevinor Rosalla (77)	B	Ch Ribbleside Ridgeman	Chevinor Rosa	A. H. Beardwood	Dr E. Rhind
Clipstone Carrots (70)	B	Dandyhow Saracen	Clipstone Dandyhow Lady	Mr & Mrs F. Jackson	Breeder
Clipstone Cetchup (73)	D	Dandyhow Napoleon	Ch Clipstone Carrots	Mr & Mrs F. Jackson	Breeder
Clipstone Chasse (81)	B	Ch Llanishen Reynard	Ch Clipstone Clicquot	Mr & Mrs F. Jackson	Breeder
Clipstone Chit Chat (83)	B	Ch Clipstone Cumin	Nelly Blithe of Clipstone	Mr & Mrs F. Jackson	Breeder
Clipstone Clicquot (78)	B	Int Nord Ch Bombax Xavier	Dandyhow Creme Caramel of Clipstone	Mr & Mrs. F. Jackson	Breeder
Clipstone Comma (73)	B	Ch Clipstone Guardsman	Ch Llanishen Illse of Clipstone	Mr & Mrs F. Jackson	Breeder
Clipstone Cumin (82)	D	Clipstone Dash	Clipstone Siren	Mr & Mrs F. Jackson	Breeder
Clipstone Guardsman (70)	D	Dandyhow Saracen	Clipstone Dandyhow Lady	Mr & Mrs F. Jackson	Breeder
Clipstone Hanleycastle Bramble (69)	B	Hanleycastle Jasper	Cawfields Ballerina	L. W. R. Clements	Mr & Mrs F. Jackson
Clipstone, Llanishen Illse of (70)	B	Ch Dandyhow Shady Knight	Hanleycastle Warbler	D. Wiseman	Mr & Mrs F. Jackson
Corburn Corn Dolly (67)	B	Dandyhow Brussel Sprout	Dr Dorothy	Mr & Mrs J. S. Heslop	J. R. Skeen
Corburn Ottercap Farm Lassie (67)	B	Dandyhow Brussel Sprout	Brown Owl	Mr & Mrs J. S. Heslop	Breeder
Coundon, Llanishen Rosemary of (73)	B	Ch Chevinor Rasamat	Llanishen Raffles	D. Wiseman	Miss Turrall
Coundon Troena (63)	B	Ch Portholme Macsleap	Ch Coundon Trudy	Miss E. A. Turrall	Breeder
Coundon Trudy (59)	B	Ch Billy Boy	Ravensdowne Roxana	Miss E. A. Turrall	Breeder
Covington Dove (57)	B	Ch Carahall Cornet	Peter's Choice O'Kim	A. Mitchell	Breeder & Mrs M. Aspinwall
Cravendale Chanter (53)	D	Ch Hepple	Hevans Sent	J. Jackson	E. Mawson
Cravendale Copper (63)	D	Ch Falcliff Topper	Wharfholm Whip It Quick	Mrs E. Walker	E. Mawson
Cribden Comet (21)	D	Sandiman	Posski	Mrs Branfoot	A. S. Watson
Cuileann Dodger (80)	D	Ch Dandyhow Humbug	Tundergarth Bonny Borderer	Mr & Mrs Mackenzie	R. Hillcoat
Daletyne Batchelor (64)	D	Daletyne Rory	Daletyne Valentine	Mr & Mrs G. Benson	Breeder
Daletyne Decora (65)	D	Daletyne Rory	Daletyne Valentine	Mr & Mrs G. Benson	Breeder
Daletyne Dundrum (64)	D	Daletyne Rory	Luck's In	Mrs M. R. Benson	Mr & Mrs G. Benson
Dandyhow April Fool (85)	D	Ch Dandyhow Nightcap	Tipalt, Scots Lass of	Mrs B. A. Sullivan	Mr & Mrs D. Fryer
Dandyhow Bitter Shandy (58)	B	Fighting Fettle	Walla Crag Wendy	Rev J. E. Johnson	Mrs B. A. Sullivan
Dandyhow Burnished Silver (70)	B	Ch Dandyhow Shady Knight	Dandyhow Solitaire	Mrs B. A. Sullivan	Breeder

Name of Dog		Sire	Dam	Breeder	Owner
Dandyhow Crofter (82)	D	Ch Uncle Walter of Dandyhow	Dandyhow Fly By Knight	Mrs. B. A. Sullivan	Breeder
Dandyhow, Duttonlea Suntan of (80)	D	Dandyhow Grenadier	Ribbleside Morning Dew	W. Wrigley	Mrs B. A. Sullivan
Dandyhow Forget Me Not (78)	B	Ch South Box	Dandyhow Millicent	Mrs B. A. Sullivan	Breeder
Dandyhow Humbug (76)	D	Ch Dandyhow Shady Knight	Polo Mint	Mrs B. A. Sullivan	Mr & Mrs. T. Mackenzie
Dandyhow Marchioness (80)	B	Ch South Box	Ch Dandyhow Margery Daw	Mrs B. A. Sullivan	Mrs P. M. Creed
Dandyhow Margery Daw (72)	B	Ch Cravendale Copper	Dandyhow Solitaire	Mrs B. A. Sullivan	Breeder
Dandyhow Nightcap (75)	D	Ch Dandyhow Shady Knight	Goodytwoshoes of Dandyhow	Mrs B. A. Sullivan	Breeder
Dandyhow Quality Street (71)	B	Ch Dandyhow Shady Knight	Polo Mint	Mrs B. A. Sullivan	Breeder
Dandyhow Sandpiper (68)	D	Dandyhow Brussel Sprout	Dandyhow Solitaire	Mrs B. A. Sullivan	Breeder & Lady Russell
Dandyhow Scotsman (80)	D	Ch South Box	Dandyhow Fly By Night	Mrs B. A. Sullivan	Breeder
Dandyhow Seashell (66)	B	Dandyhow Brussel Sprout	Ch Dandyhow Soroya	Mrs B. A. Sullivan	Breeder
Dandyhow Shady Knight (68)	D	Dandyhow Brussel Sprout	Dandyhow Solitaire	Mrs B. A. Sullivan	Breeder
Dandyhow Shady Lady (66)	B	Dandyhow Brussel Sprout	Ch Dandyhow Soroya	Mrs B. A. Sullivan	Breeder
Dandyhow Silver Ring (79)	D	Ch Dandyhow Shady Knight	Dandyhow Nickel Silver	Mrs B. A. Sullivan	Mrs P. M. Creed
Dandyhow Soroya (62)	B	Dandyhow Seamus	Cobbette	Mrs B. A. Sullivan	Breeder
Dandyhow Spectator (74)	D	Ch Dandyhow Shady Knight	Goodytwoshoes of Dandyhow	Mrs B. A. Sullivan	Breeder
Dandyhow Sultana (61)	B	Dandyhow Blue Shadow	Cobbette	Mrs B. A. Sullivan	Breeder
Dandyhow Suntan (61)	D	Dandyhow Blue Shadow	Bettes Survivor	Mrs B. A. Sullivan	A. Beardwood
Dandyhow Susette (63)	B	Kennelworth	Dandyhow Barley Sugar	Mrs B. A. Sullivan	Breeder
Dandyhow Sweet Biscuit (67)	B	Dandyhow Brussel Sprout	Dandyhow Stanlette	Mrs Dixon	Mrs B. A. Sullivan
Dandyhow, Uncle Walter of (81)	D	Ch Duttonlea Suntan of Dandyhow	Bertha's Yin	Mrs E. Hislop	Mrs B. A. Sullivan
Daphne (21)	B	Gyp (North Tyne Gyp)	Midge	Mrs D. Armstrong	D. Jackson
Deerstone Busybody (64)	B	Deerstone Duskie	Miss Black	S. A. Petty	R. Hall
Deerstone Madam					
Deerstone Debrett (63)	D	Klein Otti	Deerstone Tinker Bell	R. Hall	Breeder
Deerstone Delia (62)	B	Klein Otti	Deerstone Tinker Bell	R. Hall	Breeder
Deerstone Desirable (58)	B	Ch Portholme Manly Boy	Raisgill Radella of Deerstone	R. Hall	Breeder
Deerstone Destiny (55)	D	Ch Portholme Manly Boy	Raisgill Radella of Deerstone	R. Hall	Breeder

Name of Dog		Sire	Dam	Breeder	Owner
Deerstone Douglas (62)	D	Ch Portholme Macsleap	Deerstone Judy	R. Hall	Breeder & Miss E. Bland
Deerstone Driver (47)	D	Fearsome Fellow	Bladnoch Tinker Bell	R. Hall	Mrs B. S. T. Holmes
Deerstone Dugmore (66)	D	Ch Portholme Mr Moses	Deerstone Judy	R. Hall	Breeder
Deerstone Falcliff Ramona (67)	B	Ch Falcliff Topper	Deerstone Daybreak	E. Mawson	R. Hall
Deerstone Larkbarrow Rainbow (67)	B	Deerstone Dugmal	Deerstone Dimity	Mrs L. Farthing	R. Hall
Deerstone Realization (59)	D	Ch Deerstone Destiny	Grizella	P. Land	R. Hall
Digbrack Barley Sugar (82)	D	Thoraldby Night Owl	Barleycorn of Digbrack	Mr & Mrs G. Robson	Breeders
Dinger (31)		Gem of Gold	Beeswing	F. Beattie	J. Renton
Din Merry (76)	B	Ch Dandyhow Nightcap	Dryden Kerena	Miss Hislop & W. R. Irving	W. R. Irving
Dipley Dibs (38)		Ch Foxlair	Dipley Dinah	J. J. Pawson	Breeder
Dipley Dinghy (55)	B	Ch Billy Boy	Ch Bumble Bee	H. Pybus	J. J. Pawson
Dormic, Grenze Galanthus of (79)	B	Ch Foxtor Blue Jester	Grenze Strikalight	Mr & Mrs R. Owen	Mr & Mrs M. Rushby
Dronfield Berry (47)	B	Callum	Dronfield Ringlet	Capt E. Gorrell Barnes	Mrs J. H. Stoney
Dryburn Dazzle (53)	D	Ch Leatty Druridge Dazzler	Ch Dryburn Devilena	Miss M. H. Vaux	Breeder & Mrs G. Leatt
Dryburn Devilena (50)	B	Ch Hepple	Newminster Radiant	G. W. Sunley	Miss M. H. Vaux
Duthill, Linne of (80)	B	Ch Mansergh Pearl Diver	Chocolate Ripple	Mr & Mrs J. Bradley & Mr Rumsey	Miss A. Roslin Williams
Duttonlea Ambassador (77)	D	Ch Duttonlea Mr Softy	Ribbleside Morning Dew	W. Wrigley	Breeder
Duttonlea Lilian (69)	B	Ch Ribbleside Falcliff Trident	Ribbleside Brockanburr Mandy	A. Duxbury	W. Wrigley
Duttonlea Mr Softy (68)	D	Ch Cravendale Copper	Duttonlea Maria	W. Wrigley	Breeder
Duttonlea Steel Blue (80)	B	Dandyhow Grenadier	Ribbleside Morning Dew	W. Wrigley	Breeder
Duttonlea Sue (76)	B	Ch Oxcroft Moonmagic	Ribbleside Morning Dew	W. Wrigley	T. A. G. Knight
Dykeside Gordon Ranger (85)	D	Ch Dandyhow Crofter	Dandyhow Hot Chocolate	Mrs M. Staveley	Breeder
Eaglemount Carousel (77)	B	Ch Clipstone Cetchup	Eaglemount Sweet Genevieve	Mr & Mrs A. Barlow	Breeder
Eardiston Fettle (55)	B	Eardiston Sailor	Ch First Footer	Mrs L. Wallace	Mrs J. Brown
Easingwold Rascal (70)	D	Dryburn Dartboard	Dryburn Dark Sapphire	Miss M. H. Vaux	Mrs O. M. Bulmer
Eignwye Daletyne Santara (62)	B	Dandyhow Bonny Scot	Joygirl	Mr & Mrs G. R. Benson	R. A. Williams
Eignwye Enchantress (57)	B	Carry On	Eardiston Sally	R. A. Williams	Breeder
Eignwye Tweed (70)	D	Solway Cawfields Duke	Eignwye Queen Beaver	R. A. Williams	Breeder
Eignwye Wheatear (75)	D	Solway Cawfields Duke	Eignwye Elena	R. A. Williams	Mrs M. Lewis
Elandmead Ragamuffin (71)	D	Ch Handy Andy	Shipley Tandy	Mrs E. O. Tait	Mr & Mrs D. Fagan
Falcliff Tantaliser (66)	D	Ch Falcliff Topper	Deerstone Daybreak	E. Mawson	Breeder

Name of Dog		Sire	Dam	Breeder	Owner
Falcliff Topper (60)	D	Ch Cravendale Chanter	Falcliff Charmer	E. Mawson	Breeder
Farmway Fine Feathers (73)	D	Deerstone Despot Duty	Farmway Red Robin	Mrs M. Aspinwall	Breeder
Farmway M'Lady Robin (81)	B	Akenside Robin Hood	Farmway Warbler	Mrs E. S. Marnham	Mrs M. Aspinwall
Farmway Moneybird (77)	D	Dandyhow Nightshade	Farmway Dandyhow Brass Farthing	Mrs M. Aspinwall	S. J. Richardson
Farmway Red Robin (62)	D	Farmway Blue Raven	Farmway Jenny Wren	Mrs M. Aspinwall	Breeder
Farmway Snow Kestrel (77)	D	Farmway Woodpecker	Farmway Snow Finch	Mrs M. Aspinwall	Breeder
Final Honour (71)	D	Ch Wharfholm Warrant Stingo	Miss Georgina	Mrs P. Perry	Mr H. Jenner
Finchdale Lass (37)	B	Ch Future Fame	Stowell Away	W. Fullerton	Lady Russell
Fine Features (50)	B	Ch Future Fame	Gemma Girl	Mrs P. Hope	Mrs F. Mitchell
First Choice (50)	B	Ch Tweedside Red Silvo	Ch Rona Rye	J. Renton	Mrs F. Mitchell
First Footer (49)	B	Ch Future Fame	Fully Fashioned	Mr & Mrs A. Forster	Breeder
First Time Matamba (85)	D	Duttonlea Viscount	Tipalt Glenmelt Lady	Mrs M. Curtis	C. Heron
Foxhill Fantastic (76)	D	Ch Step Ahead	Foxhill Frolic	Mrs D. M. H. Miller	Breeder
Foxhill Feonix (70)	B	Ch Dandyhow Shady Knight	Foxhill Fabulous	Mrs D. M. H. Miller	Breeder
Foxhill Ferelith (75)	B	Ch Step Ahead	Foxhill Freckles	Mrs D. M. H. Miller	Breeder
Foxhill Fidelity (72)	B	Ch Dandyhow Shady Knight	Foxhill Fabulous	Mrs D. M. H. Miller	Mrs R. M. Urie
Foxhill Firefly (76)	B	Ch Step Ahead	Foxhill Frolic	Mrs D. M. H. Miller	Mrs C. M. Lindsay
Foxhill Firm Favourite (66)	B	Ch Happy Day	Foxhill Flirt	Mrs D. M. H. Miller	Breeder
Foxhill Fulbert (69)	D	Ch Foxhill Fusilier	Foxhill Fabulous	Mrs D. M. H. Miller	Breeder
Foxhill Fusilier (65)	D	Foxhill Fabian	Foxhill Frangipani	Miss K. A. G. Steele	Mrs D. M. H. Miller
Foxlair (34)	D	Rab O Lammermoor	Tanquair Gypsy	A. Stevenson	D. Mitchell & Mrs K. Twist
Foxtor Blue Jester (75)	D	Kes of Index	Skipster Hagg Judy	Mrs Procope	Mr & Mrs R. Hodgson
Foxwyn Shoot a Line (81)	D	Chelter Michael	Foxwyn Storyteller	Mr & Mrs R. Hodgson	Breeder
Fraxinus Diplomat (76)	B	Ch Dandyhow Nightcap	Dandyhow Cornflower	B. & Miss H. Reekie	B. Reekie
Full Toss (57)	D	Ch Billy Boy	Ch True Temper	Dr & Mrs Cuddigan	A. Halstead
Future Fame (48)	D	Fearsome Fellow	Tombo Squeak	W. B. Whitelaw	Mr & Mrs A. Forster

Name of Dog		Sire	Dam	Breeder	Owner
Gaelic Coffee (73)	B	Ch Ribbleside Ridgeman	Harvest Moon	Mr & Mrs J. Bradley	Breeder
Gatehill Copper Nob (66)	B	Sankence Smartie	Deerstone Decorative	Miss J.M. Sapwell	Mrs D. Lindley
Gay Fine (35)	D	Ch Bladnoch Raider	Red Floss	J. Johnson	Breeder
Gay Gordon (62)	D	Ch Carahall Coffee	Carahall Coralyn	D. Goodsir	Miss G. Gaddes
Gay Hussar (46)	D	Tweedside Red Playboy	Darlie's Dinah	T. Jobson	Breeder
Gay Lord (59)	D	Black Druid	Merry Moment	Mrs E. Hutchinson	Breeder
Gem of Valmyre (84)	B	Ashbrae Fleet	Dandyhow Edith	Miss M. Elliott	Mrs V. Myers
Girvanside Cruggleton Don (49)	D	Callum	Orenza	T. Buchanan	G. R. McConnell
Girvanside Sensation (55)	D	Ch Girvanside Cruggleton Don	Brownhill Wendy	D. A. MacFazdean	G. R. McConnell
Girvanside Tigress Mischief (48)	B	Rodent Lad	Barwhin Trixie	D. A. MacFazdean	G. R. McConnell
Golden Imperialist (52)	D	Fire Master	Dusty Queen	S. Ormston	Mrs G. Leatt
Golden Sovereign (48)	D	Ch Rising Light	Dusty Queen	S. Ormston (Jun)	Breeder
Grakle (30)	D	Ch Ranter	Queen O' the Hunt	J. Dodd & W. Carruthers	Sir J. Renwick
Gralene Moonlight (73)	B	Dandyhow Simple Simon	Starcyl Briar Rose	G. Pomfret	Breeder
Grenze Skylight (77)	B	Ch Step Ahead Randale	Grenze Susie Snatch	Mr & Mrs R. Owen	Breeder
Hall, Bess of the (33)	B	Ch Aldham Joker	Hunting Sally	Miss M. Long	Breeder
Hallbourne Badger	D	Ch Hallbourne Badger	Cronas Birkie	J. Kealey	Mrs E. Twist
Hallbourne Blue Val (52)	D	Ch Hallbourne Badger	Hallbourne Candy	Mrs E. Twist	Breeder
Hallbourne Bracket (49)	B	Ch Aldham Joker	Dronfield Bracken	P. J. Ratcliffe	Mrs E. Twist
Hallbourne Brick (52)	D	Ch Hallbourne Badger	Hallbourne Candy	Mrs E. Twist	Breeder
Hallbourne Constancy (54)	B	Ch Hallbourne Blue Val	Cronas Crolinda	Mrs E. Twist	Breeder
Handy Andy (65)	D	Ch Hawkesburn Beaver	Border Queen	J. Renton	Breeder
Hanleycastle Judy (63)	B	Hanleycastle Russ	Wee Willow	L. W. R. Clements	Breeder
Happy Day (59)	D	Tweedside Red Kingpin	Happy Morn	J. Renton	Breeder
Happy Mood (30)	D	Revenge	Causey Bridget	C. Renner	J. Renton
Harranby Wanda (59)	D	Ch Deerstone Destiny	Harranby Dingle	Miss A. P. Williams	Breeder
Hasty Light (48)	D	Ch Rising Light	Mosseyhaugh Jean	B. M. Graham	Miss D. Bolton
Hawkesburn Beaver (63)	D	Ch Gay Gordon	Princess Susan	T. M. Gaddes	Mrs F. L. Marchant
Hawkesburn Happy Returns (66)	B	Ch Hawkesburn Beaver	Border Queen	J. Renton	Mrs F. L. Marchant
Hawkesburn Nutmeg (70)	B	Ch Dandyhow Shady Knight	Ch Hawkesburn Happy Returns	Mrs F. L. Marchant	Breeder
Hawkesburn Spindle (73)	B	Ch Dandyhow Sandpiper	Ch Hawkesburn Happy	Mrs F. L. Marchant	Breeder
Hepple (48)	D	Fearsome Fellow	Happy Day	M. H. Horn	Breeder
Heronslea (30)	D	Styrrup	Tiot Fancy	W. Irving	A. Reid
Highgarphar Sensation (47)	D	Tweedside Red Playboy	Meikledale Trixie	S. J. Welsman	G. R. McConnell
Highland Gyp (64)	D	Daletyne Rory	Dandyhow Belle Sibelle	Mr & Mrs G. R. Benson	Mrs M. Howden
Hill Girl (52)	D	Ch Billy Boy	Woodbine Lady	J. Rochester	A. L. Waters
Hobbykirk Destiny (69)	D	Ch Deerstone Dugmore	Hobbykirk Vanity	E. M. Rowell	Mrs R. M. Urie
Hornpiece Salvia (50)	B	Swallowfield Salvo	Jannafille	Rev H. E. Jones	T. M. Gaddes

Name of Dog		Sire	Dam	Breeder	Owner
Hugill Sweep (56)	B	Hugill Ruffian	Final Flutter	Mr & Mrs A. Forster	Major G. Ion
Hulne Lass (63)	B	Ch Portholme Macsleap	Flippant	Mrs H. A. Pope	W. Newton
Himley Wild Gorse (81)	B	Ch Llanishen Red Eagle	Moon Rhapsody	Mr & Mrs F. Nicholls	Breeder
Ifracombe Dandy (54)	D	Blue Boy of Highclere	Skimp of Henshaw Green	S. E. Shore	E. B. Joel
Ivo Rarebit (30)	D	Ch Teri	Floss	Capt Silver	A. Morris
Ivo Roisterer (15)	D	Jock	Flossie	A. Drummond	Hamilton Adams
Jedworth Bunty (28)	B	Oxnam Pincher	Doodles	J. Edington	Sir J. Renwick
Jimmy Trip (58)	D	Northern Gleam	St Kevern Cindy	S. Tripcony	Breeder
Jonty Lad (58)	D	Tourist	Primrose	J. Reid	Breeder & Mrs. K. Webb
Joyden (30)		Whitrope Don	Ch Station Masher	W. Irving	Breeder
Joygirl (56)	B	Ch Joytime	Fellfoot Lass		
Joytime (53)	D	Overtime	Jessabelle	J. N. Newton	Mr & Mrs. G. R. Benson
Kathyanga (61)	B	Ch Joytime	Sun Saga	F. Searle	Breeder
Kilmeny (55)		Ch Billy Boy	Tyneside Lass	A. L. Waters	G. Diamond
Kinneton Koffey (28)		Ch Barney Bindle	Ch Station Masher	W. Irving	Breeder & Capt Pawson
Knavesmire Kopper (61)	D	Harranby Dai	Knavesmire Kelso	Mrs H. P. Longworth	Breeder
Lady Lucinda (68)	B	Ch Handy Andy	Daletyne Druidess	Mr & Mrs D. Fagan	Breeder
Lairdiarch, Thoraldby Star Appeal of (75)	B	Ch Step Ahead	Ch Thoraldby Miss Mandy	Mr & Mrs P. Thompson	Mrs M. Aspinwall
Leatty Billy Bunter (54)	D	Ch Billy Boy	Jessabelle	J. N. Newton	Mrs G. Leatt
Leatty Druridge Dazzler (49)	D	Druridge Digger	Gay Lady of Ulgham	C. D. Brewis	Mrs G. Leatt
Leatty Emblewest Betsy (62)	B	Emblewest Darkie	Emblewest Ghana	Miss D. Bolton	Mrs G. Leatt
Leatty Felldyke Badger (62)	D	Klein Otti	Daletyne Vixen	J. Harrison	Breeder & Mrs G. Leatt
Leatty Felldyke Gorse (65)	D	Ch Joytime	Felldyke Bracken	J. Harrison	Mrs G. Leatt & N. Cowgill
Leatty Joy Boy (57)	D	Bad Sinbad	Cobbette	Mrs B. A. Sullivan	Mrs G. Leatt
Leatty Juliet of Law (55)	B	Ch Wharfholm Wizard	Pepita of Rough Lea	W. Brown	Mrs M. Roslin Williams
Leatty Lace (47)	B	Bladnoch Brock of Deerstone	Leatty Sadie	A. Pethybridge	Mrs G. Leatt
Leatty Loyal Lass (55)	B	Ch Leatty Druridge Dazzler	Ch Leatty Lace	Mrs G. Leatt	Breeder
Leatty Lucky (51)	B	Ch Leatty Druridge Dazzler	Leatty Lass	Mrs G. Walsh	Mrs G. Leatt
Leatty Plough Boy (59)	D	Ch Billy Boy	Xmas Box	R. Morrison	Mrs G. Leatt
Liddesdale Bess (17)	B	Liddesdale Nailer	Pearl	J. Davidson	W. Barton
Lily of the Valley (49)	B	Blue Mickie	Redmoss Wendy	Miss M. L. Little	S. Raine & Mrs G. Leatt
Lindumwold Memory (44)	B	Osmond Fury	Hinney	A. Taylor	Mrs A. Scargall
Llanishen Penelope (71)	B	Llanishen Ivanhoe	Dandyhow Streetgate Wendy	D. Wiseman	W. R. Irving
Llanishen Red Eagle (79)	D	Ch Farmway Snow Kestrel	Llanishen Russet	D. Wiseman	Breeder
Llanishen Reynard (77)	D	Oxcroft Poacher	Llanishen Raffles	D. Wiseman	Mr & Mrs F. Jackson

Name of Dog		Sire	Dam	Breeder	Owner
Loiriston Amber (81)	B	Ch Duttonlea Suntan of Dandyhow	Thoraldby Mary Poppins	Mr & Mrs R. Wheatley	Mr & Mrs P. Thompson
Looin Saddle Up (62)	B	Ch Gay Lord	Bolt On	Mrs E. Hutchinson	Breeder
Lucky Lucy (68)	B	Ch Handy Andy	Daletyne Druidess	Mr & Mrs D. Fagan	Breeder
Lucky Purchase (49)	B	Ch Future Fame	Fully Fashioned	Mr & Mrs A. Forster	Mrs F. R. Mitchell
Lucy Gray (48)	B		Luce Ryan	N. A. MacEwan	Breeder
Ludside Chantaway (66)	D	Ch Daletyne Dundrum	Harranby Petra	L. Masserella	Mr & Mrs S. Grantham
Lyddington Lets Go (79)	D	Ch Farmway Snow Kestrel	Lyddington Lass	Mrs K. Lampert	Mr & Mrs T. A. Tuck
Lynsett Trouble Shooter (82)	D	Ch Foxwyn Shoot a Line	Lynsett Lucky Wish	Mrs L. Briggs	Breeder & Mr & Mrs Hodgson
Macmerry (46)	D	Ch Ranting Fury	Dinger Queen	T. Crozier	Breeder
Maid of Honour (66)	B	Ch Knavesmire Kopper	Beeches My Dinah	Mr H. G. Jenner	Breeder
Makerston Foxlair (65)	D	Ch Brookend Baggins	Watersplace Sally	Mrs R. M. Greenalgh	Capt H. D. O'Vigne
Mansergh April Mist (61)	B	Monsoon	Sherryripe	S. Tripcony	Mrs M. Roslin Williams
Mansergh Barn Owl (68)	B	Ch Wharfholm Warrant	Mansergh the Cuckoo	G. E. Hutchinson	Miss A. Roslin Williams
Mansergh Cushy Butterfield (75)	B	Ch Easingwold Rascal	Mansergh Muffet	Miss A. Roslin Williams	Breeder
Mansergh Dandyhow Bracken (61)	B	Dandyhow Brussel Sprout	Dandyhow Brandy & Soda	D. W. Tinkler	Mrs M. Roslin Williams
Mansergh, Froswick Button of (81)	B	Ch Mansergh Pearl Diver	Westmoreland Jessica	R. Westmoreland	Miss A. Roslin Williams
Mansergh General Post (76)	D	Mansergh Sergeant Pepper	Ragus Wassail of Mansergh	Miss A. Roslin Williams	Mrs S. K. Lampert
Mansergh, Oxcroft Pearl of (73)	B	Ch Dandyhow Shady Knight	Oxcroft Fighting Fettle	J. Price	Miss A. Roslin Williams
Mansergh Pearl Diver (78)	D	Ch Mansergh General Post	Ch Oxcroft Pearl of Mansergh	Miss A. Roslin Williams	Breeder
Mansergh Toggle (84)	B	Beenaban Bargain	Ch Froswick Button of Mansergh	Miss A. Roslin Williams	Breeder
Mansergh Rhosmerholme Amethyst (66)	B	Rhosmerholme Deerstone Damien	Rhosmerholme Rip	Mrs E. Garnett	Miss A. Roslin Williams
Mansergh Sergeant Pepper (75)	D	Ch Temeside Joss	Mansergh Muffet	Miss A. Roslin Williams	Breeder
Mansergh Wharfholm Wistful (58)	B	Ch Wharfholm Wizard	Wharfholm Hallbourne Blue Bracelet	Mrs B. S. T. Holmes	Breeder
Marrburn Morag (59)	B	Ch Maxton Matchless	Tresta	D. Cross	Mrs M. McKnight
Maxton Makrino (67)	D	Milkbank Tarka	Maxton Mhairi	Mr & Mrs W. Gardner	W. Gordon
Maxton Mannequin (54)	B	Grenor Max	Maxton Red Honey	Mr & Mrs W. Gardner	Breeder
Maxton Marla (67)	B	Milkbank Tarka	Maxton Mhairi	Mr & Mrs W. Gardner	Breeder
Maxton Matchless (56)	D	Ch Future Fame	Maxton May Queen	Mr & Mrs W. Gardner	Breeder
Maxton Miss Mink (56)	B	Ch Bargower Silver Dollar	Ch Maxton Mannequin	Mr & Mrs W. Gardner	Breeder
Maxton Monarch (63)	D	Ch Maxton Matchless	Ch Marrburn Morag	Mrs M. McKnight	Mr & Mrs W. Gardner
May Isle Misty (73)	B	Dandyhow Napoleon	Ch Llanishen Penelope	W. R. Irving	Breeder & D. Bottomley
Mister Tims (65)	D	Wharfholm Harranby Topper	Wharfholm Wistielass	Mrs M. Wood	Breeder
Motcombe Rhosdu (61)	B	Torch Light	Motcombe Liliard	J. Cobby	Breeder

Name of Dog		Sire	Dam	Breeder	Owner
Napoleon Brandy (73)	D	Ch Ribbleside Ridgeman	Harvest Moon	Mr & Mrs J. Bradley	Breeder
Nettleby Mullein (84)	B	Ch Lyddington Lets Go	Blaisdon Souvenir	Mr & Mrs T. A. Tuck	Breeder
New Halfpenny (59)	D	Klein Otti	Joyous Bet	Mrs N. E. Hartley	Miss L. Busby
Newminster Rose (35)	B	Newminster Rummy	Fairy Footsteps	Sir John Renwick	Breeder
Newsholme Modesty (67)	B	Dryburn Dunseal	Newminster Rarity	Miss M. H. Vaux	Mrs M.Sneddon
Not So Dusty (32)	B	Ch Blister	Hunty Gowk	J. Johnson	Breeder
Oakwood Pickle (32)	D	Ch Grakle	Liddesdale Nettle	T. Sedman	Miss M. H. Vaux
Osmond Braw Lad (48)	D	Osmond Fury	Osmond Fireworks	P. S. Osmond	Breeder
Oxcroft Moonmagic (69)	D	Oxcroft Rocket	Oxcroft Brandy	J. Price	T. A. G. Knight
Oxcroft Rocker (78)	D	Oxcroft Rocky	Oxcroft Ollie	J. Price	Breeder
Oxcroft Tally (80)	B	Ch Oxcroft Rocker	Oxcroft Ringlet	J. Price	A. P. Willis
Oxcroft Vixen (66)	B	Oxcroft Rocket	Daletyne Digger	J. Price	Breeder
Padmac Madrigal Singer (83)	B	Ch Lyddington Lets Go	Wandering Minstrel	Mrs L. Brown	Breeder
Plushcourt on Target (82)	B	Ch Dandyhow Silver Ring	Farmway Tawny Pipit of Plushcourt	Mrs F. S. Judge	Breeder
Polydorus Pop (83)	B	Ch Polydorus Princely Peeler	Hynerbrook Suzy of Polydorus	Mrs J. Gough	Mr & Mrs T. Carter
Polydorus Princely Peeler (77)	D	Farmway Woodpecker	Farmway Seaplover	Mrs J. Gough	Breeder
Pontbeck, Canny Crack of (84)	B	Ch Ashbrae Jaffa	Cushy Butterfield	Mr & Mrs W. Gray	Mr & Mrs W. & Miss L. Gray
Portholme Macsleap (60)	D	Portholme Mask & Brush	Ch Portholme Mirth	Mrs S. Mulcaster	Breeder
Portholme Magic (46)	B	Portholme Michael	Portholme Polly Peachum	Miss E. Lennard	Mrs S. Mulcaster
Portholme Maire (49)	B	Ribbleside Roger	Nettle Tip	E. Lee	Mrs S. Mulcaster
Portholme Mamie (49)	B	Ribbleside Roger	Nettle Tip	E. Lee	Mrs S. Mulcaster
Portholme Manly Boy (48)	D	Deerstone Dauntless	Skirden Serena	Mrs G. Edwards	Mrs S. Mulcaster
Portholme March Belle (60)	B	Montime	Xmas Box	R. Morrison	Mrs S. Mulcaster
Portholme Matinee (57)	B	Ch Portholme Merry Man	Portholme Ballarina	Mrs S. Mulcaster	Mrs I. M. Fairley
Portholme Merryman (52)	D	Ch Portholme Manly Boy	Tina O'Kim	C. Mitchell	Mrs S. Mulcaster

Name of Dog		Sire	Dam	Breeder	Owner
Portholme Mirth (53)	B	Ch Portholme Manly Boy	Portholme Mint	Mrs I. Wallis	Mrs S. Mulcaster
Portholme Mr Moses (60)	D	Portholme Mustard	Ch Portholme My Fair Lady	Mrs S. Mulcaster	Mrs I. M. Fairley
Portholme My Duskie Lady (60)	B	Ch Portholme Merryman	Dreamer	R. Ogle	Mrs I. M. Fairley
Portholme My Fair Lady (58)	B	Ch Portholme Manly Boy	Ch Portholme Matinee	Mrs S. Mulcaster	Breeder
Primrose (57)	B	Fellhouse Knapp	Jemina Lass	Mrs M. Nixon	J. Reid
Rabroy (58)	D	Tweedside Red Kingpin	Jeans Wendy	Miss J. Galbraith	W. Irving
Ragsdale Blueberry (81)	B	Ch Oxcroft Rocker	Dandyhow Blue Stilton	J. Price	F. Wildman
Ragsdale Blue Covert (84)	D	Cheltor Michael	Oxcroft Pot Black	F. Wildman	Breeder & J. Bainbridge
Ragus Dark Chocolate (72)	D	Dandyhow Bolshevik	Dandyhow Bitter Lemon	Mrs M. & Miss L. Bunting	Breeder
Ragus Warlock (73)	D	Ch Ragus Dark Chocolate	Dandyhow Wood Sorrel	Mrs M. & Miss L. Bunting	Breeder
Ranter (27)	D	Rival	Coquetdale Reward	A. Forster	Breeder
Ranting Fury (37)	D	Furious Fighter	Miss Dinah	Mrs E. Tweedie	J. Renton
Ranting Roving (57)	D	Ch Future Fame	Ch Scotch Mist	J. Renton	Breeder
Rayndale Ramona (53)	B	Ch Future Fame	Scrogmore Wendy	Mrs G. Walsh	J. Moon
Redbor Revojet (52)	B	Ch Billy Boy	Redbor Radiance	W. Addison	Breeder
Rhosmerholme Aristocrat (67)	B	Ch Deerstone Realization	Ch Rhosmerholme Recruit	Mrs E. Garnett	Breeder
Rhosmerholme, Duttonlea Sarah of (76)	B	Ch Oxcroft Moonmagic	Ribbleside Morning Dew	W. Wrigley	Mrs E. Garnett
Rhosmerholme Recruit (64)	B	Rhosmerholme Deerstone Damien	Rhosmerholme Rip	Mrs E. Garnett	Breeder
Rhozzum Tudor (77)	D	Ch Wharfholm Warrant	Eignwye Society Girl	Mr & Mrs P. Sharp	Breeder
Rhozzum Zodiac (82)	D	Cheltor Michael	Rhozzum Variation	Mr & Mrs P. Sharp	Mrs P. Ho
Ribbleside Falcliff Trident (67)	D	Ch Falcliff Topper	Deerstone Daybreak	E. Mawson	A. Duxbury
Ribbleside Ridgeman (70)	D	Ribbleside Ringman	Ribbleside Moonmagic	A. Duxbury	J. Lindley
Richies Dream (58)	B	Montime	Xmas Box	R. Morrison	Breeder
Ridesdale Highland Chief (74)	D	Ch Oxcroft Moonmagic	Tantalizing Tandy	J. N. Thomas	Breeder
Ringmaster (53)	D	Quartermaster	Ch Fine Features	Mrs F. Mitchell	Breeder
Rising Light (45)	D	Rocksand	Golden Crumb	R. Wylie	W. Irving
Road to Mandalay (80)	D	Ch Temeside Joss	Smokey Haze	Mr & Mrs J. Bradley & J. Rumsey	Breeder
Rockferry Barleycorn (81)	D	Ch Llanishen Red Eagle	Rockferry Corn Cracker	Mrs S. F. Sarll	Breeder
Rona Rye (44)	B	Frugal Friar	Byrk Tandy	Mrs W. Hetherington	J. Renton
Roserll Claudio (74)	D	Kenstaff Benbow	Princess of Oulton	Mrs R. Sorrell	Mrs D. K. Davies
Rossut Motcombe Barnbrack (67)	B	Ch Daletyne Batchelor	Motcombe Rhosdu	J. Cobby	Mrs C. G. Sutton
Rubicon Rarity (83)	B	Rubicon Resilient	Lucilady of Rubicon	Mrs R. Jordon	Breeder
Rudgate Daffodil (75)	B	Ch Wharfholm Mansergh Tinkerblue	Rudgate Dainty Daffers	J. Kilby	Lady MacAndrew

Name of Dog		Sire	Dam	Breeder	Owner
Rustic Rattler (25)	D	Crosedale Jock	Crosedale Judy	A. J. Simpson	A. M. Preston
Ryswick Ranger (81)	D	Ch Dandyhow Nightcap	Ch Oxcroft Tally	A. P. Willis	Breeder
Sally Larus (61)	B	Ch Joytime	Sun Saga	F. Searle	A. Bradley
Savinroyd President (79)	D	Oxcroft Rocky	Elandmead Pixie	J. Lindley	Mr & Mrs J. Lindley
Scarside Bell (23)	B	Ch Grip of Tynedale	Honeycomb	W. Watson	Breeder
Scarside, Betty of (24)	B	Ch Cribden Comet	Ch Scarside Bell	W. Watson	Breeder
Scotch Mist (54)	B	Neil Gow	Dinger Queen	J. Renton	Breeder
Share Pusher (36)		Stingo	Stung Again	Capt M. C. Hamilton	Mr & Mrs J. Short
Silver Sal (58)	B	Ch Billy Boy	Tiddly Winks	A. L. Waters	J. J. Holdgate
Southboro' Stray (unknown)	D	Unknown	Unknown	Unknown	
South Box (76)	D	Ch Dandyhow Nightcap	Dryden Kerena	Miss Hislop & W. R. Irving	W. R. Irving
Sprignell Crystal Bell (79)	B	Ch Dandyhow Silver Ring	Bannerdown Bush Sprite	Mrs S. W. Clarkson	Misses S. M. Coupe & R. D. Swales
Sprignell Selina (74)	B	Sprignell Sceptre	Bannerdown Bush Sprite	Mrs S. W. Clarkson	Breeder
Sprignell Spice (79)	B	Hawkesburn Little John	Ch Sprignell Selina	Mrs S. W. Clarkson	Breeder
Staple Scurry (35)		Ragtag	Staple Scutter	The Rt Hon Viscountess Portman	Breeder
Starburn Merrymaid (62)	B	Ch Happy Day	Ch Marburn Morag	Mrs M. McKnight	Breeder
Starcyl Bracken (72)	B	Dandyhow Napoleon	Farmway Sunbird	Mr & Mrs J. McCrystal	Breeder
Station Masher (24)	B	Oxnam Pincher	Jed	A. Fox	W. Irving
Step Ahead (73)	D	Ch Final Honour	Ch Maid of Honour	H. G. Jenner	Breeder & G. E. Hutchinson
Stonekite, Clipstone Tearose of (84)	B	Clipstone Dash	Ch Clipstone Chasse	Mr & Mrs F. Jackson	Mr K. Thomas
Summer Belle (71)	B	Ch Wharfholm Warrant	Miss Georgina	Mrs P. Perry	H. G. Jenner
Sundalgo Salvador (74)	D	Ch Oxcroft Moonmagic	Duttonlea Kayronta	T. A. G. Knight	Breeder
Sundalgo Serenade (75)	D	Ch Oxcroft Moonmagic	Julies Gypsy Jewel	T. A. G. Knight	Breeder
Sundalgo Slate Blue (83)	D	Ch Savinroyd President	Sunbeam of Sundalgo	T. A. G. Knight	Breeder
Swallowfield Coramine (47)	B	Callum	Todearth Calluna	C. O. Wright	Lady Russell
Swallowfield Fergus (50)	D	Ch Swallowfield Garry	Swallowfield Chloe	Lady Russell	J. K. Dryden
Swallowfield Garry (44)	D	Ch Aldham Joker	Swallowfield Solo	Lady Russell	Breeder
Swallowfield Nutmeg (47)	B	Callum	Hornbeam Heatherbell	Mrs E. Twist	Lady Russell
Swallowfield Shindy (46)	D	Ch Swallowfield Garry	Raisgill Rasta	Miss H. G. Orme	Lady Russell
Syrosa Dusty Miller (85)	D	Rockferry Barley Corn	Miss Conduct of Syrosa	Mrs J. Morris	Breeder
Teddy Boy (33)	D	Randale	April	Miss M. Long	Miss L. Cooper
Temeside Joss (70)	D	Dandyhow Saracen	Hanleycastle Rachael	G. E. Young	Breeder
Teri (16)	D	Titlington Jock	Tib	T. Lawrence	Breeder
Tertius (25)	D	Sniper	Ch Themis	G. Thompson	Breeder
Themis (20)	B	Gyp (North Tyne Gyp)	Lesbury Tatters	G. Thompson	Breeder
Thistycroft Candlelight (79)	B	Maxton Murgatroyd	Edenbrae Moon Maiden	N. Jamieson	Mr & Mrs. N. Hackett
Thoraldby Free Guest (84)	D	Ch Thoraldby Tiptoes	Ch Loiriston Amber	Mr & Mrs P. Thompson	Breeder

Name of Dog		Sire	Dam	Breeder	Owner
Thoraldby Miss Mandy (72)	B	Thoraldby Sweet Sandy	Elandmead Roberta	Mr & Mrs P. Thompson	Breeder
Thoraldby North Star (75)		Ch Step Ahead	Ch Thoraldby Miss Mandy	Mr & Mrs P. Thompson	W. M. Gillott
Thoraldby Star Quality (75)	D	Ch Step Ahead	Ch Thoraldby Miss Mandy	Mr & Mrs P. Thompson	Breeder
Thoraldby Tiptoes (82)	D	Mr Chips of Thoraldby	Thoraldby Miss Magic	Mr & Mrs P. Thompson	Messrs Rushby & Hills
Thoraldby Traveller (83)	B	Mr Chips of Thoraldby	Thoraldby Miss Magic	Mr & Mrs P. Thompson	Breeder
Thoraldby Trillion (79)	D	Ashbrae Aurora	Thoraldby Miss Magic	Mr & Mrs P. Thompson	Breeder & J. Whitworth
Thoraldby Yorkshire Lass (74)	B	Ch Step Ahead	Ch Thoraldby Miss Mandy	Mr & Mrs P. Thompson	Mr & Mrs R. Hodgson
Thrushgill Dandyhow Silhouette (68)	B	Dandyhow Brussel Sprout	Ch Dandyhow Soroya	Mrs B. A. Sullivan	Mrs K. G. Welch
Thrussington Geordie (58)	D	Browside Kim	Browside Gipsey	W. Hooton	Mr & Mrs S. Grantham
Titlington Tatler (19)	D	Titlington Jock	Gipsy	A. D. F. Patten	Mrs G. Sordy
Todgrove, John Boy of (83)	D	Ch Cuileann Dodger	Todgrove Trump	Mrs C. P. Halley	R. Hillcoat
Todhunter (30)		Revenge	Causet Bridget	C. Renner	Major Knight Bruce
Troglodyte (26)		Tornado	Ch Tertius	G. Thompson	Breeder
True Temper (53)	B	Ribbleside Rocket	Swallowfield Whisper	Dr & Mrs J. Cuddigan	Breeder
Tuppence Coloured (55)	B	Carry On	Copper Coin	Miss M. J. Lewis	Breeder & J. Whitworth
Tweeden, Ben of (25)	D	Tinker	Betty	T. B. Adamson	Breeder
Tweedside Red Biddy (46)	B	Ch Aldham Joker	Hallbourne Binkie	Mrs D. Black	Breeder
Tweedside Red Dandy (53)	D	Ch Girvanside Cruggleton Don	Ch Tweedside Red Glamorous	Mrs D. Black	Breeder
Tweedside Red Glamorous (49)	B	Ch Tweedside Red Salvo	Hallbourne Binkie	Mrs D. Black	Breeder
Tweedside Red Gloria (48)	B	Tweedside Red Playboy	Beeswing Belle	Mrs K. M. Renwick	Mrs D. Black
Tweedside Red Salvo (47)	D	Tweedside Red Silver	Tweedside Red Cherry	Mrs D. Black	Breeder
Tweedside Red Tatters (21)	B	Ch Titlington Tatler	Chip	G. Hope	Mrs D. Black
Tweedside Red Topper (23)	D	Ch Dandy of Tynedale	Ch Tweedside Red Tatters	Mrs D. Black	Breeder
Tweedside Red Type (27)		Ch Titlington Tatler	Chip	G. Hope	Breeder
Twempie Tinker (27)	D	Twempie Twink	Nanette	C. Cockburn	J. Smart
Twempie Tishie (27)	B	Ch Twempie Tinker	Twempie Nell	J. Smart	Breeder
Tynedale, Dandy of (21)	D	Gyp (North Tyne Gyp)	Otterburn Lass	T. Brydon	J. Dodd
Tynedale, Grip of (20)	D	Gyp (North Tyne Gyp)	Nell	Mrs. E. Brown	J. Dodd & W. Carruthers
Vanda Daredevil (44)	D	Moor Jock	Shesarip	W. Hancock	N. J. Fielden
Vandameres Band of Gold (70)	B	Dandyhow Brussel Sprout	Vandameres Sweet Sue	Miss J. Singh	Breeder & S. Singh
Vandameres Burnished Gold (73)	B	Ch Dandyhow Shady Knight	Vandameres Sweet Sue	Miss J. & Mr S. Singh	Breeder
Vandameres Daybreak (74)	B	Daletyne Davy Crockett	Vandameres Rainwater	Miss J. & Mr S. Singh	Breeder

Name of Dog		Sire	Dam	Breeder	Owner
Vandameres Daylight (80)	B	Ch Ribbleside Ridgeman	Ch Vandameres Daybreak	Miss J. & Mr S. Singh	Breeder
Vic Merry (48)	B	Why Not	Dinger Queen	T. Crozier	J. Renton & Miss M. H. Vaux
Wedale Jock (34)	D	Ch Heronslea	Shaws Lady	Mrs Murray	Mrs E. Twist
Wharfholm Blue Moon (60)	B	Hexamshire Gypp	Ch Richies Dream	R. Robinson	Mrs B. S. T. Holmes
Wharfholm Mansergh Tinkerblue (72)	D	Otterpot Ace	Mansergh Humming Bird	Miss A. Roslin Williams	Mrs B. S. T. Holmes
Wharfholm Warrant (66)	D	Harranby Quest	Wharfholm Wistielass	Mrs M. Wood	Mrs B. S. T. Holmes
Wharfholm Wayward Wind (63)	B	Daletyne Richie	Ch Richies Dream	R. Morrison	Mrs B. S. T. Holmes
Wharfholm Wench (52)	B	Ribbleside Rocket	Ch Portholme Marthe of Deerstone	Mrs B. S. T. Holmes	Mr A. W. Holmes
Wharfholm Wink (54)	B	Ch Wharfholm Wizard	Ch Wharfholm Winnie	Mrs B. S. T. Holmes	Breeder
Wharfholm Winnie (51)	B	Ch Deerstone Driver	Ch Portholme Marthe of Deerstone	Mrs B. S. T. Holmes	Breeder
Wharfholm Wizard (52)	D	Ribbleside Rocket	Ch Portholme Marthe of Deerstone	Mrs B. S. T. Holmes	Breeder
Wharfholm Wizardry (65)	D	Ch Brookend Baggins	Mansergh Wharfholm Wistful	Mrs B. S. T. Holmes	Breeder
Wharfholm Wonder Lad (67)	D	Ch Wharfholm Warrant	Ch Wharfholm Wayward Wind	Mrs B. S. T. Holmes	Breeder
What Fettle (35)		Ch Bladnoch Raider	Red Floss	J. Johnson	Breeder
Whats Wanted (79)	B	Dandyhow Grenadier	Early Arrival	J. Goodfellow	Breeder
Wheelton Watch That Girl (78)	B	Dandyhow Observer	Alisons Birthday Girl	Mrs T. W. Spence	Breeder
Wilderscot Beau Bell (74)	B	Farmway Dandyhow Beaujolais	Wilderscot Daisy	Miss D. E. Rumsam	Breeder
Wilderscot Morning Star (78)	B	Wilderscot Persimmon	Ch Wilderscot Silver Jubilee	Miss D. E. Rumsam	Breeder
Wilderscot Silver Jubilee (77)	B	Ch Dandyhow Silver Ring	Wilderscot Daisy	Miss D. E. Rumsam	Breeder
Winstonhall Coundon Tim (59)	D	Ch Billy Boy	Ravensdowne Roxana	Miss E. A. Turrall	Miss M. Long
Winstonhall Knavesmire Canny Lad (50)	D	Ch Future Fame	Knavesmire Lassie	Mrs H. P. Longworth	Miss M. Long
Workmore Brackon (68)	B	Ch Dandyhow Suntan	Workmore Claribelle	Mrs C. M. Walker	Breeder
Workmore Rascal (69)	B	Solway Cawfields Duke	Workmore Queenie	Mrs C. M. Walker	Breeder
Workmore Waggoner (73)	D	Coppinswell Dandy Boy	Ch Workmore Rascal	Mrs C. M. Walker	Breeder
Yak Bob (66)	D	Ch Falcliff Topper	Dandyhow Sheba	Major G. Ion	Breeder

Index